THE BROKEN LINES OF US

Visit us at www.boldstrokesbooks.com

THE BROKEN LINES OF US

by

Shia Woods

2024

THE BROKEN LINES OF US

ISBN 13: 978-1-63679-585-0

THIS TRADE PAPERBACK ORIGINAL IS PUBLISHED BY
BOLD STROKES BOOKS, INC.
P.O. BOX 249
VALLEY FALLS, NY 12185

FIRST EDITION: APRIL 2024

CREDITS
EDITOR: BARBARA ANN WRIGHT
PRODUCTION DESIGN: SUSAN RAMUNDO
COVER DESIGN BY JEANINE HENNING

Dedication

My little elephant,

I love you to the moon and back. Never stop dreaming.

CHAPTER ONE

Part of me has missed the first moments of a Manhattan snowfall, when the light flakes covering the city and park make everything look so quiet and peaceful that I can almost forget I'm in an urban jungle. What I haven't missed happens about ten minutes after that moment, when the city's grime settles into the ice on every block, and cars drive too fast down each avenue, sending up a mix of gravel, ice, and dirt onto unsuspecting pedestrians.

Maybe if I came home more often, or ever, I'd also have remembered the other constant of a New York winter: stepping off a sidewalk, not knowing if the black ground below is a puddle of ice or cement. Right now, as I shake out my wet pant leg, I'm reminded once again why I live in LA, where fifty degrees is considered freezing, and ice is reserved for overpriced lattes. Not that the weather is the reason I moved, but in this moment, as I feel the cold ice seeping into my shoe, it seems like a valid one.

Grumbling under my breath, I round the corner of 5th Avenue, and as soon as I do, I can see a green neon sign up ahead. Even though my leg is soaked and this entire city seems to put me in a bad mood, the familiar site warms me a bit. The Runaway Pub will always be an oasis for me in this city, even if the rest of it feels like a stranger now.

I'm hyperaware that being out in midtown means I could run into Jennifer's posse, or Jennifer herself, but it's a Wednesday, and Jen isn't the midweek party type. Not that I can really say, I guess. I haven't seen the woman or this city in four years.

I don't let myself think about Jen much these days, and I'm surprised by the sudden wave of anger that ripples through me. I close my eyes and take a deep breath before letting it out and looking back up at the sign.

In LA, it's easy to block out memories of her and the parts of my family I don't want to think about. But being back here on the exact street where we spent so much time together makes it hard to push everything into the "New York City" drawer I keep locked away in my mind.

As I approach the bar, I do my best to shake off the feeling. Jen and my brother aren't here, and I'm going to try to enjoy my night. After all, it's probably the only one I'll get alone until I head back to LA. If I know my sister, she'll be taking up every second I have over the next two weeks.

With new resolve, I push open the door to the place I spent more of my twenties in than my own home. Four years has not been enough time to change anything about the place. It looks as grungy and run-down as it always has, which is what I always loved about it. After spending so much of my life in homes and hotels that feel like museums, the Runaway was the first place I ever felt truly free.

I let my eyes adjust to the darkness. The first thing they settle on is the expansive brick wall across from the bar. I can't help but smile as I remember all the times I was pushed up against that wall. Or pushed someone else against it. It's easy to get away with when the bar is packed with dancing bodies at one o'clock in the morning. Now, though, it isn't even nine, and there are only a few people mingling about. Upstairs where the seating is, I can see a few more groups occupying the tables and chairs.

"Well, look what the cat dragged in. Charlie Fucking Dawson."

The moment I hear my name, I turn to the bar, knowing who I'll find. I'd recognize that deep baritone voice anywhere. I feel the first genuine smile reach my lips since I landed in New York this morning. Smiling back at me is the broad, slightly wrinkled face of Darcy Slater.

"Well, hello," I say, walking over. "You know, I expected a bit more fanfare than an empty bar."

"There would have been had we known you were coming in," Darcy replies, resting her muscular arms on the bar. "Or heard from you, like, ever." She keeps the smile, but she's an open book, and I see a flash of hurt cross her features.

Four years ago, I didn't think twice about the people I left behind. I just needed to get out of the city and somewhere new. Somewhere that didn't remind me of Jennifer or my parents around every corner. And I'll be leaving again as soon as I can. "You know me." I wink. "Too busy wining and dining the rich and famous out west."

Deflection is easier to me than breathing, and luckily, the hurt in Darcy's eyes is gone as she lets out her familiar bark of a laugh. "Of course," she replies. "It's good to see you, Charlie."

"You too, Darcy." I move onto one of the barstools while she grabs a bottle of bourbon. She holds it up in silent question, and I give a quick nod. "How's Alice?"

"She's good. I'm sure she'd love to see you. How long are you in town?" She slides the drink in front of me and clinks it with her own.

We both down our drinks in one gulp, and she moves to pour me another. The entire scene is so familiar that it almost feels like I never left. As if things never changed and the old crew could come barging in any minute.

I take a sip before answering. "Three weeks. I'll be tied up with family stuff, but I'll try to stop in. Kat's getting married."

I hate lying to her, but this is the only time I'll be in the Runaway while home. I barely convinced myself to come home in the first place, but I love my sister and would never miss her wedding. Even if it means I'll have to spend an extended period with my brother.

Darcy gives me a long look, as if she can read the truth behind my words, but she doesn't say anything. She's never been one to push a conversation, probably from being a bartender for so many years. If Alice was here, she would push, so I'm thankful it's only Darcy tonight. Wednesdays are quiet at the Runaway.

It was in this bar that I met Darcy and her wife, Alice. Ten years older than me, they, along with their crew, liked to think of me as their lesbian protégé. They were there to witness everything: my early days of fumbling through horrible pickup lines that never worked and the polished woman I am now.

Guilt washes through me. I could have at least texted every now and then instead of dropping off into oblivion. I make a promise that I'll try to stop by one more time before leaving town.

"And how is the family?" Darcy asks.

I buy myself some time by taking a sip, but a knot forms in my stomach at the mention of my family, something that doesn't happen as much in LA, where I'm surrounded by people who know nothing of my last name. There, I'm Charlie Scott, my mom's maiden name. Dawson is nowhere to be found. I've only been back for seven hours, and yet, everything here reminds me of my parents. This city will never let me forget it was theirs.

And they're gone.

"Fine." I turn on my stool and look around the empty bar.

Darcy doesn't push. "And are you on the prowl tonight? Should I warn the masses?"

I turn and smile. "I've moved on to the LA market now."

"Oh, you mean blond yogis who drink green smoothies for all their meals?"

"No," I say defensively. "They're not *all* blond."

She lets out another loud laugh. "Well, whether it's the sun or the smoothies, you look a hell of a lot better than when you left here. So cheers." She pours me another drink. I hold up the glass in thanks right as a group of women comes in laughing. As they approach the bar, Darcy puts out some coasters before turning back to me. "You going to stay awhile?"

"Yeah, I thought I'd drink this upstairs and watch the parade for a bit."

She gives me a quick nod before turning her attention to the women. One, a pretty redhead with loose curls, gives me a not-so-subtle once-over and a lingering smile. I return the smile but don't stop on my journey to the staircase. Maybe I'll come back down and chat with her in a bit, but that wasn't my plan for tonight. I've shared enough drama with this city for one lifetime.

An hour later, the alcohol warmly courses through my body. Switching to beer was a good idea, considering I have to be up early to do a fitting for Kat's wedding. The Runaway still isn't as busy as a Saturday night, but a handful of women are on the dance floor downstairs, giving me something to watch. I've heard that most lesbian bars in Manhattan have closed, so I suppose even on a Wednesday, this is the only place for women to come where they won't be hit on by clueless men.

I should stop drinking, even if it's only beer. The more I consume, the more the idea of talking to the cute redhead sounds appealing. She hasn't stopped glancing at me since I came up here, and I'm not one to hold back when a woman is so obviously interested. Especially one whose shirt keeps moving lower and lower, leaving her cleavage on full display from my vantage point.

When my self-control loses to the alcohol, I direct a flirtatious smile at her, but as soon as I do, I hear Darcy's deep voice behind me:

"I'd stay away from that one. Bit of a loose cannon. She dated Jessie." She nods to the redhead as she sits and sets down two fresh pints of beer. "On the house," she says, clinking her glass against mine again.

"No, you should let me pay. Might as well use my family's money."

"Except your brother cut you off."

"Just from the trust. I still got the money from the sale of my Manhattan apartment and gallery. He can't touch that."

"Don't you think your parents would have words to say about him taking your inheritance?"

I'm not surprised she asked. I left so quickly four years ago that my friends probably have a lot of unanswered questions. But the last thing I want to do tonight is talk about all that. "It doesn't matter. They're dead."

She is quiet for a moment, but I can feel her eyes on me. "And how's the gallery?"

I take a sip before answering. "Turns out, when I can't milk the Dawson name, it's a little harder to get visibility with the right buyers. It took a couple years to get any real names in, but it's doing well now."

I'm again grateful that it's Darcy sitting here and none of my other New York friends, who would be peppering me with questions. After a moment, we fall into an easy silence as we watch the dancing women. The redhead is now blatantly staring at me and doing some odd dance that I assume is supposed to be enticing but only makes her seem like she can't control her limbs.

Darcy lets out a small snort. "So little Kat's getting married? It seems like yesterday she was a sixteen-year-old asking me to serve her booze."

"She hasn't been sixteen for twelve years, Darcy."

"That means I'm twelve years older, too," she says with a headshake. "Let's just pretend."

"I'm good with that."

"Have you met the groom?"

I nod. "They've both come out to LA a few times. Jake's cool. He's a veterinarian, too, which is kind of cute and kind of gross. They opened a clinic together downtown. But he's great to Kat and hates Ian, so he's good in my book."

"And how's the hotel business?"

I take a deep breath instead of doing what I want to do, which is roll my eyes, as I seem to do anytime my family's company comes up. "I get updates I don't need through my uncle," I say once I let my breath out. "But my brother runs that show now, and you know how I feel about him."

She gives me a knowing smirk. "I assume things haven't improved on the Ian front?"

"He is still a spoiled, conservative jackass. Nothing will ever change that. How's the gang?" I ask, hoping to change the subject.

Like always, her wise eyes convey more than she says, but she takes my cue. "They're good. Everyone's being super gay. Making babies and growing urban gardens and shit."

"Wait, who?"

"Nora and Flo on the babies and Jessie on the garden. Oh, and Cam moved to Long Island, so we see her almost as much as we see you."

"What about you and Alice? Any baby making?"

She laughs and holds her arms up. "We have one. You're sitting in it."

We continue to catch up, and though the conversation flows easily, I can feel an unspoken tension. I've felt so disconnected from New York and equate it so heavily with my parents and Jen that I don't know how to feel at ease, even with someone I've known for so long.

"Everyone misses you," Darcy says.

I let out a harsh laugh. "I'm sure that's not the case. I was an asshole for leaving the way I did."

"We all understood. Are you happy out there?"

"I think I am, yeah." I shrug. "As big as Manhattan is, it's always felt a bit suffocating. Now, I have a new gallery that's all mine and women who are interested in me for more than my family's money."

"They must be desperate artists because we both know it's not your face they're after. I see you only got worse looking."

I smile, knowing she's just teasing. I would have to be blind not to notice the way most women react to me, and LA doesn't seem any different to New York. Growing up, I was always jealous of Kat and Ian's resemblance to our mom. As twins, they both have gorgeous dark hair, dark eyes, and pale skin that gives them a sophisticated, elegant look.

I'm my dad's daughter through and through, with messy, dirty blond hair and light brown eyes. Kat says I look like I belong in California, and now that I'm older, I've come to appreciate my resemblance to our dad more. "Did you forget that I'm both attractive and charming?" I tease back.

"True. But what I really love is your modesty."

I glance at my watch again. It's almost eleven. I need to leave before I drink too much more and make a bad decision, a feeling that only intensifies when my eyes land on the drunk redhead again. But right as I'm about to say good-bye, a woman enters the bar alone.

All at once, the time, my reasons for being in New York, the redhead, and even Darcy fade into the background of my mind. My body feels like it's been in a coma and has come to life.

I scoot forward against the rail, trying to get a better view. She gracefully sits at the bar and orders a drink. Everything about her screams sophistication and class. From her straight back to the hands resting politely in her lap, this woman doesn't fit in at the Runaway, and I'm not sure where she would. She has an elegance that most modern women don't possess. My quick analysis is solidified when the bartender slides over a glass of white wine. I love Darcy and the Runaway, but ordering wine here? No, thanks.

She seems to have an easy confidence and authority. She glances about with an expression of subtle boredom, almost as if she's beyond the silly women dancing and laughing together. And to be fair, with a face that perfect, she probably is. And though I promised myself I'd behave and keep a low profile in New York, I hadn't counted on someone like this walking into the bar tonight. I can't remember anything I've wanted to feast my eyes on more, and I work in the art world. Her face is impossibly beautiful, as if every feature was meticulously designed.

I can't see the color of her eyes, but I can tell that they're light. Her face is angular but not fierce, and her long, flowing brown hair looks like it was styled by a professional. Her black pants and emerald blouse are simple, but I can tell even from here that they're expensive.

"Who's that?" I ask, trying to keep my voice neutral.

Darcy looks down as she finishes her beer. "Haven't seen her before." She raises her eyebrows. "But I know that look."

"I don't have a look."

"She looks like Jennifer."

I scoff. "She looks nothing like Jen."

"Different hair style, much taller. And brunette. But she's got that same snooty vibe."

The beautiful stranger is now watching the dancing redhead and her friends with an amused expression. She must notice the redhead look at me because a moment later, she's looking directly at me. It's a good thing we're across the room because the second our eyes meet and I see the clear blue of hers, a noise I don't even recognize comes out of my mouth.

When she doesn't look away, I lift my drink in a silent toast and try to stop the slight shake in my hand. Her eyes dance with amusement, but her lips remain stoic. *Kissably stoic.* She turns her back to the crowd and drinks her wine.

"Smooth." Darcy says. "I think you got rejected before you even asked. You must be losing your touch."

I shrug and remind myself that I'm not after a hookup. Besides, I'm surrounded by beautiful women in LA. Maybe not this heart-racing-dry-mouth-inducing kind of beautiful, but I'm not hurting for female attention.

"I have to head back. I'll send Lee up with another round when you give me the sign." Darcy points to my half-empty beer as she stands.

Half an hour later, I have a fresh beer and am one step past tipsy. I continue to steal glances at the brunette, but she still has her back to me. When I've resigned myself to the fact that she isn't going to turn again, I know I should head home. But right as I'm about to stand, the redhead approaches my table.

"You made me walk up a staircase to get to you," she says, leaning against the rail in front of me. Her eyes are glassy, and her sweaty hair falls into her face as she smiles.

"Am I not worth a few stairs?" I ask, trying not to be too annoyed that she's blocking my view of the beautiful stranger.

She gives me an appraising look, and by the way she wobbles, she is very drunk. "You certainly are. I haven't seen you here before. You seem to know people, though." She nods toward Darcy.

"I used to live here." I'm already bored.

She isn't picking up on my obvious disinterest and sits in the seat Darcy vacated. "You're really beautiful." She leans into me.

I roll my eyes at the unoriginal line. I'm being harsh, but her presence is beginning to grate. "Thank you," I say, doing my best to sound polite but not interested.

"Can I buy you a drink? I'll even walk up those stairs again. Or we could grab a cab and walk up to my apartment."

I can't help but be impressed by her boldness. The way she's leaning forward causes her cleavage to lift, giving me a view of her curves. I allow myself one glance as I weigh my options. This would certainly be an easy outlet for the night, but as Darcy's warning rolls around my head, I bring my eyes back up and give her a tight smile. "I'm very flattered. But I think I'm going to drink alone tonight."

She stares for a moment before she moves her chair back and stands. "Suit yourself. Have fun...alone." She gives a mocking laugh as she heads back down.

I sit back with a sigh of relief; that woman is a walking red flag.

The bar has filled up even more, and after the awkward exchange with the busty redhead, being somewhere public has lost its appeal. As I make my way downstairs, I move through the small group of people at the bar so I can pay and head out. I try to catch one last glance of my beautiful stranger, but she's gone. I try not to be too disappointed.

"Heartbreaker, then?" A low alto voice close to my ear sends a pleasant shiver up my arms.

When I turn, I'm rendered speechless by the brightest eyes I've ever seen. Now that the brunette is in front of me, I can tell that they're not quite blue, more of an aquamarine. She sits on the stool next to me. Her drink now a neat brown liquor that dangles sexily from one hand as her eyes roam my body.

"Sorry?" I ask, only able to form one word as my eyes take over all brain activity, leaving my mouth useless.

She nods at the corner of the bar, and I reluctantly tear my attention away from her. The redhead is leaning against the far brick wall, surrounded by her drunk friends. Her arms are crossed, and she's directing a scowl my way.

I'm again relieved that I didn't let that conversation go any further, and I feel a rush of excitement around the fact that the brunette was watching me. I turn back and am met with a sexy, amused smile. The air feels thicker here than it did upstairs, and I can't tell if that's due to the dancing bodies or the woman in front of me. But for some reason, I feel nervous. I don't remember the last time a woman made me feel that.

"I think she'll survive," I squeak out. I clear my throat, not quite sure why I sound like a hormonal boy.

She gives me another smile and turns back to the bar. The quick flirtation and abrupt stop have me staring dumbly. "If *you* asked to buy me a drink, I'd have a different response," I blurt out.

Darcy decides that's the moment to come over, and when she hears my comment, she gives an eye roll and walks away.

"Is that your way of conning women into buying you alcohol?" the woman asks, turning again, which I consider a small win.

I feel a surge of my usual confidence. "Do I look like someone who needs to con women into things?"

She takes her time checking me out, giving me an opportunity to do the same. If I thought she was beautiful from upstairs, it's nothing compared to what she's like up close. I feel torn between looking at her piercing eyes, the adorable sprinkle of freckles over her nose, or her entirely too kissable lips.

She doesn't hide her blatant appraisal, and I don't mind the attention. She looks at my tight black jeans and slowly moves up to my soft white T-shirt. "You look pretty good from here." As I realize she's flirting, I can't help but smile. Something about what I'm feeling seems fresh and new, as if I've never been flirted with by a beautiful woman. "Where did the pretty girl go wrong?" She takes a small sip and nods toward the redhead again.

"You think she's pretty?" I ask, making sure not to break eye contact.

"I think you're prettier."

The compliment gives me a different feeling than when the redhead said it only ten minutes ago. Or when any other woman has ever told me. "Thank you," I reply with a small smile before glancing back at the sulking redhead. "I'm not interested in anything serious right now. And something tells me she's easily confused."

The brunette flashes a quick smile, and the way her lips part so perfectly over her teeth has me swooning. "She does have a Stage Five Clinger vibe," she says before leaning in closer. "Just so you know, I'm not easily confused."

I'm not sure if it's the confidence, her musky perfume, or the fact that her eyes are on my lips, but my pussy gives a sudden, almost painful throb. As someone squeezes behind me, I use the excuse to move closer. My thighs are grazing her knees.

"So you're alone on a Wednesday night. Are you celebrating something or forgetting something?" I ask. "Unless you're meeting someone," I add with haste, scoffing at my verbal clumsiness.

"I'm not waiting for anyone. But are those my only two options? Forgetting or celebrating?"

"Oh no. There's a third." I lean down so my mouth is closer to her ear, and I swear I hear her gasp. "Getting laid," I say quietly.

She regards me but doesn't say anything. I wonder if I am being too bold, too fast. But her hand grazes the inside of my thigh. The touch sends another shot of electricity right to my center, and I can't help but close my eyes and focus on not moaning. I only open them when she pulls her hand back.

"Which one do you think it is?" she asks in such a low quiet voice.

I take a few breaths before answering. As sexy as she is and as much as her touch affected me, I have more game than to almost come in my pants from one graze. I give her body a dramatic look up and down and twist my mouth as if analyzing her. "Usually, people celebrate with others," I say, relieved that my voice sounds normal. "And you're drinking something dark and strong…so I'd say this isn't a celebration." I cock my head before I continue. "The liquor might imply you're trying to forget, and you look like you just came from work, and work always makes people upset. As for the third option, something tells me you don't have to try too hard. Plus, it's a Wednesday, hardly the best pickup night of the week."

"Tell that to your sulking friend," she says with a smirk.

I laugh. "I'm not sure I'd put you two in the same category."

"Well, thank you. I appreciate that."

"So how close am I?"

"Very logical reasoning so far. But which one is it?"

I tap my lips as I look her over once more. "Number three is intriguing since you *did* start talking to me. But I'm irresistible, so I'm going with door number two. Forgetting."

She gives me a smile and tilts her head as if considering. "Interesting logic. But I'm afraid you're incorrect."

I gasp in mock offense. "You mean, I'm not irresistible?"

She lets out another low laugh, and I feel a rush of silly satisfaction. "Incorrect in your choice," she replies. "You assumed it couldn't have been more than one. And the truth is, I'm here drinking alone, as you *so generously* pointed out, to celebrate and to forget."

"But not to get laid?"

"I haven't decided on that part yet." She lightly plays with the tips of my free hand.

My lips part at our sudden contact, but I'm able to stop the gasp. I clear my throat. "Do you want to go get a drink somewhere with me?" I glance at Darcy. The lesbian rumor mill is strong, and I don't feel like dealing with that this week. "Somewhere other than here."

She looks at my lips before nodding slowly.

"My hotel is close. They have a bar."

"Hotel?"

"I'm just here for a visit. But we can go to another bar if that's more comfortable."

She's quiet as she looks around, the first time she's seemed nervous since coming in. It makes me feel better that she isn't completely impenetrable, considering my own heart feels a tad fast for someone standing in place. "Let's go to your hotel." She stands and puts on a long coat. "Do you need to settle your tab?"

I look at Darcy and nod toward the door, indicating my departure. She gives me a knowing smirk but simply nods back. I have to remember to send her a thank-you text. "No, I'm good."

We move toward the exit of the bar, and I can't miss the daggers from the long-forgotten redhead now dancing between two very drunk women. I open the door to let the brunette through. As we begin walking, she casually slides her arm through mine, and I try my best not to smile like an idiot.

"It's just up on 51st. The Dawson Midtown," I say, as we turn the corner. Her pace slows, so I stop and turn. "Like I said, we can go somewhere else. Or I can walk you to a cab…" I trail off because that's the last thing I want.

She steps into my space, so close that I can feel her warm breath on my face. "Take me to your hotel," she says quietly, her eyes never leaving my lips. "I want to go."

It would be so easy to lean in and kiss her, but I don't want to rush, especially when she just agreed to go with me. I simply turn and pull her arm back through mine as we continue walking. Now that I have this gorgeous woman on my arm, Manhattan feels hotter than July.

CHAPTER TWO

Every promise I made to myself when I got off the plane this morning is in the process of being broken as I sit across from my beautiful stranger in the hotel bar. If I was in town for any reason other than Kat's wedding, I wouldn't be thinking twice about this, but my sister is the most important person in my life, and I'm not going to ruin that by fighting with Ian the whole time. Which is exactly what would happen if he saw where I'm currently sitting.

It's not that he doesn't know I'm staying here. I assume my uncle Neil told him. But Ian has always had a conservative stick up his ass, and I know what he'd say about keeping my personal life out of *his* line of hotels. Not that they're his; the Dawson Hotel Group was our parents' pride and joy, and both Ian and I know that they never intended him to take over.

But here I am, sitting across from the most beautiful woman I can remember seeing, a woman whose name I don't even know. So far, there's been some unspoken agreement between us not to get too personal. And I can't deny how much I enjoyed our flirty, entirely unsubtle banter at the Runaway. Banter that seems to be missing now as I watch her look around nervously.

"Are you okay?" I ask as the bartender comes over with our drinks. "You seem nervous."

She takes a breath and gives me a smile. "Maybe you make me nervous."

"I doubt that. I assume you own a mirror. I'm the lucky one to be sitting here with you." I know it sounds cheesy, but I hope she can sense my sincerity.

"Based on the way some of the women were looking at you, I think you do okay."

"How long were you watching me?"

"It's hard not to look at someone who keeps staring at you."

"And I thought I was being subtle."

"I'm glad you weren't."

"And what did you see while you were watching me watching you?"

She takes a moment to roam her eyes down my body "You flip your hair to the other side when it falls into your face. Your smile doesn't flash, it grows slowly. You seemed distracted, which produces a slight crease between your eyes. You were comfortable in there but detached. When I first saw you, I pictured you standing on a tropical beach, holding a surfboard as you geared up to race into the waves. Wearing that easy, confident smile that makes my pulse faster. You look foreign to snow, as if you should be in perpetual sunlight. And you may be the prettiest girl I've ever seen."

I wasn't expecting all that, and all I can do is stare. "I don't surf," I say, eliciting a laugh.

"Maybe you should learn."

"I'll add it to the to do list." I take a sip as I try to control my smiling, hard now that she's admitted being attracted to me. "So you're out to celebrate and to forget. That's an interesting dichotomy. What are you celebrating?"

I regret asking when the humor dancing behind her eyes dims. "I was promoted."

"Congrats," I say carefully, considering she said the word *promoted* like it was toxic.

"Thank you."

"You don't seem happy."

"It's not what I want to do."

"What do you want to do?" As soon as I ask, she looks around, and I can tell I've hit a sensitive topic. "It's okay if you don't want to talk about it."

"I don't," she says in the most serious tone she's used all night. But a second later, her face softens. "You never told me why you were drinking alone on a Wednesday. I'm guessing it wasn't a celebration."

"No."

"It's okay if you don't want to talk about it," she repeats.

"It seems like neither of us really wants to talk."

"That doesn't mean the night has to end." The tension lifts as she gives me a playful smile.

Relief rolls through me, which seems silly since I just met her. But her words offer us a chance to give in to whatever this crazy chemistry is without telling our life stories. In an instant, I realize how much I need this: one night of raw, hot, no-strings-attached sex before I enter a parade of never-ending events with my family and memories I haven't wanted to revisit.

When her smile grows, I realize that I've been staring in my hazy daydream. I see a yearning on her face that I know is mirrored on my own. "Do you want to get a room so we can continue to not talk?" she asks.

"Meet you by the elevators," I say, a little too quickly. "I'll take care of the bill."

She gives me one nod and comes closer to my side. She pushes some of the hair that's always falling into my eyes out of my face. "I can't wait to see what that hair looks like even more tousled." She trails her fingers down my cheek.

I watch her walk away and know my mouth is hanging open like a cartoon, but I don't remember the last time I met a woman who's as beautiful as she is bold, and the swagger is sexy.

My legs feel shaky as I walk, and I'm not sure if that's from the beer or the brunette, but I have a feeling it's not the alcohol. My entire body feels on fire from a simple touch to my cheek.

The Dawson Hotel rooms haven't changed much since the last time I was in one. The curtains look a little different, but things seem the same as they were four years ago. When I was younger, I always looked forward to the Christmas party. I'd get to stay in a suite with my cousins and siblings. Once it was bedtime, my parents, aunt, and uncle would break out the expensive liquor and put the kids to bed in the rooms upstairs while they carried on downstairs.

Some of my favorite childhood memories are running through the halls as fast as we could, eating way too much junk food from room service, and then sneaking into the kitchen for more. Even Ian was fun on those occasions.

I don't usually think about my brother this much, and I don't want to ruin this sexy turn of events by giving him any more energy. I also don't want the brunette to notice my wandering thoughts. It's not that I'm hiding who I am, but telling anyone that I'm the absent heir to the Dawson throne only brings up questions I don't want to answer. Tonight, I don't want to be a Dawson. I just want to be a woman taking another woman back to a hotel room and hopefully, fucking her thoroughly.

From the hungry expression she is directing my way as she shuts the room door, I can tell she feels the same way. Leaning against the door with her hands behind her back, she looks so sure and sexy. Whatever nervousness she exhibited downstairs is nowhere to be seen.

All I've been able to think about since I first saw her is getting my lips on hers, and I still can't believe this is how the night is ending. A few years ago, I'd already be at the door, pushing her up against it. And part of me wishes I could be the roguish, carefree woman I used to be. But the one thing everything with my parents' death and the breakup with Jennifer has taught me is that I need to grow up and realize that not all messes go away with a snap of my fingers or a swipe of my credit card. Leaving drama in New York isn't something I'm here to do, and I want to make sure the brunette is on the same page. "I'm only in town for a few weeks."

She pushes off the door before turning to secure the deadbolt. The only light in the room is coming from a small lamp in the corner, and when she turns, I can see an intensity in her eyes that wasn't there before. I can practically feel the desire radiating off her as she takes a step closer. "Good," she replies. "I won't be giving you my number."

Emboldened, I take a step as well. "You'll never see me again after tonight."

Now we're close enough to touch. "Good. I'm a very busy person."

I take one more step so our fronts are lightly touching, and I can feel the gentle press of her breasts against my own. We're both breathing heavy, as if we already exerted ourselves. "Just tonight," I whisper as I stare at her mouth.

"Just tonight."

"I don't think I've ever been with a woman and not known her name."

"It's Annie."

Despite how turned on I am, I lean my head back and smile. "You look like an Annie."

"Really? Most people equate that name to a redheaded orphan."

"Well, I won't do that if you promise not to ask me if I enjoyed the chocolate factory. I'm Charlie."

"Deal," she says with a smile. "Now that we have formalities out of the way, can we get back to getting to know each other nonverbally?"

I respond by closing the distance between our lips. At first, the kiss is tentative as we softly brush against each other, familiarizing ourselves to the new taste and feel. I can faintly taste bourbon on her breath, but more than that, she tastes sweet, as if she just devoured a handful of candy. I pull her closer and deepen the kiss.

As our tongues meet, all softness and hesitation dissipates. I tighten my hold as she moans into my mouth. Everything I thought I knew about first kisses flies out the window as this magnificent woman takes control, moving her tongue in and sucking. If this is how Annie fucks, I can't wait to get her naked.

Something about kissing her feels so different to anything I've ever experienced. She kisses like she was told she'll never get to kiss a woman again. She's thorough and sensual, and if all we did was kiss, I'd probably feel more satisfied than I have with any other woman.

Her hands move up my body and snake into my hair, pulling my mouth even closer. When she rolls her hips, the moan that comes out of me almost surprises me. I'm so turned on already, and we're both still fully dressed.

As we break apart for air, Annie whispers, "Wow," as she pinches my bottom lip. "I thought you might taste good. But not this good."

I can't find the words to reply, not with her fingers on my lips. I nod and take those same fingers into my mouth. I massage them gently with my tongue, causing Annie's eyes to close. She takes her fingers out of my mouth and moves backward. I do my best to hold in a whimper from the loss of contact, but based on her smirk, I'm pretty sure I failed.

Without saying anything, she lifts her shirt over her head and throws it to the ground. Soft curves spill out of a black lacy bra, and all I want to do is to bring her against my body again. Something seems to have shifted. My own breathing increases, but I can't control the trembling mess I've become. And it seems she can sense that she has complete control.

I'm not exactly a top. Though, more often than not, I've directed the flow and pace of my sexual encounters. But with Annie so brazen and confident in just her bra, I feel hopeless to control anything. For the first time, all I want to do is give. And give and give and give.

When she stays where she's standing, I start to take my shirt off since it only seems fair.

"Don't," she says in a soft but commanding voice. "Let me." She makes quick work of removing my top and bra, tossing them aside like she did her own shirt moments before. As she grips my waist, she makes no show of hiding her blatant ogling. The look of desire, mixed with the sexy way she licks her lips, has my nipples hardening almost painfully. "God. You're so sexy. I wanted you the moment I saw you," she whispers as she places her lips on the spot right below my ear.

As she begins sucking down my neck, I can't keep in a moan. I want to respond, talk dirty to her, let her know how sexy she is, but all that seems to be able to leave my mouth are small gasps and moans as her lips continue to familiarize themselves with my body. When she latches on to my nipple without warning, I let out a gasp and jerk forward. She cups my tits as she sucks, and I don't even know how long she's at it until my legs begin to shake.

Needing to anchor myself to something, I lace my hands into the silky hair. I feel a primal need to taste her lips again, and I don't know how much longer I can stand as she focuses her hot mouth on my tits. For the first time, I take control and pull her mouth off my nipples so I can kiss her. She lets out a frustrated grunt, but once our lips touch, she leans back into the embrace. She is so sexy, so sure in her desire, that I may come as soon as my pants are off. Even if I never see her again, I won't let her leave this room thinking I'm some inexperienced teenager who fumbles her way around women.

As our tongues flick against each other, I reach behind her and remove her bra with one quick movement, earning me a satisfied moan that vibrates in my mouth. The touch of our bare breasts together removes the last vestiges of control for both of us, and we fall into a sloppy embrace of roaming hands and wet kisses. I break away so that I can let out two raspy words:

"Bed. Now."

Without missing a beat, she gently pushes me back, and I'm forced to sit on the edge. She stands before me as she unbuttons her pants and removes them, along with her underwear. Everything seems to slow, and I can't do anything but stare, even though my fingers itch to touch her. If tonight is the only night we have, I want to sear the image of something so beautiful into my memory. Like I would a sunset or a rare painting.

"You should be on a canvas," I say dreamily. She stops, making me immediately regret saying that. "I'm sorry. Did I say something wrong?"

"No." She looks more serious than she did only moments before, but after a beat, she continues until she's right in front of me. "Feel," she says, pulling one of my hands up to the inside of her leg.

My eyes snap shut, and I let out a low moan at the wetness coating the inside of her leg. She sets my hand in my lap again. "That's what your words just did to me."

"You're neat and tidy compared to the mess in my pants right now," I tease back, gazing up at her.

She smiles as she kneels and moves between my legs. "Poor baby," she says as she unbuttons my jeans and pulls them down. "I'm sure I can help you clean that up."

Once my clothes are completely discarded, Annie grazes up my legs until her hands settle on my upper thighs. She looks at me, and even though we're both naked and she is in a submissive position, she's still in control. All I can do is stare at her and try to temper my breathing.

"What do you like?" she asks.

"Everything?"

If I wasn't so turned on, I'd probably cringe at my clumsy response, but I'm so desperate to feel more of her that I don't care how it happens, as long as it happens soon.

She has a mischievous smile. "That would take more than one night, but I'll see what I can do."

CHAPTER THREE

I watch the smile fall from Annie's face as her hand trails down my inner thigh and touches my dripping pussy. When one of her fingers slides easily through my folds, she closes her eyes and lets out a sigh, almost as if in relief. I can only mirror the action as she brings her finger up the length of me.

After only a moment, she pulls away, causing my eyes to open. "You were right. You are very, very wet. May I taste?" she asks.

"You can do anything you want."

Her request for consent is sexy, but I can't imagine saying no. About anything. By the tone of the question, I can also tell that she knew what my answer would be. I don't think I've ever been with a woman who bypassed the rest of my body so quickly, but Annie is on a mission. And that mission seems to start with my pussy.

Without teasing me any longer, she lowers her head and places one soft kiss on my center. She repeats the action, carefully placing kisses up and down my length, as if she's becoming familiar with me in the same way she did when we first kissed. She takes a long breath as if inhaling my scent as she makes her way down.

I can feel myself getting wetter by the minute, and I'm tempted to push my hips up to demand more, but she doesn't need the encouragement. As her tongue makes contact with my opening, my eyes slam closed again, and I let out a long, deep moan. My hands fall back onto the bed so I can hold my shaking body upright.

Annie begins circling my opening with her tongue but doesn't enter. Instead, she brings it back up, taking her time to lick up as much of the flowing juices as she can. When she reaches my clit, she only flicks it once before pulling back.

I open my eyes as soon as her tongue leaves my pussy, but I'm too aroused to form even one word. I let out something between a grunt and a gasp. But when I see her face, all glossy and wet, I don't mind that she stopped. She looks drunk on her own arousal, and the sight is as hot as anything a tongue can do.

"You taste better than anything I've ever had on my tongue," she says with that same dazed look. "So sweet. Almost like you belong in a *chocolate factory*."

It takes a moment for her words to sink in, but when her smile becomes more of a smirk, I let out a low laugh. "That's the weirdest yet hottest thing anyone has ever said to me."

"You'll need to tell me when to stop. I won't be doing that of my own volition," she says as she lowers her head again.

This time, she doesn't tease, and she doesn't kiss. She devours. I don't think I've ever felt someone's mouth explore me so thoroughly, and the sensations are so overwhelming that I don't know if any other tongue will ever satisfy me again.

The only other woman that I've been with who has taken such control was Jen, but that always felt more like a competition, as if asserting dominance in the bedroom asserted it over all aspects of our relationship. Annie demands control in such a different and sexy way. It's as if she needs this, has been waiting desperately for it.

When she lets out another moan, the vibration, mixed with the idea that she's enjoying this as much as I am, causes me to let out a series of gasps and moans, and I can already feel myself barreling toward an orgasm.

Annie's lips come away again, and the lack of contact causes another involuntary groan of protest, eliciting a small laugh from her. "Don't worry," she says. "I'm not finished. Lift your legs over me."

I feel paralyzed by the pleasure flowing through my body, and I don't think I could even lift a finger, let alone my legs. Annie seems to pick up on my dilemma when she lets out another laugh and guides my legs over her shoulders. She pulls me as close as she can, and I wrap myself around her neck. She keeps her hands on my legs as she moves her tongue back onto my dripping folds. My body starts to shake as my orgasm gets closer. I place one hand on Annie's head, and based on the way she moans in response, I can tell it's a welcome move. "I'm getting close. I'm going to come." As soon as the words are out, two fingers enter my opening as Annie continues to swirl her tongue around my clit. And as her fingers sink deeper, she begins a steady pace of pumping in and out while her tongue flicks against me, as if she knows exactly what to do to push me right over the edge.

"Fuck, that feels good." I moan when she thrusts faster. Her enthusiasm is intoxicating. I won't last much longer.

"Come for me," she says, taking her lips off my clit for only a second before resuming her attack. "Come for me, now," she demands, and that's all I need before I can feel my walls clench tightly around her fingers.

"I'm coming. Fuck. Don't stop," I scream as I grip her hair, trying desperately to soak up as much of her mouth as I can.

When her tongue swipes against my clit again, my body jerks from the overstimulation. I move my hand from the top of her head so I can stop the movements of her mouth and indicate that I can't handle anymore.

She lets out a small groan of protest but stops, resting her head against my thigh as I attempt to catch my breath. When I feel like I can move again, I sit up.

Annie's hair is a complete mess, and her eyes are glassy, but it's the confident smile on those lips that has my pussy clenching all over again. I haven't fully recovered from my orgasm, and part of my body just wants to collapse, but there's something about the sexy look that erases any need or desire for rest. And while I love the way she has taken control so far, I also want to wipe that smile off her face and turn it into something else.

"Come here." I pull her up. "Straddle me."

She seems as enthusiastic about receiving as she is about giving because she doesn't hesitate to move up and wrap her legs around me. For a moment, I'm distracted by the perfect pair of tits in front of me, and I cup each before lowering my head to suck on her nipples. I swirl my tongue around them, reveling in the moans before bringing my head up again.

I lace my fingers through her hair so she's anchored around me. Our faces are close as I hold us together. "That was fucking amazing. May I return the favor?"

She leans in and places a sensual kiss on my lips, sliding her tongue in to allow me to taste myself there. When she leans her head back, I realize that my grip on her hair has loosened, and she has once again taken control. "If you don't, and now, I'll do it myself. At this point, it won't take much," she says right before she swipes her tongue across my lips.

"Fuck that." I grab her back with one hand and move the other so I can dip my fingers into the pussy that I can already see is as perfect as the rest of her body.

We're far past the point of teasing, and I can tell by the way she grinds that she doesn't need things to be soft and gentle. But I also don't want to rush getting to feel her for the first time, so before pushing my fingers inside, I explore just how wet she is.

As my fingers become soaked, I drop my forehead to hers and let out a low groan. "You are so wet," I whisper against her lips.

She simply nods vigorously. As I flick her clit, she lets out gasp after gasp, and I can't help but stare at the beautiful way she accepts pleasure so openly. Seemingly unable to speak through the moans, she grabs my wrist and pulls my hand down. "Inside. Please. Fuck me," she says almost incoherently.

I grip her back harder and lift her so I can get two fingers inside and begin to pump in and out.

"Yes, yes, yes," she cries. "You feel so good, Charlie." She pulls me in for a messy kiss that she continues to moan into. She's taking my mouth so thoroughly that all I can do is accept it and focus on what my fingers are doing. "I'm getting close." She gasps, breaking her wet mouth away from mine. "Add another."

"Gladly." I add a third finger, pushing in as much as I can. None of it is graceful, but this moment doesn't call for that, and she seems to agree. She's breathing heavily, and there's a slight shake to her body.

"I'm coming, Charlie, I'm coming," she shouts, leaning into the headboard.

I feel her come just as much as I hear the words, but I continue to thrust until I can feel her begin to slow. When she stills, I slide my fingers out and allow her body to fall into mine.

After a few minutes, we move up the bed so we're lying next to each other. She drapes one hand across my middle and nuzzles my neck. I know all too well how high emotions can run after sex, but I can't help but think that she fits perfectly with my body, both during sex and as we cuddle.

"You," she says as she presses her lips into my neck. She doesn't say anything else, just continues to place soft kisses there.

"Me, what?" I reply with a small laugh.

"You are really sexy. And good at that."

"Right back at ya." I turn so we're facing each other.

Throughout my life, there have always been things I've wished I could memorialize: sunsets or beaches or scenes that move me. Perhaps that's why I love art so much; it captures a moment forever. And as I lie here, tracing Annie's face, I feel that once again. Her skin is flushed, her lips swollen, and her hair is falling in different directions, but I can't tear my eyes away, as if her face was made for my gaze. "You are so beautiful. I'm glad we did this."

"I am, too. But I'm not done."

"You're not?" I lean over until she's pressed onto her back under me.

"Charlie No-last-name, if you think you can fuck me and then just throw me out without at least one more orgasm, we're going to have words."

"I wouldn't dare. But just so I know, is there an orgasm minimum tonight?"

Her face scrunches up adorably. "I'm not leaving this room without three."

"You could have at least given me a challenge," I tease.

"Your confidence is very sexy."

"As is yours. Now, are there any other rules I should know about? Am I allowed to drink? Eat? Use the bathroom?"

"In an hour, I'll let you have a sip of water." She grazes my sides, leaving a trail of goose bumps in her wake.

"You're so generous," I reply, but even the light touch causes my voice to tremble and my eyes to close.

"And don't forget it," she says right before she pulls me down for another passionate embrace.

I let my body sink onto hers, knowing we won't be talking again for some time. And I'm perfectly fine with that. Because Annie is right. We're not done with each other yet. Not even close.

CHAPTER FOUR

"Thirsty?" Annie says with a laugh as she watches me finish off an entire bottle of water in less than a minute. I don't even care that some of it is dripping down my body. I feel like I haven't had anything to drink in days.

"Your fault. You may be the death of me." I place the empty bottle on the bedside table next to us.

"I don't think anyone has ever died from too much sex." She takes a small sip of her own bottle.

We've just come up for air from our last round and are leaning against the headboard. The sheet is under Annie's body, and I'm trying not to stare at the bare tits teasing me, but my body needs a break, so I keep my hands to myself.

"There are, like, seven billion people in the world," I say. "I'm sure someone must have died from sex at some point. Like in a nursing home."

"Oh my God, that is so sad."

"Yeah, sorry. Bad example. But my point remains."

"And you're right. I am so very sorry for endangering your life tonight."

"I accept your apology. But only because you're hot and naked."

"That's fair."

Our moment is interrupted when her phone buzzes on the bedside table where the waters now sit. She reaches over and reads something on it, her brows scrunched in a way I haven't seen yet. Whoever is trying to reach her isn't welcome. I have the urge to smooth the lines so the fresh, happy expression comes back, but I allow her a moment to herself.

"Sorry." She locks her phone and sets it on the bed.

"Is everything okay?" But I'm distracted by the image I saw on her lock screen.

"It's fine."

"Was that a photo of your grandma or someone?" I point. We've made an agreement not to share personal details, but my curiosity gets the better of me. And after the passionate sex maybe that rule can loosen.

"No. It was someone I saw in Hungary. She let me take her picture."

"It's a beautiful shot."

She gives me a serious look before unlocking her phone and passing it to me.

"Annie, it's stunning. Her expression, it's haunting."

"She was just sitting there on that dusty doorstep, and I took the shot. She smiled at me, and I walked away." She stares at the image and seems lost in thought. I don't know her expressions well, but this one looks sad.

"Are you a photographer?"

She lets out a harsh laugh before taking the phone back, locking it, and setting it on the table again. "No. I had to take a prerequisite photography class in art school, but it was never my thing. I just like to take photos on trips."

I feel a sudden rush and push myself off the headboard so I can see her face better. "You're an artist?"

"No. Not really."

"But you went to art school? Which one?"

"It doesn't matter, Charlie," she snaps, causing me to lean against the headboard again as if her words pushed me back.

I don't know how to respond to the tension that's settled over us, but it's clear I'm not going to get anything personal out of her tonight, and if I keep pushing, she'll probably leave. A question about art school seems benign, but her reaction wasn't.

"Sorry." She puts a hand on my leg. "I don't like to talk about it."

I have so many questions, but I hold my tongue. I don't want this night to end. "That's okay." I lace my fingers with hers. "We don't have to talk about it."

She seems like she's battling with something in her head. "I meant what I said," she says in a quiet voice. "I can't see you again after tonight."

I pull my hand away and look around the room for a distraction, landing on the room service menu on the bedside table. I know it's petty, but I'm also annoyed by the implication that I'm being needy by asking a couple of simple questions. The truth is, I'm hurt by the fact that she is so against seeing me again when we clearly have a connection.

An awkward silence takes over, and I can feel her eyes on me as I stubbornly read the menu.

"Charlie," she says softly, sliding to my side so she can put her hand on my leg again.

"It's fine." I hate how stiff my voice sounds. I don't want to care that she's basically rejecting me, but even if I hadn't technically asked her out, I do care. And caring, especially after only a few hours, is not normal for me.

"Are you hungry?" she asks tentatively when I don't add anything else.

"I may order a drink. Do you want anything?"

She glances over to the clock on the nightstand. "Are they still open? It's past three in the morning."

"The kitchen stays open twenty-four hours a day."

"How long have you been staying here?"

"I got in this morning."

"Then, you've stayed here before?"

"Once or twice." I hand her the menu. If she isn't going to expand on her life, I'm not going to tell her that we just fucked in a bed owned by my family.

She sets the menu in her lap. "Look, Charlie, I've had an amazing time. I don't think I could find the words to describe *how* amazing. They'll probably come to me in weeks as I think back on how you made me feel. But my life is complicated."

I'm taken aback. As soon as I heard the word "look," I expected another unwarranted rejection, but what she said was sweet and almost romantic. The annoyance dissipates, and I give her a small smile. "I get it. But you know what's not complicated? A cheese plate." I point to the menu.

She returns my smile and seems relieved that the conversation is moving on to something less intense. I do my best to ignore the knot in my stomach and try to remind myself that I live in LA, and even if Annie was interested, it wouldn't work. I should follow her lead and move back into the land of sexy and casual.

"I'll call down." She leans over for the hotel phone. "What would you like to drink?"

"Bourbon," is all I manage to get out with her body pressed against me, causing another wave of arousal to hit me.

When she finishes talking to room service, she's basically draped across me. The look she's giving me is the same hungry one she had when we first entered the room, and my body is buzzing with anticipation again.

"How long did they say it would take?" I lace my fingers through her silky hair.

"Forty minutes." She closes her eyes and leans into my hand.

"That is so much time."

A smile grows on her face as she slowly opens her eyes. She puts both legs on either side of me, and straddles my lap. "Know any jokes?"

"Nope."

"Scary stories?"

"Nope."

"Tongue tricks?"

"A few."

"I guess that will have to do until our cheese arrives."

"Let me show you my first one." As I capture her mouth, it feels as if I belong there, as if our lips were built to kiss each other. But once again, I push that thought aside as I let my tongue slip into her mouth. If I can't have a tomorrow with Annie, I'll make sure that whatever time I do have is memorable.

CHAPTER FIVE

I down the rest of my coffee as I read the latest text from my sister, an easy feat now that I've been sitting here for so long it's gone cold.

I've been waiting in our favorite Upper West Side coffee shop for more than an hour, but I've never known Kat to be on time for anything except her job. That's why she's late now. Her latest text said something incoherent about a "cat emergency."

Not only did I expect my sister to be late, I also don't mind. Once she gets here, I'll be in wedding mode for the next two weeks, and Aunt Sandra has already warned me that she's putting me to work. Though I suppose being busy with whatever "maid of honor" duties are is better than sitting in my hotel room alone, stewing in memories that continue to press in on me.

With the exception of the time I spent with Annie last night, this city is one big reminder of my parents. Being back doesn't feel healing; it just reminds me of how much I miss them. I'm not sure New York will ever feel truly comfortable again, and it certainly won't feel like home. Something is missing. Or two things, to be exact.

It seems different for Kat and Ian. They were born five years after me, and by then, my parents' company had taken off. The hotel line was expanding, and the twins spent a lot more time with nannies than I ever did. I'd accept that as the reason Ian turned out how he did, but Kat still managed to inherit everything that was good about our parents.

Despite my many issues with Ian, I'll forever be grateful the twins were born. With their birth, I got a best friend in Kat and freedom from my parents' business with Ian. My parents never hid their desire for me to be involved in the Dawson Hotel Group. They both came from struggling families but worked their entire lives to build the company into what it's become, and apart from their children, those hotels were their life. While I always respected their work ethic and seamless ability to run a company, I never shared their passion for hospitality.

But Gail and Charles Dawson were special and so unlike the parents of other affluent kids I met growing up. They wanted me to follow in their footsteps, but they never pushed. When I started to show an aptitude for art, they bought me all the supplies I could ever need. And when they saw me flirting with my first crush at my sixteenth birthday party, the next day, they asked if I'd kissed her.

When it became clear that Kat shared my lack of interest in the hotel business, Ian became the beacon of the future, even if he and my dad never saw eye to eye. About anything.

"Can I get you another?"

I look up to see a barista staring at me. I was so caught up in thoughts about my family that I didn't see her approach. "Oh, yeah, thanks. Black, please."

When I hand her my cup, we make eye contact, and her light eyes remind me so much of Annie that I have to force myself to look away so I don't end up staring like some creep. While the barista is very pretty, she's not Annie.

Annie. It hasn't even been twenty-four hours, and yet, everything reminds me of her. I've had plenty of one-night stands—more than I'd like to admit—but images of Annie are stuck on repeat in my mind. And not the images I would normally fixate on after a night like that. Yes, the sex was mind-blowing, but it's so much more. She felt special. Being with her felt special. An experience that I could never replicate, even if I searched my whole life.

But since she made it crystal clear that she didn't want anything more than last night, I do my best not to think about the what-ifs. Even as we fell asleep, and she nestled so perfectly into me, I held a sliver of hope that maybe she'd change her mind and stay. But when I woke to an empty room, reality settled in. One night is all I'd ever get.

But while I may have woken up alone this morning, she didn't leave my bed completely empty.

The barista sets a new cup of coffee on my table. I wait until she's gone before reaching into my pocket and pulling out the piece of hotel stationary I've been carrying all morning. I've already memorized the note, but ever since I saw it lying on Annie's pillow, I keep looking at it again and again:

I will never forget this night.
xx
A

It's not her words that keep me coming back or prove just what last night meant to her. It's the small sketch of me asleep in the bed. I've always been a heavy sleeper, and I have no idea when she managed to sketch it, but it's the most romantic gesture I've ever received. I haven't always been the best at deciphering my feelings, let alone someone else's, but the drawing feels intimate, as if I'm getting to see a rare side to Annie that nobody else gets to experience.

Her denial that she's an artist is futile, considering the talent on the page. And with a hotel pen. Kat has always claimed that art is my "love language." Right now, I have to agree. But as much as the note and sketch mean to me, I can't escape the emptiness. There's a hole in my heart that feels unique to Annie, as if nobody else can fill it.

"I'm sorry, I'm sorry, I'm sorry."

I stuff the note back into my pocket when I hear my sister's voice boom across the coffee shop. When I look up, Kat is racing to my table, her unruly brown hair flying around her face as if it's windy in here. Before I can say anything, she's pulling me up from my chair and into a tight hug.

"I'm so happy you're here," she shouts, not letting go.

I can only laugh as I hug her back. Kat is a tornado of energy, opinions, and noise, and her personality is infectious. I'm far less excitable and pretty relaxed. But somehow, our differing personalities have always worked well together, and being away from her has been the hardest part about living in LA. "It's good to see you," I manage to get out when she releases me.

As we sit, she attempts to put her hair to one side, but it ends up falling into her face like it always does. That may be the only thing we share, wild hair that refuses to be tamed. "Things at the clinic have been crazy. It took me forever to get out of there. Remind me why I decided to go out on my own?"

"Because you're a Dawson. And *Dawsons deliver*," I repeat the family mantra I heard so many times throughout my childhood.

"We have fifteen minutes before we need to leave, or we'll be late, so drink up." She points to my cup.

I roll my eyes. I'm not the reason we'll be late to anything, but I keep my mouth shut because she doesn't look like she's done talking. Typically, she is *never* done talking.

"We'll go next door for the final dress fitting," she continues. "Then, we need to go to SoHo for your fitting. A designer down there is handling the bridesmaids' dresses. And then, we'll have lunch."

I wait a moment to make sure she's done. "I can't wait to see you in your dress. Are you nervous?"

"A little. But the alterations were minor, so it should be fairly the same as the last time. Aunt Sandra is an angel for the strings she pulled. You won't believe how gorgeous the design is." She pauses her rambling to steal a sip of my coffee, but as soon as she does, she puckers her lips like she tasted something terrible. "That needs milk. And sugar. And heat. Anyway," she says. "This entire day is going to be about me, as it should be, so let's talk about you."

I smile as she finally takes a breath and drinks the rest of my coffee, cringing the whole time. "I talk to you every day. What do you want to know?"

"What did you do last night without me? I'm sorry I had to work."

"It's fine. I checked into the hotel and then went to the Runaway."

"The Runaway?" She smirks. "Well, that's a throwback. Did you meet anyone, missy? Isn't that what you do there?"

"I meet women every time I go out, Kat. Nothing new. I was just stopping in to say hi to Darcy." She continues to stare at me in a very annoying, sisterly kind of way. "Get that smirk off your face. And don't call me 'missy.' It's weird." I force myself to maintain eye contact, knowing she can sniff out a lie in a second.

"You seem a bit shifty. One might even say *defensive*." She has a huge smile at this point, and I'm not surprised at all. Teasing me about my dating life has always been one of her favorite pastimes, partly why I never brought girls home from school. Kat always had a way of embarrassing me and making everything into a bigger deal than it was. But I love her. Despite her inability to chill the fuck out. "Okay, fine. We'll come back to your love life later. How's the hotel?"

"It's a Dawson hotel room. Ian hasn't changed *that* much. Same old."

"I'm surprised he isn't charging you."

"I don't even think he knows I'm staying there. Uncle Neil set it up."

Kat lets out an exaggerated gasp. "He never gives me free rooms."

"You live in the city. On the Upper West Side."

"How would you know? You haven't been here."

"Oh. Burn," I reply sarcastically.

"Uncle Neil's probably only doing it so he can butter you up and convince you to stay."

"He knows my answer won't change."

"Maybe. But you never know with *Dawson determination*."

I smile at the throwback to our dad. He loved to use our last name with any other D word that made sense in the moment. As a kid, I found it beyond embarrassing, especially when he did it around my friends. But now I'd give anything to hear one of those stupid alliterations again. "It would be a *Dawson debacle* to try."

"You could have stayed with me instead of being all weird and alone in a hotel room."

I'm not as loose-lipped as Kat, who can't keep a secret to save her soul. I'm not about to tell her that I wasn't alone last night. Not at all. "The last thing you need before your wedding is your big sister all up in your business," I say instead.

"*I* don't mind as long as *you* don't mind me screaming Jake's name at odd hours. Vets fuck when they can."

"Makes sense. Have you guys ever done it in the clinic?"

"That's for me, Jake, and a room of rescued hamsters to know and you to never find out."

"You can rescue a hamster?"

"You can rescue almost anything."

"You've always had Mom's compassion," I say, surprising myself. It's rare I let myself utter the word "Mom" anymore.

She gives me a thoughtful look before smiling. "I guess I was never cut out for the corporate world."

"I think Mom and Dad figured that out the day we found you in the security tent at the zoo."

"The so-called 'natural environment' those meerkats were in was horrifying. I was just expressing my feelings about it, as any normal person would do."

"You picked a fight with a zookeeper and crawled into that so-called 'natural environment.'"

"It's not like it was the tiger exhibit."

Her specialty is making me laugh. "You were born to be a vet. Mom and Dad knew that. And we all love you for it."

She's unusually quiet as she stares at me. "This is the most I've heard you talk about them since the accident," she says, causing my stomach to tighten.

I take a moment to glance out the window at the traffic and pedestrians crowding the streets. She is right. I rarely let myself even think about my parents anymore, let alone talk about them. It doesn't come up in LA, and I never volunteer it. But sitting here, knowing I'm about to face so many people from my past, a constant reminder of what I lost, it's hard to do anything else.

Kat seems to be in her own thoughts. She looks so much like our mom. Bright and beautiful and full of life. But right now, she also looks young. I need to remind myself that she lost parents that night, too. And I'm her big sister. It's my job to be here for her like she's always been there for me.

"They'd be so proud of you," I say. "I wish they could be here to walk you down the aisle."

"Me too," she whispers before a soft smile grows on her face again. "But I'll take Uncle Neil and Aunt Sandra as backups. Pretty good ones."

"Very good ones."

She swats my arm playfully. "I've missed you. And I know you miss me, too, Choo Choo."

"Only because you haven't used that nickname since we were ten."

"We like that nickname."

"No, we don't," I laugh. I don't care what my sister calls me as long as it isn't Charlotte, my birth name.

She looks thoughtful again before she speaks. "Dinner is at eight tonight."

The statement sounded simple enough, but we both know that a Dawson dinner is never simple. "And I assume our dear brother will be there?"

"Uncle Neil is making him."

"Uncle Neil has authority over Ian? Since when?"

"Ian gets how influential Uncle Neil is within the company. He's not going to rock the boat now that he's gotten what he wants."

I'm silent as I try to shake the anger that flows through my body. Ian has never been a warm or kind person, but he showed exactly who he is after our parents died, and I won't ever forget it. Maybe it's a twin thing, but Kat has always been more forgiving of his antics than I have. Though, everything happened so quickly after our parents' death that I don't know if Kat even knows how Ian executed the will. I left town right after, and we've never discussed it.

"We all know the company should have gone to Uncle Neil," I say, not able to hold back the sentiment I've felt since I found out Ian took over the hotel group.

Kat looks surprised, and I don't know if that's because I'm talking about it or because of what I said. She puts her hand on mine, releasing the tension there. "I guess we'll never know why Mom and Dad made certain decisions."

There's so much she has the right to know that I haven't said, but I stop from going into it further. The past is the past, and what Ian did doesn't matter now. I'm as far away from New York and the Dawson Hotel Group as I can get. I care more about the people I lost than the way Ian executed the will. The next two weeks should be about Kat, and I'll do my best to behave around Ian because that's what she wants and what my parents would have wanted.

I scrunch my nose, trying to lighten the mood. "Can't you, me, and Jake just get pizza tonight?"

"We have to go for Aunt Sandra and Uncle Neil. Besides the rehearsal dinner and wedding, this is the only time you'll have to see Ian."

"Do you see him often?"

"Only when Uncle Neil makes him come to family dinners, which is rare."

"Is he still trying to sleep with all of New York?"

"From what I hear, yes."

"Gross."

"Says the lesbian catnip machine," Kat replies, making herself laugh.

"You spend too much time around animals. Anyway, enough about him. When is the bachelorette party?"

"You're a terrible maid of honor. You don't even know when the bachelorette party is?"

"This is why I'm a co-maid of honor with Holly. She organizes the party, and I bring my charm and good looks. Everyone has a good time." I spread my hands.

"Whatever. It's Saturday. And you do need to bring your charm. Because there's someone I want you to meet."

I cringe. "Please don't set me up."

"Are you still hung up on Jen?"

The only thing I can think about is Annie staring into me. But I can't say that. "We were engaged. You don't just get over that."

"She left you when you were at your lowest. Seems like the kind of girl you get over quickly."

"I don't want to talk about her. And I don't want to be set up."

"You'll like her. I promise. She's a new tech at the clinic, and she's gorgeous. Newly single. Not into astrology and the vegan lifestyle."

I roll my eyes. "Not all lesbians are vegan."

"But they're all into astrology?"

"Only when Mercury is in retrograde."

"Aw, I forgot you could be funny," she says with a laugh. "Are you done? Because we need to go."

"You literally just drank the rest of my coffee. We can go." Just as I'm about to stand, the same barista from before is back at the table and smiling at me.

"Can I clear that for you?"

I nod and allow her to clear the table before looking at Kat, who's watching with a small smile. "What?" I ask.

"I've been coming here for over a decade and have never gotten table service."

"Maybe she's into blondes."

Kat scoffs. "You're hardly even a blonde."

"Maybe she can sniff out your heterosexuality."

"I don't think it has a smell, Charlie."

"Hamsters do, though."

"I wasn't with the hamsters today. It was a cat."

I smirk. "There's a pussy joke in there somewhere."

"And yet, we don't have time to hear it. Let's go, Casanova."

CHAPTER SIX

S andra said I'd find you hiding in here. Now I know why."
I look up from the bourbon I've been nursing to see my
uncle in the doorway of his study. I've been holed up here since
arriving at my aunt and uncle's Upper West Side townhouse,
knowing I'd need a moment alone and a drink before facing my
brother at dinner.

"Hey, Uncle Neil." I stand from the expansive mahogany desk.
"Of course I'm in here. Holly and I have been breaking into your
bar since we were teenagers. Did you expect anything less tonight?"

He laughs before shaking his head, causing some of the messy
blond hair that's so much like mine and my dad's to fall into his
face. "I prefer you two doing it at this age."

"It was more fun using a paper clip to get in," I joke, but this
time, he doesn't laugh.

He moves farther into the study until he's on my side of the
desk. Once he's in front of me, he grabs my hands and squeezes. "I
wasn't aware of the paper clip. Now I know why my lock was all
scratched up. Welcome home."

The soft smile causes a wave of unexpected warmth to flow
through my body that has nothing to do with the bourbon and
everything to do with the man in front of me. My uncle is one of
the people I've missed the most, and now that I'm seeing him in
person, I'm realizing just how much. As hard as it is to be in New
York without my parents, being back in this townhouse, only blocks
away from the one I grew up in, doesn't hurt as much as I thought.

"Thanks," I barely manage to get out before he's pulling me into a hug.

I tense as his arms wrap around me, but when he tightens his hold, I begin to relax. Besides my sister, I haven't hugged anyone in my family since my parents were alive. Not even at the funeral. But hugging my uncle feels familiar and safe, like I have a tiny bit of my dad left.

He releases me but doesn't pull too far away. "It's good to see you, Picasso. We've missed you."

I smile at the silly nickname. Ever since I was a kid and showed an interest in art, he's done that. He tries to pick a new artist each time, but he doesn't know that many, so it's usually Picasso or Monet or some other obscenely famous artist. I was Van Gogh for an entire year when I was fourteen. "I've missed you, too. Can I get you a drink?"

He walks to the bar on the other side of the small room. "I can get my own drink. You relax. You're our guest."

"I spent as much time in this house as I did my parents'. I'm hardly a guest." I pick up my drink and lean against the desk.

"I haven't seen you in it in four years. It certainly feels like you're a guest."

As I watch him pour the same bourbon I'm drinking, my stomach tightens. I know his words aren't meant to be malicious, and I'm not surprised by his comment. He's the most direct and honest man I've ever met, and he's never been shy about his feelings on my move out west. Partly because he misses me and partly because he is a New Yorker through and through and has a biased disdain for LA.

"When will we see Holly and Logan?" I try to move the conversation onto safer ground. It seems to work as he gives me a fatherly smile. My aunt and uncle are so similar to how my parents were. If anyone gives them the chance to talk about their kids, they'll take it.

"Holly just finished her winter break, so you'll see her soon," he says, moving back over. "And I guess we'll see Logan whenever he decides to check his text messages." He rolls his eyes, but I know he's not serious. If there's one thing he's proud of, it's his kids. It doesn't matter if it's Holly's teaching or Logan's acting career, he'll brag about them to anyone who will listen.

"Good. Because I have a feeling Holly will be much better at this whole maid of honor thing than I will."

"She manages twenty-five seventh graders every year. I think she can handle a little wedding planning."

I let out an exaggerated scoff. "A *little* wedding planning? You aren't being sent email after email about it. Literally, all day long."

"Sandra said you haven't answered one." His stern expression reminds me of my childhood.

"Exactly. Kat should have made Holly the sole maid of honor in the first place so I can drink at the wedding in peace."

"Kat loves Holly. But you're the most important person in your sister's life. She needs you now."

I stare at my drink so I can avoid his soft, thoughtful expression. If there's one thing being home has done, it's made me realize that leaving the way I did was more selfish than I was ever willing to admit. And if there's anyone who's going to make me remember that, it's Uncle Neil. "I know."

There's a moment of silence as we both drink before he speaks again, this time in a much lighter tone. "And how's the room? Are they treating you like a Dawson over there?"

"They didn't roll out the red carpet, but beyond that, the room is perfect. Thanks for setting that up."

He makes a small hum. "I'll have to speak to management about the red-carpet miss. But you don't have to thank me. That hotel is as much yours as it is mine."

"Tell that to Ian."

"Or you could."

I regret my comment and let out a long sigh. "You know I don't want to get into this again."

"You don't even know what the will says."

I close my eyes for a moment. "Mom and Dad made him the executor. If they cared about me seeing the will, things would be different." I hate how defensive I sound, but this is the exact topic I wanted to avoid tonight. I feel like a broken record.

He gives me another serious look before setting his glass down and putting his hands on my shoulders. "Your mom and dad knew their children very well. I'm sure they assumed Ian would deal with that part of things the easiest. But, Charlie, they would have never wanted things to happen as they have."

I set my own drink down and put all my effort into keeping my eyes dry despite the tears I can feel pressing in. We have already talked about this. But not in person, and feeling his loving, familiar touch is making me lose my resolve to avoid the topic altogether.

"They loved you more than anything," he continues in a gentle voice. "And so do we. I know why you left. I loved them, too. He was my brother and my best friend. But maybe it's finally time to face things here."

"I'm not sure Ian would agree."

"Ian isn't the only person in this family." He puts his fingers under my chin and tilts my head until I'm looking into brown eyes that are so much like mine. So much like my dad's. "Have lunch with me while you're here, and we'll talk more. But for tonight, no more serious talk. This is a Dawson dinner. Let's drink and eat until Sandra has to roll us away from the table. It's what we do best."

I give him a small smile. "Lunch sounds great. If you can convince your wife to let me out of wedding duties for a bit."

"I've never been able to convince my wife of anything. But I'm sure Holly can hold down the fort for at least one afternoon."

"It's your grave," I reply, causing him to laugh again.

"Speaking of graves, I told your aunt I'd come help set the table, and you know how demanding she is. I better head in."

"Oh, yes," I reply sarcastically. "You really should look into getting a new wife."

He sighs dramatically. "Perhaps. But at this age, I don't think I can be bothered."

"Let me come help—" I start to say before he puts a hand up.

"Just relax in here. I know tonight won't be easy." He picks his drink up before placing a quick kiss on my forehead. "Someone will come get you soon." He's halfway through the door when he pauses. "We've really missed having you home. This is home, Charlie."

He has always been free with his emotions, and I can see so many feelings broadcast across his features. That's all I need to lose my resolve. The tears that I've held at bay have no chance of staying put. I let them fall freely as I stare at the man I've always considered to be a second father.

He's one of the most constant and reliable people in my life, but it became too hard to be around him after my parents died. He was a constant reminder of what I've lost. But now, all I want to do is run back into his arms for another hug, an emotion I didn't expect to feel tonight or in New York at all.

Before I can reply, he gives me a more playful smile and points at the bar. "Help yourself. Not that I need to tell you that. I'll see you soon."

As soon as he's out of the study, I lean back and wipe the tears from my face. I have no idea when I'm going to see Ian, but I'm not about to let him see me cry. When my face is dry, I take a deep breath and let it out slowly. My uncle put me at ease in an unexpected way. I'm still dreading dinner with Ian, but I'm also trying to remember that this house is full of love. Kat, her fiancé, Jake, and my aunt and uncle are all happy to have me home, even if my brother isn't.

I take the last sip as I think about my uncle's request for lunch. Maybe he's right, and it's time to face everything I've compartmentalized for four years, including the aftermath of my parents' death and what happened with their will. But I don't know what it will change. It won't bring them back, and I don't care about their money or their company.

My uncle's stake in the situation is different. Not only does he work for the Dawson Hotel Group, he's also their chief operating officer and was an integral part of helping my parents get it to where it is. He's always been convinced Ian didn't honor my parents' wishes. While I tend to agree, there's not much I can do outside of taking my own brother to court, and I won't do that to Kat.

I'm lost in my own thoughts when the big clock in the corner chimes, indicating it's seven. I look at my empty glass and make the quick decision to visit the bar cart one more time. Even if he put me at ease, I figure another drink before I get called to dinner can't hurt. Being sober around Ian is what hurts.

I look around the room I spent so much of my childhood in. Everything about this house is nostalgic, but this room was always the one Holly and I spent the most time sneaking into. Because this is where my uncle keeps his liquor but also because it had an air of mystery to it with its dark walls and lush green couches. We liked to pretend we were in some fancy Victorian house as we lounged around, gossiping.

Logan is closer to Kat and Ian's age, so I didn't hang out with him as much. But the five of us still spent plenty of time together. In fact, every Friday was a Dawson dinner, and we switched off which family hosted. It's not an exaggeration to say I grew up in this house.

I take a sip and close my eyes as the alcohol burns my throat. If I'm honest, this trip isn't turning out how I thought it would. I didn't want to believe that it could feel good to be home. It's easier to justify leaving if I don't. But it does feel good. And there are happy memories here. It's only now that I'm back that I realize how much my grief has become a crutch I've stubbornly held on to.

Hiding in this study feels ridiculous now. After all, it's just a family dinner, not a war. Just like so many I've done before. I take one more deep breath as I make the decision to be a mature adult and see if my aunt needs help in the kitchen.

But as I open my eyes, everything changes. Because standing there in the doorway, staring with her mouth hanging open, is the last person I expected to see in my aunt and uncle's house. Or ever again.

Annie.

CHAPTER SEVEN

C harlie?"

I hear the shock in Annie's voice, but I can't answer or even move. I'm paralyzed by the face that has been haunting my every thought for the last day as my mind tries to unscramble what I'm seeing.

Her expression matches her voice, but she seems to have more control over her body than I do. While I continue to stand there, she moves slowly into the room. "What are you doing here?" She stops a few feet away.

All I can do is hold my drink limply and take in her face; she has only gotten more beautiful since the last time I saw her. Maybe it's because her eyes are shining, and my gaze is fastened to them.

"Charlie?" she repeats, this time in a whisper. "What are you doing here?"

I open and close my mouth a few times before I'm able to get words out, and even as I do, I feel like I'm watching the scene from above. "This is my aunt and uncle's home. What are *you* doing here?" I barely recognize the raspy whisper that comes out of me, but with the shock I'm feeling, it's the best I could do.

Annie looks confused for a moment before an entirely new expression settles on her features, and her eyes get as wide as I've ever seen them. "Charlotte?"

I've never felt the blood drain from my face until this moment. My confusion mixes with dread, and I know I'm as white as a ghost.

There's only one person on earth who calls me that. "What did you just say?" I whisper.

She shakes her head, and before she has a chance to respond, I hear another voice from the doorway, the voice I've been avoiding since arriving in this house:

"There you are, Annie," Ian says.

She whips around like she's watching some horror movie. Her face is so white that the freckles across her nose are standing out in stark contrast. But that must not be anything compared to the complete bewilderment I feel. *How does Ian know Annie?*

"Oh, and you," he adds when he notices me. "Welcome home." He walks into the room, and now I feel like I'm watching a horror movie as he places a kiss on Annie's cheek. "Did you get my drink like I asked, darling?"

I repeat the word *darling* over and over in my head as the cold realization of why Annie is here starts to sink in. She doesn't look at him, just slowly shakes her head.

"I told Uncle Neil that I'd grab him one as well." Ian moves to the drink cart and pours two bourbons. One thing that has never changed about Ian is that he's completely self-absorbed. The fact that he hasn't noticed the intense stare down Annie and I are engaged in is evidence of that. He barely even acknowledges me, despite the fact that we haven't seen each other in years. Not that I expected a warm welcome. I know he'd prefer it if I never came home.

He turns back to us and points at me. "Annie, this is my older sister, Charlotte. Charlotte, this is Annie."

I look between them again, almost not believing what is unfolding right in front of me. "Annie," I manage to get out in a shaky voice, but that's the only thing I can muster. I've had some big surprises in my life, but this tops the list. I don't know how to act normal right now. "Annie," I repeat before I can stop myself.

The room is quiet as we continue to stare at each other.

"My girlfriend," Ian adds when the silence carries on.

"Girlfriend," I repeat in the same shaky voice.

"Are you just learning English? What's the matter with you?"

His annoyed tone causes me to snap out of my paralysis. I send him the best big sister glare I can before turning my attention back to her. Despite the situation, I'm not going to let Ian get the upper hand. Especially in front of Annie. "Hi, Annie. Ian's *girlfriend.* Call me Charlie. All my friends do."

She continues to stare in horror, and for a second, I think she may even pass out.

"What friends?" Ian says sarcastically.

I decide to ignore his immature jab. "Where did you two meet?" I ask her.

"I'm doing some work with her father," Ian interjects before walking over to her and putting his arm around her. "He's in real estate. Not that you care." He points his drink toward me. "Charlotte is an artist."

Apparently, being gone for four years wasn't enough time to soften him or his opinion of me. His comment has nothing to do with my question and everything to do with the disdain he feels for anything culturally fulfilling.

But that isn't really what bothers me about the moment. I'm used to his rude comments about my work. It's his arm around Annie that bothers me. I feel a wave of jealousy and anger I've never felt before.

"You're an artist?" Annie asks before glancing at Ian. "You never told me that."

"Why would I?" he asks. "She must not have been that good. She's just a gallery owner now."

She looks at me quickly, and I try to ignore the spark across her eyes. "You own a gallery?"

"Yes. And Ian's right. I couldn't cut it as an artist. But I have an eye for talent. A very *discerning* eye." I stare right into her eyes when I say it, and by the intense look, I have a feeling she knows I'm talking about the sketch she left me.

"Careful, darling," Ian interjects. "Or Charlotte will have you throwing your career away to socialize with out of work painters in Brooklyn."

She remains quiet as he laughs at his own joke. I might have only gotten a handful of hours with her last night, but so far, this isn't the Annie I experienced. This one seems shy and reserved, and I can't imagine the woman I shared a bed with last night allowing someone like Ian to talk to her the way he is.

"Dinner is almost ready," I hear from the doorway. Aunt Sandra stands there, wisps of auburn hair flying about her face as they always do when she spends prolonged time in her kitchen, one of her favorite activities. "Oh, hello, Annie. I didn't know you had arrived. You look lovely."

"Thank you, Sandra," she replies in a voice that sounds as shaky as mine. "It's nice to see you."

My stomach tightens again at the familiarity between them. This is starting to feel like some nightmare I can't wake from.

"Ian, I could use some help with the platters in the top cupboard. Would you mind?" my aunt asks.

He seems hesitant to go but quickly gives his fake-charming smile. "Of course, Auntie. See you at the table." He kisses Annie's cheek before moving. It takes everything in me not to flinch.

Despite the questions rolling through my head, my desire to run and avoid the entire situation is even stronger. But I can't, so I give my aunt a hopeful look. "What can I do to help?"

"Just relax. Come to the table in five minutes. You're the guest tonight," she responds with a warm smile, repeating my uncle's words from before.

Ian gives me a dirty look. He doesn't say anything, just leaves for the kitchen.

The moment they leave, there's a heavy silence. I have so many questions. So many things I need to know. But I can't bring myself to make eye contact with Annie. Not because I'm angry, which I am, but because her presence overwhelms me. If there's one thing I'm best at, it's running when I'm overwhelmed.

"We should head to the table. Aunt Sandra has a thing about food getting cold," I say, heading to the door.

"Charlie, wait."

I feel her hand on my arm. The contact stops my movement, and I turn to look at her hand. As soon as I do, she drops it as if I burned her.

"You have to let me explain."

"So now you want to give me personal details?" I take a step back. I need to create some space. My arm feels on fire where she touched it, and I hate how the rest of my body craves more. "You were pretty tight-lipped last night."

She takes a deep breath and glances at the door. "It's complicated."

I let out a harsh laugh. "I can see that."

"I didn't know I'd see you again."

"I'm terribly sorry for the inconvenience," I snap back.

"That's not what I meant." She closes the distance between us so we're inches apart. As her perfume hits me, I feel a wave of longing. "The moment I left that room, I wanted to go back. I wanted to see you again."

"But you have a boyfriend."

"And you're a Dawson."

"What does that mean?"

"It means we both lied. Why didn't you tell me that you own the hotel we were in?"

"Because I don't. My family does."

"I'm just saying that we both weren't honest."

"Maybe that's true. So, tell me, what else weren't you honest about? Are you straight, Annie?"

She takes one tiny step so the front of our bodies are touching and looks at my lips. "Did I seem straight last night?" she whispers, not moving her eyes off my lips.

My brain and my body are at war. Part of me wants to forget the mess we're in and kiss the lips I've been thinking about nonstop. But the other part is screaming at myself to stop and think. "No," I say, not able to mask how thick my voice is. "But you also seemed single."

"Let me see you. Somewhere else. Let me explain."

"Ian is an asshole, Annie. He's never been faithful to any woman in his life."

"Let me see you," she repeats. "I *need* to see you."

"If you're worried I'll tell him, I won't. We don't have that kind of relationship."

"I'm not worried. I need to explain."

"Why?"

"Because I care about what you think."

"Last night, you made it clear you didn't want to see me again."

"I made it clear I *couldn't* see you again. But now you're here, I feel like I can breathe again."

Her words scare and confuse me all at once. This is my brother's girlfriend. And yet, our bodies are pressed against each other, and I can do nothing to move away. "You don't owe me an explanation."

"Yes, I do."

Despite how close we are, I've managed to avoid looking at her lips. But now that a new silence falls over us, I lose the battle and fixate on her mouth. And just like last night, her lips are the most kissable ones I've ever seen.

As I continue to stare, her lips part, and I see her take in a quick breath. "Charlie," she whispers. Her eyes appear heavier than before, as if she's drunk.

My entire body feels like it's vibrating. No woman has ever affected me like this. It's visceral. I can feel it all over like a light caress. Maybe in the height of passion, I've felt this kind of physical connection, but Annie and I are barely touching.

The tips of her fingers graze mine, but as soon as they do, there's a shout from down the hallway:

"Charlie! Annie," my aunt's voice rings out. "Dinner is ready."

I'm pretty sure Annie isn't a vampire, but the speed with which she runs to the other side of the room is impressive. Her obvious fear of being caught provides a quick reminder of the situation. Almost like a cold bucket of water over my head. And I can't believe I was just about to kiss my brother's girlfriend. *Again.*

Now that we have more space between us, I can think clearly, and all I want is to be alone in my hotel room. Or even better, in my apartment in LA. I never thought I'd see Annie again despite how much I wanted to. And now that she's here, so fully entrenched in my world and yet untouchable, I can feel my heart ache.

I can't function properly when looking at her perfect face, so I start for the door. "I'll see you at the table," I mumble.

"Charlie, wait," she calls, but I don't hear anything else she says because I'm moving down the hallway as fast as I can.

Maybe it's childish, and maybe I should stay and tell her that we can meet up. But right now, I can only focus on getting through dinner without my entire family knowing that in one night, I fell for my brother's girlfriend.

Because if there's one thing seeing Annie again has made clear, it's that I have absolutely fallen for her.

CHAPTER EIGHT

Everyone is at the table when I come in, and as they all look up, I do my best to school my features. It doesn't matter if it's been four years, my family, and especially Kat, can read me annoyingly well.

"Sufficiently drunk?" Kat asks from the end of the table.

"Not even close."

"Leave your sister alone," Jake says from his spot beside her. "She's on vacation. She can drink all she wants."

She lets out a noise that sounds like a snort. "Then what's her excuse for the other three hundred and forty-four days of the year?"

"Wow. Fast math," I reply. "You must be a scientist."

"Damn right." She does an exaggerated hair flip.

"Ignore her and come hug me," Jake says.

I stick my tongue out at my sister, which she smiles at. Though we like to tease each other, it's vastly different to the way Ian teases me. Her humor is wrapped in affection while his is wrapped in disdain.

I give Jake a quick hug before taking the empty seat next to him. Despite the roller coaster of emotions I'm feeling about Annie, my sister's fiancé is one of the warmest and kindest humans I've ever met. The sight of his face is always a welcome one. "It's good to see you, Jake. I hope my sister hasn't been driving you crazy with wedding stuff."

"No, that would be me," my aunt says proudly from across the table.

As Jake blows my aunt a kiss, Annie walks quietly into the room, sending my body into another frenzy. She stops close to the table, making my own stomach drop. There's only one free chair, and it's the one next to Ian.

Across from me.

She stares at the empty seat and then at me before walking over to sit. She keeps her eyes down, and looks so sad and defeated that even though I'm mad and confused, my heart aches all over again. But without her attention devastating my entire body, I'm able to appreciate just how pretty she is. Given the circumstances, that's the last thing I should be doing, but there's something that causes me to lose all control with her. Even knowing what I know, I can't help but be affected. When I first saw her at the Runaway, I was convinced there was no woman on earth more beautiful. And tonight, despite everything, that belief is only solidified.

Her outfit is similar to last night, but tonight, her blouse is a cream color that complements her skin perfectly. Her long hair is down, and it takes everything in me not to picture it sprawled across the pillows of my hotel room.

Ian has always dated beautiful women, so I'm not surprised. But even with his striking angles and full, dark hair, he pales in comparison to Annie. I just can't see them together. They don't fit.

My attention is pulled away when my uncle clears his throat and raises his glass in a toast. He has always opened our family dinners, and it seems things haven't changed much. While my dad and uncle shared many physical traits, in personality, they couldn't have been more different. My dad was a confident, intelligent man but rather quiet and reserved. He never minded letting his brash younger brother take the reins in social settings.

"Let's raise our glasses," he starts. "I can't believe the day has come that we're celebrating one of you three getting married." He pauses to give a pointed look to Kat, Ian, and me. "Kat and Jake, many congratulations. I know the next two weeks will be busy, but

I hope you can take a step back and remember why you're doing it. Even if your aunt does drive you nuts."

"I'm sitting right here, dear," she chimes in.

"Yes, dear. I know." He laughs, gazing at her with adoration. "And Charlie," he continues, "what a blessing it is to have you home. Families may not always see eye to eye, but I know your parents would want to see all three of you sharing a meal to celebrate our Kat. Here's to the Dawson family." He looks at Ian as he finishes, and I can't help but think it's targeted. After all, the rest of the family has never had any trouble "seeing eye to eye."

Once he's done, I lose the game of chicken I've been playing with myself, and my eyes drift back to her. Her expression is so intense, it's as if she's not even trying to hide her feelings. I may be a mess inside, but I think I've done an admirable job at keeping my shit together. It's *Annie* who's being obvious, and if people weren't so busy piling food onto their plates, I'm sure they'd notice something.

"Potatoes, darling?" Ian asks her, causing her to jump.

"No, thank you," she responds in a quiet voice.

"Women and carbs," he jokes as he passes the potatoes to my uncle.

My uncle gives him a long, serious stare before taking the bowl, successfully wiping the smug expression off Ian's face. Once he puts the bowl down, my uncle directs his gaze at Kat. "How was the fitting?"

"It was fabulous. My dress is a dream. The bridesmaids' dresses are a dream. It's all a dream. Thanks to your wife."

"I only coordinated with the designer," my aunt says. "You came up with the inspiration, and you wear it. It's gorgeous, honey. I'm so glad you're happy."

"Maybe now that Charlie has seen it, she'll give me a hint as to how much I'll cry when Kat's walking down the aisle. Sandra won't tell me a thing," Jake says, leaning toward me.

"Baby, you are so cute," Kat says before I can reply, pulling him in for a quick kiss.

I make the mistake of catching Annie's eye. She turns red, and I can only imagine she's thinking about us kissing, too. "You two are disgustingly cute," I say, tearing my eyes away. "And you will be crying your eyes out when you see her, Jake. But that's all I'm going to say. I may be older, but Kat can still kick my ass."

"You know it." She playfully narrows her eyes. She turns back to Jake. "Wait until you see Charlie in her bridesmaid's dress. She looks like a model."

I can feel myself grow red, which is not normal for me. I'm painfully aware of Annie's attention. "I'm pretty sure Jake's eyes will be glued to you, Kat. He won't notice me or any other bridesmaid."

"Of course he won't," she says. "But there will be plenty of women there whose eyes *will* be on you and that fabulous dress. You can thank me later for all the numbers you get."

I smile, even though my stomach is tightening. I don't want some random wedding guest to look at me. I want one specific woman to look at me. A woman I can't have. Annie looks as happy about Kat's comment as I feel.

"A dress?" Ian asks. "I figured you'd wear a suit."

"When have you ever seen me in a suit, Ian?"

"I just thought that's what your people wore. Apologies for the confusion."

"Ian," Aunt Sandra warns in the tone she's used since we were kids.

His smarmy smile sends a wave of anger through my body. But despite how upset I am about the entire situation, plus his homophobic comment, I choose to take a deep breath and not engage. I know him well enough to know that he's trying to bait me.

He turns to our aunt and gives her a much more genuine smile. "Honest mistake, Aunt Sandra."

I turn to Jake, trying to move things back to an amicable place. "And what will you be doing Saturday night when we all go out for Kat's bachelorette party?" The wedding seems to be the safest subject and will hopefully keep Ian and me from getting into one of our usual fights. I can tell by the look on Kat's face that she's already starting to feel awkward, and I promised myself that I wouldn't let that happen.

"The Syracuse boys are taking me out on a pub crawl," Jake says. "Kat tells me you're in charge. Should I be worried?"

"That depends. How many strippers are too many?"

He laughs. "Zero, I think."

"Then, yes, you should be worried."

"As long as the same goes for you," Kat interjects, leaning into him and poking him in the ribs. "Zero seems like the perfect number."

"It's not the same for men and women." Ian looks around the table, and when everyone just stares at him, he continues. "I wouldn't allow my fiancé to have male strippers—"

"What about female ones?" Kat interrupts, and I'm glad I didn't have anything in my mouth because I would have spit it out. Kat is just being Kat, but she has no idea how ironic her joke is.

I'm too scared to look at Annie, but I assume the comment wasn't lost on her.

"Men and women's bachelorette parties should be different," Ian continues.

"Maybe in 1954 when you were apparently born," I snap, losing my resolve not to engage.

"Annie, how are you doing?" my aunt asks in an obvious way.

"She's better than good," Ian says, not letting her speak.

"And why's that?" my aunt asks.

"She's just been promoted at work. To senior project manager." He doesn't even look at her as he brags about her. The whole thing reminds me of an owner bragging about his finest racehorse, not a man talking about his girlfriend.

"Does Annie get to answer herself?" I ask him.

He snarls. "Don't be rude, Charlotte."

"Don't be a hypocrite, Ian."

He rolls his eyes and turns his attention back to my aunt. "She'll be running that department in no time. And probably taking over for her dad at Astor Properties shortly after that."

"Astor? Is that your last name?" I ask, too curious to stop myself. She nods "And you work for your father?"

"Do you want her social security number too?" Ian asks.

"That won't be necessary," I reply in a monotone.

"Well, that's very impressive, Annie," my aunt says in another attempt to keep the peace. "Congratulations on the promotion."

"It's not a big deal. My dad owns the company, after all," she says quietly, staring at her plate.

I once again don't recognize the Annie sitting in front of me. The confident, sassy woman I spent the night with seems to have been replaced by a subservient shell who sits quietly by her man as he drives the conversation.

"The world is built on nepotism, Annie," Ian says, giving her a condescending smile. "Take advantage of it."

"You would know," I say, again not able to hold my tongue.

"And you wouldn't?"

"As much fun as this is, will you two please stop?" Kat asks. "Annie will think we weren't raised right."

I give Ian one last glare, but Kat is right. This trip is about her wedding, and I know how much it upsets her when we fight. I take a deep breath and shoot her an apologetic smile. "Sorry, Kat. We're done."

"Yes. Sorry, Kit Kat," Ian says before he sends another glare my way. He then turns to my uncle. "Speaking of Astor, the first franchise contract is ready. We just need to meet with the lawyers. I'll need your help with the final presentation to the board."

"I didn't realize we'd made a final decision on franchising." My uncle puts his fork and knife down. I know him as well as I know anyone, and besides the day of our parents' funeral, I don't remember a time I saw him this tense. But when my aunt puts a hand on his arm, he smiles and picks his silverware back up. "Right. No work at the dinner table. We can talk about it on Monday, Ian."

I can tell Ian wants to say more, but he gives a fake smile and turns back to his plate.

"Charlie, anything exciting happening in the art world?" my uncle asks.

Annie looks up as the question is asked. It's the first time since we sat that I've seen the familiar spark in her eyes.

"Quite a bit. The last exhibition got us some nice exposure."

"What's your gallery called?" Annie asks, surprising me.

"The Scott Collection. I used to own a gallery here in Manhattan, but I've moved."

"Right. You're only in town for a couple weeks." She's repeating my words from last night.

I set my fork down, not able to think about food when her attention is on me and only me. I have no idea if anyone at the table has noticed the intensity, but I can't bring myself to care when she's showing me glimpses of the woman I met last night.

"Where do you live?" she asks. Her voice is steadier than I've heard all night, and I can see some more of her confidence emerge. It's as if we're having the first-date conversation we should have had last night. In front of my whole family.

"LA."

"What kind of artists do you feature?"

"Typically, contemporary. I feature a lot of local artists but also some international up-and-comers. My last exhibition featured Luis Ortega."

"Nobody here knows or cares who that is," Ian says. "What about the no work talk at the table rule?"

"The Mexican sculptor?" Annie asks, pointedly ignoring him.

I chance a glance at him before looking back to her, and I have to stop myself from smirking at the shock on his face. Apparently, the Annie he knows is very different from the one I know, and I'm guessing she doesn't often ignore her boyfriend. "Yes," I reply with a smile. "It was his first west coast showing."

"Wow. He's amazing."

"Have you seen his work in person?" I ask, now fully engrossed.

"No, I wish. But I've seen photos."

There's a tense silence at the table. I'm so confused about everything. Part of me wants to keep this going, to talk to her about art like two people discovering they have something in common on a first date. But I glance over and see Ian's bored, annoyed expression, and the cold truth sets in again. A truth that only brings about more questions. How is this interesting woman with *Ian*, of all people?

"The gallery is amazing. It's this beautiful open space. Kat and I got to see it a few months ago," Jake says when the awkward silence goes on.

I'm grateful for his ability to move things along since Annie seems to be swimming in as many thoughts as I am. She gives me an almost pleading look.

"Thanks, Jake." I turn to him. "When does your family get in from Ohio?"

As he starts to talk, my aunt and Kat begin chiming in on wedding details, and I'm relieved that the topic isn't focused on me anymore. While I half listen about the seating arrangement, I allow my eyes to drift back to Annie.

I've never believed in anything beyond the physical world. But right now, as I sit across from the person who has consumed my every thought since last night, I have to believe that the universe is against me for putting her in front of me as if she belongs there. Like we were always supposed to meet again. And yet, making her completely forbidden.

There's an uncontrollable force pulling me to her. In one short night, she became everything. I don't even think I realized how numb I'd become before meeting her. She ignited something in me, and for the first time since my parents' death, I *feel*. And, I'm desperate to keep feeling it. I'm desperate for more of her.

My daydreams are once again interrupted when Ian taps his empty glass against the table. "My drink is low, darling."

I can't help a scoff at what he's implying. And when she reaches over, takes his glass, and begins to rise, the last of my control flies out of the room. "Is that how you let him treat you?"

Both Annie and Ian snap their eyes to me. But while she stands there looking shocked, he looks defensive. "Asks the relationship expert," he says. "Didn't your girlfriend leave you?"

"Ian. Stop," Annie says.

He looks up at her in surprise, and it again seems as if he's not used to pushback from her. "It's just banter," he says, giving me a challenging look.

I know I can't stay at this table and not give myself away. Ian has always had a special talent for getting me to my breaking point, and with Annie by his side, that ability is exaggerated. The only thing I can think to do is what I should have done from the moment I saw Annie standing in the doorway of my uncle's study.

I push my plate away and stand. "Aunt Sandra, the food was amazing, as always. But I'm still jet-lagged. I haven't slept much since getting to New York. I'm going to head out."

She stands. "But we haven't even had pie."

"Save me a piece? I'll be at Kat's tomorrow for the—" My mind goes blank as I try to remember what random wedding task my sister told me we're tackling tomorrow.

"Gift bags," she chimes in.

"Right. The gift bags," I repeat, having no clue what she means.

In attempting to avoid Annie's gaze, my eyes fall to my uncle. I regret it when I see the disappointment on his face. I know he thinks I run anytime things get hard, but he doesn't know exactly how hard tonight is.

My sister gets up and comes over. "You don't have to go," she whispers in my ear as she pulls me into a hug.

"I'll see you tomorrow." I give her a quick kiss on the cheek.

Annie is standing there holding Ian's glass like she doesn't know what to do. She looks like she wants to say something; that would be bad with my entire family staring at us.

"It was nice to meet you, Annie," I say. "Maybe I'll see you again sometime."

She gives me a small nod, and I wish I could read her better. There are so many emotions flitting across her features, but I don't know if it's because of what I said or if she's upset I'm leaving or both.

Once I'm out of the house, I take a deep breath of the cool night air and head down the street, deciding that I'll walk to my hotel instead of catching a cab. I could use the air to think. I feel worse with every step that takes me farther from my aunt and uncle's house. For leaving Kat like that. For fighting with Ian when I promised myself I wouldn't. But mainly, for going to the Runaway last night. If I hadn't gone, I would have just met Annie as my brother's girlfriend. I would have never known what it felt like to kiss her and hold her and fuck her.

But I do, and as childish as it may have been to leave, I couldn't be in that room any longer. Not without giving myself away. So I did what my uncle would say I do best: I ran.

Now, I just need to figure out how to get through the next two weeks so I can go back to my haven in LA where I may feel numb most of the time, but at least I don't feel *this*. And the only way to do that is to avoid Annie Astor.

CHAPTER NINE

"W hy don't you have a wedding planner?" I throw down
the infuriating ribbon I'm supposed to be tying around
a gift bag. I've been working on the same one for ten minutes, and
I've lost my patience with the whole project.

"I do," Kat says from next to me on the floor where she's
putting her own stack of gift bags together. "But I'm handling the
gift bags myself. They need a personal touch."

I roll my eyes. Everything in Kat's life needs "a personal
touch." When she was a kid, she would make the most elaborate
cards for her class. And not just on Valentine's Day. *All year long.*
She got her big heart from our mom, and it is one of the things I love
most about her.

But after two hours of sitting in her living room, putting bags
together, I am not finding it so endearing. "I thought the bride and
groom were the ones who got gifts. Why are you giving gifts to
people?"

"It's perfectly normal and considerate to give gifts to the guests
but especially the wedding party," my aunt says from the couch.

"Fine, but how is it personal if I'm the one putting them
together? Shouldn't *you* be putting your touch on all of them?" I
direct to Kat.

"Stop complaining, Charlie. This isn't hard labor," my aunt
chides.

"Besides, one Dawson is the same as the next. Your touch is as good as mine," Kat says cheerily, humming like this is the most fun activity in the world.

"Does that mean I can marry Jake?" I throw a ribbon at her.

She throws it back. "Do you want to marry Jake?"

"I love your fiancé, but, no."

"Good. He's taken."

"Anyway, one Dawson is *not* the same as the next," I say. "If I'm anything like Ian, I quit life."

Kat gives my aunt a significant look, but she doesn't say anything. I'm sure she's doing her best not to relive the disaster that was our family dinner last night.

"Why can't I have Holly's job?" I ask. "She's just looking at her laptop."

"I'm not just *looking* at my laptop," Holly scoffs from next to my aunt on the couch. "I'm working on the very delicate challenge of keeping Jake's conservative family away from our family."

I almost tell her to seat them at Ian's table, but I know Kat has had enough of the Ian drama, so I bite my tongue.

"We gave you the easy task," she continues. "You're putting things into a bag and tying them."

"You try to work with these ribbons." I wave one in front of me. "I don't think lesbians were made to work with ribbons."

"I sleep with women, too, and I'm fine with ribbons," Holly argues, not looking up.

"You also sleep with men, so I don't think you have a say in this."

"Ignoring your casual biphobia, I have full faith that you can manage those bags. I really do."

"And that means the world to me," I deadpan.

Holly glances up from her laptop and gives me an exaggerated wink. Lately, she looks so much like my aunt. She is much taller, which she gets from my uncle, but with their bright green eyes and curly auburn hair, Aunt Sandra and she have always looked more like sisters than mom and daughter.

"Or you could switch jobs with me," my aunt says as she stands. "I'll handle the gift bags, and you go pick up Jake's mom and dad from the airport."

I scrunch my nose. From what Jake has told me, his parents are nice enough but probably wouldn't be the most accepting of someone like me. He once told me that before he sees them, he jots topics into his phone so when the conversation eventually stalls, he has something to talk about. Thinking about being in a car with that all the way from JFK to the city doesn't sound appealing at all.

"But I'm having so much fun with the bags, Aunt Sandra. Please don't take them away from me. They're all I have," I joke from my seat, eliciting a sigh and a tired smile.

"Hmm. That's what I thought." She leans down to place a kiss on Holly's head. "I'll see you three later. I'm going to take them to the hotel, and then Neil and I will have dinner with them." She gives Kat and me a kiss on the head as well.

When I'm in LA, my aunt texts me almost daily; she's always been more like a mom than an aunt. But it feels different being in her presence again. I forgot how wonderful she is to us all. I can see how much she's supported Kat, and I'm grateful for it. She treats us like we're her own kids.

"And don't forget, we're all having brunch tomorrow at the hotel," she says as she walks through the living room. "Eleven o'clock. Charlie, you only need to walk downstairs from your room, so I expect you won't be late."

"Or drunk," Kat jokes, earning a glare from me.

"At eleven o'clock?" my aunt asks. "Yes, I suppose you should come sober as well. But that's up to you. Just be on time."

"You know I'm the oldest, right?" I ask, trying to sound offended.

"I do know that, honey."

"And you know that it's Kat and not me who's always late?"

"Not with Jake's mom," Kat chimes in. "She scares me."

"She shouldn't," my aunt responds. "Her son is lucky to have found a woman as amazing as you."

"Thanks, Aunt Sandra." She smiles up from the floor. "You're the best."

"I just love you all. And I'll see you tomorrow. Charlie, you're not leaving this apartment until those bags are done." She points to the mess of bags with a stern look on her face.

"Oh, so Kat gets the sweet comment, and I just get lectured?" I tease.

"She's the bride. Get married, and I'll be nicer." My aunt sends me one last smile before walking out.

I know her comment was a joke, but my entire stomach is now in knots. Mentioning my nonexistent wedding only makes me think about the thing I've been trying to avoid all morning: Annie. Now all I can think about is what she would look like in a white dress.

I give myself an internal shake and pick up the last bag. Thinking about marrying Annie is pointless and will only make my heart hurt more than it already does.

"Now that she's gone, can we pull out the mimosas, and you guys can tell me about last night's drama?" Holly asks, leaving the room before we can answer.

Kat gives me the same look she gave my aunt but doesn't say anything as she picks up one of the gift bags and begins tying a ribbon. A few minutes later, Holly comes back carrying a tray with three drinks on it. She hands two of them to us, sits on the couch, takes a long sip of her mimosa, and gives me the look she's been giving me since we were kids. I'm about to be grilled. "Spill. What happened last night?"

With my aunt's throwaway comment about getting married, plus the fact that talking about last night makes me ache for Annie, I can't even think about putting something in my stomach. I set the glass on the coffee table and let out a sigh. "Just a normal Dawson dinner, Holls. Nothing to report. Just Ian being Ian."

The fact that I'm intently working on one of the gift bags should have told her everything. But I know her well enough to know she isn't going to let things go that easily. "Mom said it was worse than normal."

I shrug and continue working.

"I know it's been years since you've seen him, but you did seem even more agitated than you usually do," Kat adds tentatively. "Before dinner even started. Did he say something?"

I can tell I'm not going to get out of this, so I decide to answer vaguely before moving the conversation along. "You heard him. He was being an asshole. A particularly annoying asshole. I don't want to talk about him anymore. Let's talk about the bachelorette party."

"You must really not want to talk about him if you'd rather talk about wedding planning, but fine," Holly says. She's always been like my uncle, direct and to the point.

I'm honestly surprised she's letting the whole thing go so easily. "The bachelorette party is hardly 'wedding planning,'" I argue. "It's a party. I'm good at parties."

"Which is why you've helped plan so much of it?" Holly rolls her eyes before taking another sip.

I can already tell we're heading to an early afternoon of tipsy Holly Dawson. "Why would I stop you from doing what you do best? You're a planner. I'm a socializer. My job comes later."

"And it sounds like Kat has someone for you to *socialize* with," she says suggestively.

"Kat, I've told you not to set me up."

She shrugs innocently and continues working. "She's already invited. What are you going to do, ignore her the whole night?"

It was one thing when she mentioned this woman yesterday. That was a simpler time, when all I was dealing with was being back in a city that haunts me. Now, I also have to deal with the emotional disarray Annie has caused. I can't wrap my head around hitting on some technician who works with my sister. "Who else is coming?" I ask, desperate for this not to turn into some gossip session about my love life, as things are prone to do with Holly and Kat around.

"Well, the gorgeous Lily from work who you're going to ignore all night," Kat says. "And the three of us, obviously. Lena and Juliet. And a couple women from my book club who I've gotten close to. Am I forgetting anyone?" she asks Holly.

"Annie."

I should get used to that name casually coming out of the mouth of family members, but hearing it still causes my heart to accelerate to an unhealthy rate. Just like the first time I saw her, I go from relatively calm to being able to feel my pulse in every part of my body. There is no topic or thought that doesn't lead back to Annie now. My entire life will forever be pre-Annie and post-Annie. "What do you mean Annie?" I ask a little too loudly.

"I invited her," Kat says simply, seemingly not noticing the wild emotions coursing through me.

I take a subtle breath and try to control the intensity in my voice. "Why would you invite her?"

"Don't judge her just because she's with Ian. Poor girl. I feel bad for her. She has no idea what he gets up to."

My hand tightens on the gift bag. "You think he's up to something?"

"It's Ian," Holly says. "If he's being faithful to that girl, I'll name my first daughter Ian."

"You'd have to go out with someone for more than two dates if you want kids," Kat jokes.

"Plenty of people have children without having a partner," Holly responds.

"True," Kat replies. "And then, you wouldn't have to negotiate with them on naming your daughter Ian."

"He doesn't deserve that honor anyway." Holly gets up and leaves the room. She's back soon after with an open bottle of champagne and refills her glass. Apparently, for my cousin, the pretense of orange juice isn't needed anymore.

"I think Ian likes the idea of Annie's family." Kat's so blasé in how she says *Annie*. She has no idea how the name flows through my body like an electric current. "To him, it's the perfect match. You know, a big real estate family merges with a big hotel family. Plus, you can't deny that they look good together. Like Barbie and Ken."

"But with an actual penis and vagina," Holly offers. "Those dolls are anatomically confusing."

Kat makes a fake sick noise. "Gross, I don't want to think about my twin's penis."

"I wouldn't mind thinking about Annie," Holly says playfully.

My hands pause on the bag. I put all my energy into not reacting to her words, something that is becoming increasingly difficult by the minute. Her comment was flippant, and I'm not even with Annie. Why should I care if Holly thinks she's hot? She *is* hot.

"Why are you being so serious?" Kat asks when I don't contribute anything to their banter. "Who cares who Ian's dating?"

"I don't care," I say, way too defensively. "I just thought it was weird you invited her."

"Look, this is probably the girl he's going to marry. We may as well get to know her."

I'm glad Kat's attention is on the bag because her words feel like they flew out of her mouth and straight into my gut. *Annie marrying Ian?* I can't think of anything I'd rather do less than attend that wedding.

I knew coming back would be hard. It was inevitable that being back would make me feel things only this city can. What I could never have predicted was experiencing an entirely different kind of heartache. The kind only a woman can induce. Even after Jen left, I never felt this discombobulated. And I knew her for six years. I've known Annie for three days. But as I sit here with these damn ribbons surrounding me, I'm having to hold back tears.

Minutes of silence pass with Kat continuing to work until Holly clears her throat loudly. "Well, I think it's very sweet you invited her." She puts her laptop down and claps. "But that's not the important thing we need to discuss. What are you guys wearing tomorrow?"

I feel an instant sense of relief as the topic changes. "Are we supposed to be dressing up? I had planned on skinny jeans."

"You're not wearing skinny jeans to your sister's bachelorette party," Holly says.

"Why? It's not like it's the actual wedding."

"I'm just happy you'll be there," Kat says to me. "Wear whatever you want."

She sends a warm smile my way and again reminds me of our mom. She's so uninhibited with her love, and in New York, and even LA, that's a rare quality.

"If you want me here so much, can we do something more fun than these stupid gift bags?" I ask hopefully.

"Oh God, move aside," Holly says, coming over to sit next me. "You pour the drinks, and I'll bag. That way, my mom won't yell at us, and we can get drunk faster."

"How about Holly finishes the bags, Charlie pours the drinks, and I show you my outfit options for tomorrow night?" Kat skips out of the room toward her bedroom.

"I think you Dawson sisters just manipulated me into doing all the work," Holly says.

"But you're *so* good at it, Holls. I've never seen anyone master ribbons like you. Your students must be in awe."

"Yes, Charlie, my seventh-graders can't believe their teacher can *tie* things."

"I see rhythmic gymnastics in your future."

"Just pour the champagne, asshole."

CHAPTER TEN

The first thing I feel this morning is the pounding in my head, as if some tiny little person is hitting my brain repeatedly with a hammer. I keep my eyes closed as I let the events of the previous night come to my memory. I should have known that mimosas with Holly wouldn't end with just mimosas. The last thing I remember is her doing solo karaoke after we both took shots of tequila.

I vaguely remember her leaving my hotel room at three in the morning, and I'm pretty sure I could hear her singing in the hallway. I should text to make sure she got home okay, but I can't seem to open my eyes, let alone grab my phone.

Kat was the smart one and left before midnight, claiming that she hated karaoke and wanted to save her energy for the bachelorette party. Now that I'm on the other side of that decision, I can see her point. On both karaoke and getting drunk the night before her party. But mainly the karaoke, which was atrocious.

When the pounding against my skull gets unrealistically loud, I lift my body and realize that while my head does hurt, the pounding is a knock on my hotel room door. I force my eyes open so I can look at the clock, and that's all I need to get moving. I have a feeling I know exactly who's on the other side of that door. Aunt Sandra was very clear about being late this morning, and it's already ten minutes past eleven.

Luckily, I passed out in all my clothes last night so I'm not naked. I run to the door and don't even bother to check who it is, assuming it's family ready to lecture me on punctuality.

"I woke you," Annie says, looking fresh-faced and beautiful in a simple pair of jeans and a black V-neck T-shirt.

Maybe it's because I just woke up, but I have trouble forming words. Instead, I allow my eyes to rake over her body. This may be the most casual I've seen her, yet she still renders me speechless.

"Charlie?"

Looking at her face makes it harder to process the fact that she is standing here. Especially when my hangover is starting to settle in. "I meant to set my alarm."

"I thought coming in the morning was the best way to catch you. I didn't have your number. But now I see that was a bad idea. It's Saturday. You probably went out last night."

"My cousin and I had a late night."

She gives me a small smile. "Cute morning voice. Can I come in?"

"That would be good. Considering my whole family is downstairs."

"What?" The smile drops from her face.

I pull open the door. She doesn't hesitate. She moves about as fast as she did at my uncle's house when we were called for dinner. I close the door and move farther into the room. We both stand there silently for what feels like a full minute, and I can't help but wonder if she's thinking about the last time she was here. I never thought I'd see her again after she walked out of this room. Having her back feels surreal.

"Why is your family here?" she asks when the silence goes on.

"Jake's family flew in yesterday, so we're doing brunch."

"Shit. I'm sorry. I didn't know."

"That's because Ian doesn't come to most family things."

"And you do?"

"Why are you here, Annie?"

"I wanted to talk to you. I thought it would be better to do it before your sister's bachelorette party tonight."

"As you can see, now is not a good time."

"Because you're late to family brunch, or because your hair is sticking up like Alfalfa's?"

Her smirk and confident, casual behavior reminds me of the Annie I met on our first night. The one who stood in that exact spot and took control of me.

"Nice to see the docile version of you that I met at dinner was only temporary." I attempt to smooth out my hair.

She takes a few steps closer. "The real me hasn't gone anywhere. You know who I am."

"No. I don't know you at all. And I need a minute." I force myself to move into the bathroom, trying to ignore the hurt on her face. If I don't get downstairs soon, my aunt will be up here, or she'll send someone else. But more than that, I feel like I've been on an emotional roller coaster, and I don't know what to make of Annie's Jekyll and Hyde act.

I do my best to tame my wild hair since I don't have time for an actual shower and quickly brush my teeth before walking back into the room. Annie is sitting on the edge of the bed, but when she sees me, she stands.

"Better?" I ask, pointing to my hair.

"Even with bed hair, you look beautiful. You always look beautiful."

I've never been affected by a woman calling me pretty, but I can feel my whole body warm. I turn to the closet so she can't see my face. "You can't say things like that to me."

"Why not?"

"Because you're with my brother."

"And you won't let me explain."

I grab a pair of pants and a T-shirt that I'm sure Jake's mom won't think is dressy enough, but I'm too distracted to care. I consider it a win that I'm not going down in yesterday's clothes. "Are you going to explain at what point you'll be breaking up with him?"

She takes a step, but the bed is between us, and she can't go far. "No. I mean, not yet. I want to. Soon. But it's complicated with my family."

"Will you turn around?"

She looks confused, so I point down to the fresh clothes I had set on the bed. When she realizes my meaning, she smiles. "You weren't this shy on Wednesday."

"I wasn't that aware on Wednesday," I snap.

The playful expression falls from her face, and she turns. Part of me wishes I could forget everything and engage in the flirty banter she falls into so easily. But I can't flirt with her. Not now that I know she's with Ian. And not because I owe him anything, but because I can feel myself falling for her every time I see her, and that can't happen.

She stays quiet as I put on my shirt. "What family things?" I ask to her back.

I can hear her inhale. "My dad owns a property investment company that's in deep with Ian to franchise the Dawson Hotels. My family's company needs this deal."

I think about that as I button my pants. I vaguely remember something about that deal coming up at dinner and the way my uncle reacted to it. "You're using my brother to help your family business?"

She whips around, seemingly not caring if I'm dressed, which I am. "No more than he's using me."

"But that's who he is. Is that who you are? Does your dad even know you like women?"

Of all the things I've said or asked, of all the ways I've snapped at her in the past two days, nothing has made her face fall quite like my last question.

Her eyes fill with tears. "There's more to it," she whispers.

Before I can ask, the hotel phone on my bedside table is ringing, making me jump. If I don't answer, whoever is calling is going to come up to my room. I walk over to the table and pick up.

Kat's voice speaks loudly on the other end. "I was late, but you're even later. Get your butt down here before Aunt Sandra comes up and drags you down."

My eyes don't leave Annie as my sister talks. She's looking at the ceiling, and it seems as if she's trying to keep her tears from falling. "I'm coming now," I say. "Cool your jets."

"They're cool. Freezing, in fact. It's our darling auntie whose panties are in a bunch." Kat drops her voice. "I think Jake's parents stress her out. Not to mention me. Get down here. *Please.*"

"Okay, okay. I'm coming. Is Holly there?"

She laughs. "The shell of Holly is here. But that's about it. How much did you guys drink last night?"

"I don't want to talk about it."

"Fine. Just get downstairs. I'll order you a water with a side of water."

"You're a gem. See you soon." I hang up, and there's a heavy silence before Annie begins to move toward the door.

"You have to go. I shouldn't have come. I'm sorry. That was stupid."

"Annie."

She stops.

"Let's just talk later tonight."

"At your sister's bachelorette party?" she asks, turning.

"Right. Maybe not the best place. Tomorrow, then. We can find somewhere safer than here."

"I know where we can go," she says, and I hate how the hopeful look on her face makes my body feel all kinds of things it shouldn't.

"I guess I'll see you tonight, then."

The hopeful look is gone as she begins to chew her lip, an act that doesn't help the things I'm feeling. Because now, I'm staring at her lips and wishing they were on mine. "I don't have to go tonight."

I pause, not knowing what to do. Partly why I got so drunk last night was that it was easier than focusing on the prospect of spending Kat's entire bachelorette party with Annie. Now, she's offering a way out of that situation, yet I don't want to take it. She's like a drug, and I want more, even though I know it will hurt me. "Kat wants you there. Don't cancel on her."

"Do you want me there, Charlie?"

"Yes, but I shouldn't."

"Why?"

"You know why."

"And if I wasn't with Ian?"

"Is this something you do often?" I know I need to leave, but there are questions I can't wait to ask, questions I didn't get to ask at my aunt and uncle's house.

"What do you mean?"

"I have a feeling you weren't lost when you found yourself in the Runaway. You certainly knew what to do with a woman once we got back here."

She looks hurt before her features harden. "No. It's not something I do often. I haven't been with a woman since college. But I could say the same thing about you. You seemed comfortable in the bar."

"Yes, but I'm single. You're not."

"I know, Charlie," she says in a loud voice. She puts her hands through her hair as if she's exasperated. When she speaks again, her voice is quiet, and she sounds broken. "I just wanted to pretend for a night, okay? I wanted to be in a lesbian bar and think about what I could have but am too scared to get. I didn't plan any of this. I didn't plan to meet anyone that night."

"You started talking to me, not the other way around." Maybe I'm not good at reading her expressions, but she's looking at me like I'm the most irritating thing she's ever seen.

The hotel phone rings again.

"Nothing good will come of answering that. But I do have to go." My legs don't want to move, but I force them toward the door. When I get next to Annie, I stop. "I'll see you tonight?"

She gives me a long, intense look. I know I should be running downstairs but she has me rooted to the spot. I'm not sure I'll ever be able to leave when she's gazing into my eyes. "I talked to you because I've never been so instantly attracted to someone," she says quietly. "Not dating women hasn't been easy for me. But I've managed because it made things easier at home. Until I saw you, and all that carefully constructed control came crashing down." She touches my hand, and I allow our fingers to lace together. "I came back here with you because I've never wanted anyone more, and I had to have you. I had to taste you. I left because I'm scared of losing my family."

I'm so engrossed that I don't even notice her moving slowly into me until my back hits the door. This is the Annie I met: confident, sultry, and intoxicating. "And now?" I whisper.

"And now I feel right back at the start. Staring at something I desperately want but I know I shouldn't."

"And what will you do about it?" I've lost the power to stop the inevitable.

She unlaces our fingers and grazes up my arm until her hand is resting behind my neck. Our faces are so close that I can feel her breath, and my eyes are fixated on her parted lips. "I'm powerless against you." She places a small, torturous kiss against my lips.

Even that small touch sends my brain into overdrive. The only thing I can process is the need to feel her lips again. She must feel the same because before I can decide to kiss her again, her lips are back on mine. This time, the kiss is not small.

I don't even have to try to push rational thoughts aside. Every single one flies out of my head as I feel her hands in my hair. We don't have long, but all I've been able to think about since Wednesday is kissing her. I have a desperate need to feel my tongue slide against hers. She seems to have the same need; she pushes my mouth open and doesn't hesitate to push her tongue inside.

We both moan, and right now, I may give anything to be allowed to keep kissing her. She explores my mouth like she did on our first night, and I know why she seemed so thorough, so desperate to feel and taste me. For a woman who *really* seems to enjoy being with a woman, not being with one since college must have been torture.

I'm ready to rip her clothes off and disconnect the hotel phone for the rest of the morning. But before I can, Annie pushes gently off me and takes a small step back. She wipes her thumb against my lips and does her best to straighten my wild hair that probably looks about as good as it did when I woke. "Have a good brunch," she says with a smile. "I'll see you tonight. Maybe go downstairs before me. Just in case."

She walks confidently to the door, opens it, and tilts her head. I have no idea how she's so cool and collected when I feel like I'm on fire, but the last thing I need is my aunt or sister seeing her standing there holding the door. I give her a small nod and walk through on incredibly wobbly legs.

I'm shaking as I walk into the elevator, and I'm thankful nobody else is in there so I can lean against the wall and breathe deeply. Hopefully, my family will think I'm just flustered from rushing, not because I was pushed up against a door by Ian's girlfriend.

I close my eyes and sink to the floor. My legs have given out, and I don't know what else to do with myself in this state. "*Fuck*," I say. "I am *so* fucked."

Chapter Eleven

In a family full of big personalities, I've always been one of the more understated members. But if anyone could see me now as I pace back and forth on a quiet sidewalk, they wouldn't believe that.

I smooth out my jumpsuit for the hundredth time as I glance down the street, waiting for everyone else to arrive. In LA, the fashion leans toward intentionally casual, and I'm not used to dressing up. But this is Manhattan, and not only did Holly text me four times to make sure I didn't wear jeans, I'm also hyperaware that Annie will be here.

I shouldn't care what she thinks of my appearance. And I absolutely shouldn't want her to want me. But I'm far past lying to myself. I *do* care. And I *do* want her to want me. My mind and body have been on overdrive since our kiss this morning, and there's nothing I can do to calm it.

So as much as I pretended to resist Holly's fashion advice, I took more time getting ready than I have in years. As I pace past the hotel again, I'm able to catch a glimpse of myself in the lobby window and stop to make sure my hair is still intact after all my moving about. It's rare that I try to tame the wild mess atop my head, and we'll see how long the low bun holds. I doubt it will be long. It never holds.

I take one more look at my black jumpsuit and heels, tilting my head at my own reflection before rolling my eyes at myself. If

I'm going to keep Kat and Holly from thinking something is going on, I need to get a grip. Fretting over my appearance is out of the ordinary.

I turn from the window when I hear a car pull up. Holly climbs out, and if I felt like I was dressed up, it's nothing compared to my cousin. Ever since we were teens, Holly has known how to dress, and tonight, she does not disappoint. With her red curly hair flowing over a skintight green dress, she looks glamorous. Most people who see her like this won't assume she's a teacher by day.

"You don't get points for being early," she says as she walks over. "Nobody but me is here to see it."

"Being on time this morning wouldn't have made Jake's mom like me any more than she did."

"Maybe it's because you showed up looking like you just rolled out of bed."

"Says the woman who came in slippers."

She smiles and takes a step back so she can make a show of analyzing my outfit. "You decided against skinny jeans. Glad to see you still clean up nicely."

"More like I was guilt tripped out of them. By you. If that wasn't clear."

"Still. I did not expect eyeliner. And cleavage."

I self-consciously look at myself. My jumpsuit isn't tight, but the top does cut down my chest, so an ample amount of cleavage is on display.

"You seem nervous," Holly says. "Is it because Kat is bringing her hot friend? Is that why you're in heels?" She smiles widely.

I do my best not to scowl. I may be able to avoid talking about my love life with Kat since she's so much younger, but Holly grew up pestering me about women. We even came out to each other on the same night when we were sixteen. Talking about who we're dating has always been a consistent part of our friendship. "I'm in heels because you told me not to wear my Vans, and that's the only other thing I brought. Besides, how do you know Lily is hot?"

"Kat showed me a photo."

"Why don't you date her? You live in New York and don't have perpetual baggage."

I meant the comment as a joke, but Holly's face becomes uncharacteristically serious. "Or you could let go of that baggage and move home, Charlie. All you have to do is get your head out of your stubborn ass."

I can't help but smile. "You're so much like your dad sometimes."

"And you're like yours. Brilliant and stubborn."

Even with the pretense of teasing, I can tell where this conversation is going, and it's a place I don't want to visit on Kat's bachelorette night. I make a show of looking at my phone so I don't have to answer, and though I can feel her eyes on me, Holly doesn't push the topic.

"Anyway, Lily isn't my type," she says, seemingly reading my mood, which is one of the benefits of hanging out with someone who's known me for so long.

"Not enough tattoos?"

"None, from the photo I saw. She's your type, though. Believe me."

"Everyone seems to think they know my type, yet I don't even know it. Maybe I don't have one."

"You like them feminine but not overly girly. Long hair. Light eyes. Polished. Somewhat sophisticated and cultured. Clean."

"As opposed to dirty?" I laugh at her simplistic description.

"I like a little grit and grunge. Your type is more like…" She trails off as she looks down the street. "Annie."

My stomach drops as soon as the name is out of her mouth. "What? No, it's not," I say, far too defensively, but when Holly turns, she seems confused.

"What are you talking about?" she asks. "Annie," she repeats, pointing down the street. "She's here."

I turn and see Annie walking toward us. Even if Holly wasn't calling me out, that realization does nothing to temper my racing heartbeat. And now that I'm with Annie again, I know that I lied before. I do have a type. And she's walking toward me now.

This part of 10th Avenue is long, and she's still pretty far away, but that gives me more time to stare.

"Now, there's a woman who transcends type," Holly says. "How the hell is *she* with Ian?"

"That's a good question." Until now, I concluded that my major mistake in all of this was going to the Runaway. As if everything would have been fine if I had met Annie in a different context, one in which a "we" was never a possibility. But as she walks toward us as if the entire block is her personal runway, I know that it doesn't matter how I met her. I would have wanted her regardless. My entire body vibrates with desire.

As she gets closer, my breathing becomes shallow, and I'm glad there's enough street noise to cover it up. Annie always affects me strongly, and she's always gorgeous, but tonight, she is literally breathtaking.

Beneath her long, open peacoat, she's wearing an elegant, very short, midnight blue dress, and since our night together, this is the first time I've gotten to see her bare legs. It doesn't help that she's wearing a pair of silver heels that accentuate their length. It takes all the self-control I have not to blatantly stare.

I force my eyes up, landing on an intricate bodice that fits tightly over her breasts. Her hair is swept up high, and though I crave to see it down, flowing in perfect waves over her shoulders, this new view of her exposed neck and pronounced clavicles causes a wave of arousal to hit me.

Once she's in front of us, Holly pulls her into a quick hug, and I'm thankful because now that I can see her and smell her familiar perfume, I'm a useless puddle. "Hey, Annie," Holly says, taking a step back and looking at her outfit. "You look gorgeous. This dress is incredible."

"Wait until you see the back," she says, her eyes moving to me with a heated expression. "But thank you, Holly. You look beautiful, too." Though she's talking to my cousin, her eyes are on me, and I can't help but think the words weren't meant for Holly.

I should act normal and say hello, but my mind is fixated on what the back of her dress looks like. Soon, a silence falls over us with Annie and I staring at each other.

"And you remember Charlie from dinner?" Holly says, breaking the awkward moment with a laugh. "I mean, how could you not? Sounds like it was eventful."

Annie gives me a small smile before her eyes rake down my body. And not subtly. "It was indeed. It's good to see you, Charlie." Her eyes stay on mine for only a moment before she's looking at my outfit again. Or more accurately, my chest. "You look amazing."

"She won't admit it, but she's trying harder tonight because Kat is bringing a hot friend she wants Charlie to meet," Holly chimes in, oblivious to the sexual tension.

Though I can't read Annie's expression, the heat that emanated off her a moment ago is gone. I wish I could say that the only person I dressed up for is her. But even if Holly wasn't here, that would be inadvisable. "I see," she says simply. "Playing matchmaker at her own bachelorette party? That's ambitious."

"Kat has a lot of energy," Holly says.

"Where is she?"

"She'll be here any minute. Two of her childhood best friends got ready with her and planned some surprises."

"And where is your date?" Annie asks, bringing her intense gaze back to mine.

"It's not a date."

"You might change your mind once you see her," Holly says.

"Why? Is she pretty?" Annie asks.

"Very." Holly pushes my shoulder lightly. "Charlie is just being boring. She used to be more fun."

Annie narrows her eyes at me and smirks. "Did she? That's interesting." She points up at the hotel we're standing in front of. "Isn't it against the family rules to eat at a non-Dawson hotel?"

"I'll tell my dad it's for competitive analysis." Holly shrugs. "Besides, the hotel doesn't own the restaurant, and it's one of the best in the city. You have no idea what I had to do to get us a private room."

"Do I want to know?" I'm relieved that the conversation has moved on from my nonexistent date.

Holly shakes her head slowly. "Nope." She turns to Annie. "Kat thinks she's a foodie, even though she works so much that she never eats anything but store-bought ramen. All she said she wanted tonight was a good meal with a small group of friends."

"Well, I'm honored to be invited."

"Of course. Besides, you need to see that not all Dawson dinners end in fights." They both look at me, but as they do, a limousine pulls up to the curb. I've never been more thankful to see obnoxious opulence. The last thing I want to do is talk about Ian.

A giggling Kat, along with her friends, Lena and Juliet, tumble out of the limo. Their loud voices and chatter make me think they had a couple drinks as they got ready. Though I haven't seen Lena or Juliet in seven years, they haven't changed at all. Kat met both in first grade, so I've watched them all grow up. And as much energy as Kat has, it's nothing compared to Lena and Juliet.

"Hello, ladies," Kat shouts far louder than is necessary. "Hello, sister," she says, giving me a hug. "You look so good."

"Hello, sister," I repeat, smiling at her silly mood. "You look even better."

"That's true." She twirls in her dress as she laughs.

"Wow. Charlie Dawson. I haven't seen you in years," I hear before I'm being pulled in for a hug by Juliet.

"Not without me," Lena shouts and throws her arm around Juliet so I'm being smothered by them.

"It's nice to see you both managed to grow up and stay out of prison," I say when they let go.

"Who said we've stayed out of prison?" Lena asks.

"I figured Kat would have told me if her two best friends were incarcerated."

"We don't tell Kat everything," Juliet says, causing Kat to turn from where she's talking to Holly and Annie.

"Honestly, you two tell me *too much*." Kat points at them. "Annie, this is Lena and Juliet. I've known them for, well, forever. So don't listen to a thing they say." She gives her friends a wink. "Guys, this is Annie, Ian's girlfriend."

They pull Annie into a hug, eliciting a laugh. The mention of Ian causes my stomach to tighten as it always does, but I'm almost glad. With Annie looking the way she does, I'll need every reminder that she's untouchable.

"Chloe and Laura are already in the lobby," Kat says once everyone has said their hellos. "And Lily should be here soon," she adds, looking pointedly at me.

"We should head in to make the reservation time," Holly says, showcasing once again why she is the real maid of honor. She may be a bit of a party girl, but she's also neurotic about logistics.

"Sounds good." Kat turns to me. "Charlie, why don't you wait out here for Lily and bring her in when she arrives?"

"I'm sure she'll be able to find her way." I give her a sisterly glare that I know she'll recognize. If she's trying to be subtle, she's failing.

"Personal touch, Charlie," Kat repeats from yesterday.

I can't get a sober Kat to understand why setting me up during the few short weeks I'm home is a bad idea, so I certainly won't be able to get this overly tipsy Kat to see reason. And it doesn't matter because a moment later, she is shuffling the others into the hotel.

"Take the elevator at the back of the lobby up to the 56th floor," Holly says as she follows. "They'll show you to the table."

Annie is the last to follow, and before she goes, she looks at me with a serious expression. I wish I could pull her into a kiss and tell her that this silly "setup" means nothing. The only person I want to date is her. But for so many reasons, I can't.

I'm left standing on the street alone, wishing Kat had listened to me for once in our lives. I spend the next few minutes regretting the flimsy jacket I wore. Luckily, I don't have to wait long. Soon, a yellow cab pulls up, and a light-haired woman with the longest legs I've ever seen steps gracefully out of the car.

"You must be Charlie," she says as she walks up to me.

"I am." I put my hand out. She ignores it in lieu of leaning in to kiss my cheek.

When she pulls away, I'm able to get a better look, and Holly is right. Lily is hot. Beautiful, in fact. She has on a simple, short black dress and heels and seems like the type of woman who could get into any Manhattan nightclub with just a flip of her long blond hair and turn around to run a *Fortune 500* company the next day.

"Kat said you'd be waiting. How chivalrous."

I can already tell she's in flirt mode. It's clear that she is confident, and I'm guessing she has no trouble finding dates. "Not really," I say with a small smile that I hope isn't too inviting. "Ready to get out of this cold?"

"Absolutely. Lead the way, gorgeous."

In normal circumstances, I would recognize my in and take it. Especially with those beautiful blue eyes giving me a not-so-subtle look of desire. But my mind is still in Annie-land, and I don't know if it will ever leave. I lead the way into the building. The sooner we get upstairs, the sooner I can see Annie again.

Zenith, the restaurant that sits on top of the hotel, is known for its superb food but also its stunning views. As we step off the elevator, I can see why. The entire room is lit by small, twinkling lights hanging delicately from the ceiling, and the large windows allow us to see the full effect of the New York skyline. Everywhere I turn, I'm gifted with a different view of Manhattan and beyond. I can't remember the last time I saw the city like this.

After getting my name, the hostess leads us through the main room to a private dining room with a long table and the rest of our party, including two new women who I assume are Chloe and Laura.

Just like the main part of the restaurant, this room feels majestic, with floor to ceiling windows. But even with a clear view of the Empire State Building, plus the elegant ambience of the room, I can't tear my eyes away from Annie at the end of the table.

Now that her coat is off and I can see her whole dress, I'm grateful the reveal didn't happen in front of Holly. I would have given myself away. My mouth goes dry, and I have no idea what she meant when she mentioned the back. There *is* no back. In fact, with both her back and her long legs exposed, there isn't much dress to speak of. The only thing that might save me from drooling is the fact that the only two empty chairs are on the other end of the table.

"Oh, good, you're here," Kat says loudly, holding up a drink she's already consumed most of.

I take the seat next to her, that still gives me a good view of Annie, while Lily moves into the chair across from me. As we settle, Kat introduces us to Chloe and Laura, and though I say a polite hello, I'm so consumed by Annie that I can't even remember who's who.

Kat leans into me. "Isn't the view amazing?"

"It is. I know you've been wanting to come here."

"I'm sad Jake can't be here." She pouts. "He's been dying to try it."

"None of that tonight," Juliet says. "You get him for the rest of your life. Tonight, we party."

"By eating," Kat says with a giant smile.

Holly, sitting on the other side of Kat, lets out a loud laugh. "You didn't think we were just having dinner tonight, did you?"

"We're not?"

"This is a bachelorette party. This is just stop one."

"I don't remember the last time I went out past ten."

"That's because you work too hard at the clinic," Lily chimes in before looking at the rest of the table. "Believe me, I see her do it daily."

"How about you just take over for me?"

Lily smiles. "I'm not qualified for that."

The conversation is interrupted when a server comes into the room and takes another round of drink orders. As I hear Annie order a bourbon, I'm thrown right back into my hotel room and memories of how that dark liquor tasted on her lips. It's not until I hear my name that I'm shaken out of the moment. When I look back to Lily, her eyes are on me.

"Sorry, what?"

"I asked if you're an animal lover like your sister is," she says.

"Oh. I guess." I try to temper the blush I feel creeping up my face after getting caught daydreaming. "Not like Kat. I don't want to see them when they're sick."

"Charlie is scared of dogs," Kat says playfully. "When we were younger, a dog sniffed her, and she never recovered."

"The dog didn't *sniff* me. He tried to eat my underwear."

"It was a teacup chihuahua," Kat says, fully laughing. "I don't even think it was capable of doing that."

I hate how warm my entire body feels when I see Annie laughing along with Kat, but the sight makes me smile despite myself. "Whatever." I roll my eyes and turn my attention back to Lily. "How long have you worked at the clinic?"

"A year. Your sister has taught me so much. And she's become a very good friend."

"I couldn't have gotten through this year without you." Kat blows her a kiss. "And I'm very happy you two are finally meeting." Even if she wasn't tipsy, Kat wouldn't be subtle, so I'm not surprised by her comment or the pointed look she's directing at Lily and me, even if it does make me squirm.

"I'm glad, too," Lily says, and her eyes roam from my face to my chest. I feel a wave of annoyance.

"What's your next exhibit?" Annie asks. The question is so abrupt that it takes me a moment to realize she's talking to me.

I look at her before answering and wonder if her intention was to end my conversation with Lily. Either way, I'd rather be talking art with her than past canine trauma, and her slight show of jealousy makes me happier than it should. "We're featuring a few different local artists who all focus on geometric abstraction. Each one uses a different medium. One of my favorites uses recycled products to create models and then photographs them. They're beautiful."

"That sounds fascinating." She leans forward. "One of my favorite courses was about cubism, and I've always been intrigued as to how it's evolved."

I open my mouth to ask her about school, but I'm cut off by Lily. "Are you an artist too?" she asks Annie.

She wrestles with a response as a round of drinks and appetizers are delivered. I know she's not comfortable talking about her own experience in the art world, so I'm curious as to what she'll say.

"No, not really," she says as the group starts digging into the food. "But I went to art school."

"I didn't know that," Holly says, looking between us. "I guess you two have that in common."

"Among other things," I say.

Holly's brow furrows slightly, but everyone else is too inebriated and distracted to think anything of my comment. Annie doesn't seem shocked or upset. Her expression sends a shiver down my body, and if there was any question as to which version of her is here tonight, there isn't any longer. This one owns the room, and I catch myself thinking of this her as *my* Annie.

"You're pretty sexy when you talk about art," Lily says to me.

"Damn, girl. Can I borrow some of that confidence when I hit on men?" Lena asks from beside her.

She directs a flirtatious smile at me, not bothered about being called out. "You just have to set your sights on someone and go for it."

"Do you like art, Lily?" Annie asks.

A look of surprise crosses Holly's face. I'm not sure if she sensed something's off or if she's just not used to such a vocal, confident version of Annie.

Lily hums as she takes a sip of wine. "Well, sure. I like to go to the Met now and then, and there was this fabulous photography exhibit at the Guggenheim recently. Kat and I went. But I can't remember the artist's name. Something to do with poverty."

"That was good," Kat says. By the way her S slurs, I can tell she's getting drunker by the minute.

"That was Peggy Jackson's work. I saw it, too." Annie looks like she just won some contest, and her confident look goes straight to my pussy.

A group of servers enters with several family-size entrees, but despite how good it all smells, I feel like I have the freedom to ask Annie more about herself, and I don't want to miss the opportunity. "What kind of art did you make?"

She gives me a thoughtful look. Tonight, she doesn't seem guarded like she did the night we first met. Her expression is open, and I can see the spark that first drew me to her flashing in her eyes. "I've dug into a few. But lately, I focus on portraits using charcoal."

My eyebrows rise and not because of her medium. I'm surprised she's speaking about it in the present tense. "How do you keep your fingers so clean?" I smile.

"It's groundbreaking. I use soap. Clean and ready," she says, wiggling her fingers.

I open and close my mouth, and it's not because I can't think of anything to say. I just can't think of anything *appropriate* to say.

"Now, portraits are an art form I can get behind," Lily says. "When I see modern art, I don't really know what I'm looking at. Like, anyone could have thrown some paint on a canvas, you know?"

Out of the corner of my eye, I see my sister flinch. If there was anything Lily could have said to turn me off, she just said it. It's not that I need to date an art expert. But someone who lumps all modern art into one category and can't see the beauty in so many of its forms isn't for me.

"Try these scallops," Kat says, pushing something onto my plate. "They're amazing."

I know she is trying to smooth over the moment, but I wasn't going to respond to Lily's comment anyway. We're not on a date, so it doesn't matter if we're compatible. I take a bite as the rest of the table starts talking about the dishes. I'm relieved that food has taken over as the center of attention. As much as I enjoy talking to Annie about art, it's exhausting trying to balance my desire with needing to keep it a secret.

As we eat, the Zenith servers make sure that our glasses are never even close to empty, and by the time the dessert is being cleared from the table, I can feel a heavier buzz.

"So where is stop number two?" Kat asks Holly.

"You'll see," she replies as she signs the bill and puts on her coat.

Kat rubs her stomach in an exaggerated way as she leans back. "Well, at least tell me that stop number two is the last stop. I'm so full, I could sleep for a week."

"Yes, I know you very well." Holly puts her arm around Kat's chair. "Dad secured us a suite at the Dawson Midtown. We can pass out there later."

"Does Jake know I'm not coming home tonight?"

"Yes, he knows."

I catch Annie's gaze as I put on my jacket, and I know she's thinking the same thing I am. The only thing the Dawson Midtown will ever remind me of is my night with her, and I'm desperate to know if she's planning on joining the group there later. That seems too tempting and risky.

"Are we all ready?" Holly looks around the table.

"Are we all getting into cabs?" Laura—or Chloe—asks as we all start to stand.

"No, no," Juliet replies. "The limousine is ours for the night. It's our gift to the bride for her bachelorette party."

"I have the best friends," Kat says.

"Remember that sentiment tomorrow when you're nursing your massive hangover," Lena replies.

"Let's do it, then. Our next reservation awaits. And ladies," Holly says before looking dramatically around. "I hope you're ready to dance."

CHAPTER TWELVE

Tunnel?" Lena asks as our limo pulls up to a club. "I've wanted to come here for ages, but the line is always so long."

"That doesn't seem to have changed," Juliet replies, looking at the line that goes from the front door all the way down the block.

"What's Tunnel?" Kat asks, pressing her face against the window.

I'm sitting between Lily and Annie, and I'm such a mix of uncomfortable and turned on that I just want to get out. I don't care if it's a fancy club or a bowling alley, as long as I'm not sandwiched between these two for much longer.

"It's a very popular club," Holly replies. "Huge dance floor. Amazing cocktails. You'll love it."

"You had me at dance floor," Kat says. "But will we get in?"

The door of the limo opens, and Holly motions for everyone to get out. "My dear cousin, who do you think I am? Of course we'll get in."

Like I've seen her do so many times before, Holly marches to the front of the line and whispers something in the bouncer's ear. He looks at a list, gives her a nod, and then says something into a walkie-talkie. I've never seen her turned away from any door in this city, and I'm not surprised that hasn't changed.

After a minute of waiting in the cold, a woman comes out the door and motions for us to follow. "Well, this feels very VIP," Lily says as we follow Holly into the club.

"I told you," Holly replies, looking over her shoulder with a wink. She's so in her element. "Only the best for our queen tonight."

"I'm so glad I made you one of my maids of honor," Kat says, practically skipping. "We'd be at Hooters if Charlie was in charge."

"I can hear you," I call from the back of the line.

"Love you, Choo Choo," she shouts back.

I hear a low chuckle next to my ear. When I turn, Annie is standing there with a small smile on her perfect lips. "Choo Choo?"

I narrow my eyes but can't help a smile at the playful look she's giving me. "Don't even think about calling me that."

"But why?" She lets out a louder laugh. "I think it suits you. Very sexy."

We're side by side, and her fingers brush against mine. "Are you into trains, Annie?" I ask, allowing my fingers to touch hers again.

She gives me a heated look. "No, Charlie," she says in a low voice. "Just you."

Our eyes lock, and we both stop walking. Something tangible vibrates between us that has nothing to do with the music pressing against my eardrums and everything to do with our explosive chemistry. But as I begin to lace our fingers, someone grabs my arm.

"Come on," Holly says, moving me toward the front. "You're going to want to see your sister's face when we get in there."

I've never been to Tunnel. Big clubs aren't my scene anymore. But Holly has been talking about it nonstop. As we enter, it becomes clear how the club came to its name. We walk through a long dark tunnel that's only lit by colorful strobes bouncing off the walls. The whole experience feels like walking into some kind of gay funhouse.

That feeling only intensifies in the club itself as we are greeted with an explosion of lights, noise, and dancing bodies. The club is huge, three stories, all centered around a main room on the ground floor that features a large dance floor and DJ booth. Along the side of the club are roped off VIP booths.

The sheer magnitude isn't the most eye-catching thing. Plastered all around the room, including on a huge poster on the DJ booth and the shirts the bartenders are wearing, is Jake's smiling face. I turn to Kat's wide eyes as she sees her fiancé's face on every surface.

"That's a lot of Jake," someone shouts behind me. It was either Chloe or Laura, but I still can't tell the difference.

When we follow Holly to the edge of the dance floor, the music gets quiet, and a spotlight hits my sister.

"Ladies and gentlemen," a voice booms from the DJ booth. "We have a bachelorette party in the house tonight! Everyone give it up for Kat and her fiancé, Jake. I'm sure you know him. Or are drinking on his face right now." He pauses as the crowd, including our party, lets out a loud cheer. "Now, make sure you get a good look at this bride. Because as of tonight, this one is off the market. Kat, this jam is for you. Party hard tonight. The first round is on Tunnel."

The music picks back up, and the spotlight dims, allowing me to see Kat's glowing, smiling face. "I can't believe that just happened." She turns to Holly. "How did you manage all this?"

"Dad knows the manager," Holly responds, shrugging as if this was nothing.

"Ladies, if you'll follow me, I'll show you to your booth," the club employee says before moving along the side of the room to the VIP section.

We follow her into a roped off area full of large leather booths that face the dance floor. Scattered around the table is more alcohol than we'll be able to drink, especially considering how much the group has already consumed.

"Put your coats down and come dance your faces off," Kat shouts before flinging her coat into the booth and grabbing Lily and Juliet's hands so she can pull them to the dance floor. Lena, Chloe, and Laura all follow.

"I'm going to have a drink first," Holly says, sliding into the booth.

"Coming?" Annie asks, looking at me and gesturing to the dance floor.

I glance at the packed area. "I think I'll join Holly for a drink first."

"Let me guess, you don't dance," she responds.

"I *can* dance," I reply with a smirk. "I just prefer to watch other people do it."

"Well, then," she replies with her own smile. "Enjoy the show." Without another word, she turns toward the dance floor and walks off, swaying her hips.

I didn't know I could feel so many conflicting things at once. Even if Annie wasn't with Ian and in the closet with her family, I don't live in this city. There's nothing but obstacles in the way for us. But as I watch her step gracefully onto the dance floor and twirl, I don't think I've ever wanted something or someone more. And I'm now realizing how ironic this entire situation is. I left this city to get away from Ian and memories that hurt too much. And now, because of him, I can't imagine leaving.

"Are you going to sit here all night?" Holly asks as she slips her sweaty body into the booth and pours herself a drink.

"We all have our parts to play. Mine is sitting here making our VIP section look so good."

Holly rolls her eyes before she takes a long sip and sets her drink down on a coaster with Jake's face on it.

"This is amazing, Holls," I say, flicking one of the Jake coasters at her. "You've done an incredible job."

Her face lights up as she looks at Kat dancing. "Thanks. I'm just glad she's having fun." We're both quiet for a moment. I'm in no rush to break the silence now that we're both looking at the dance floor, and I feel like I have free rein to watch Annie. "I saw you sitting next to Miss Lily in the limo. How's that going?"

I take a deep breath. The limo ride just reminds me of being close to Annie, her bare leg pressed against me. But I can't say any of that, so I shake my head. "She's very beautiful. But that's not going anywhere."

"It was the modern art comment, wasn't it?"

"I mean, that didn't help. But the whole thing was a bad idea to begin with. I can't start a long-distance relationship."

"Your sister just wants to see you happy. You haven't dated in a while."

"I've been busy," I say, which isn't a complete lie. Moving to LA and making sure the gallery is a success without being able to lean on my old contacts has been hard enough. I haven't had the time or energy to put into dating again.

"Has there been anyone? Even casually?"

We were so drunk when we hung out the other night that we didn't get into any real conversations. I'm not surprised she's curious; these are the things we're used to talking about. Maybe it's the alcohol or that I miss having someone to confide in, but I don't mean for my next words to slip out. "There's been one person. But it's not an actual thing and never will be."

Holly's eyes snap from the dance floor to my face. "It's not Jen, is it?"

"Jen? God. No."

"You're back in New York. Old memories come up."

"Not good ones."

"Then you won't care if I tell you that I heard she's engaged?"

"I couldn't care less. She did us both a favor."

"Good. I never liked her anyway."

"Who's she engaged to?"

"Some social media influencer."

"That's not surprising. She only ever wanted me for my parents' money and name. Evidenced by the fact that she left me the moment it was all gone."

"You can do a lot better." Holly holds up her drink in a toast. "Good riddance to greedy lesbians."

I laugh and tip my glass against hers, relieved that the conversation became about Jen and not the revelation that there's someone I'm interested in.

"Who's the greedy lesbian?" Annie asks from beside our table.

I didn't see her leave the dance floor. She slides into the booth beside me, and I have to remind myself once again not to stare, despite the way the perspiration coating her skin causes the hair to stick there, reminding me of our hot sweaty night.

"We were just talking about Charlie's ex," Holly responds.

"And now we're done," I say, trying to give Holly a pointed look that will get her to shut up.

"Oh, come on, Charlie," she replies with a smile. "Everyone loves hearing about lesbian drama. Right, Annie?"

She looks hesitantly between the two of us. "Is there drama?"

"No. There hasn't been ex drama for years."

"Perhaps. But she was just about to tell me who she's been crushing on." Holly seems entirely too pleased with herself, and I should have known she wouldn't let my comment pass. She lives for romantic gossip.

"Really?" Annie asks. I can't tell if she's concerned. More than anything, she looks amused.

"I wasn't about to tell you anything. I was about to change the topic."

Annie gives me a smile. "I'll help. How's Logan, Holly?"

"You two are boring." She rolls her eyes. "But he's fine."

"I've been gone for years, and he didn't even bother to show up for our family dinner," I say, jumping on any opportunity. "Some cousin he is."

"That's my brother for you. Logan lives in his own world. He just started rehearsals for a show downtown, so I expect to see him even less than I already do."

"When will I see him?" I ask.

"The rehearsal dinner, I suppose. He's wearing a kilt."

"Why?"

She lets out a long sigh. "Because I told him he couldn't wear one to the wedding."

"Are you guys Scottish?" Annie wonders.

"Not enough to warrant a kilt," Holly says. "But Logan is Logan. I've given up trying to make sense of his whims. He wore a beret to his high school graduation."

"I forgot about that." I laugh at the memory of my cousin in his red beret among a crowd of white caps.

"And it could be worse," Holly continues. "He could be Ian."

An awkward silence falls over the table before Holly's eyes go wide. "Shit, I'm sorry, Annie. I'm an asshole. Don't let me drink any more." She makes a show of pushing her drink aside, but Annie simply smiles and waves her hand.

"It's okay, you can drink," she says, leaning over me so she can push Holly's drink back in front of her. "I know how challenging brothers can be."

Holly looks relieved before her face morphs into confusion. "I thought you only had a sister?"

Having little to no actual knowledge of Annie's life, I'm fascinated to know more about her family, but her face has taken on a serious, almost sad expression. She's quiet for a moment as she pours some water.

"I have both," she answers in a quiet voice that's hard to hear over the music.

"I'm learning all kinds of new things about you tonight," Holly replies. "In fact, I think this is the most I've ever heard you speak. I had no idea you were an artist."

"I'm not really," she says, staring at the water.

"Are the portraits you do ever nudes?" Holly asks.

I roll my eyes. "Holly's mind is perpetually focused on sex. Ignore her."

Annie turns, and the serious expression is replaced by a heated one. She brings her gaze from my face slowly to my chest. "And yours isn't?" I can feel my face grow warm, but I don't need to say anything because Annie is turning back to Holly as if nothing happened. "I've never done nudes. Just faces. And they're not all realistic. Some of them are quite abstract."

"What art school did you go to?" I ask.

"Art Institute of Chicago."

I don't know what I was expecting, but her answer surprises me. "Impressive."

"Where did you go?"

"Pratt."

"Impressive," she replies. "What kind of art did you make?"

"Everything. But I wasn't that good. It's my eye that's the talent."

"Yes, I've heard you speak of this eye."

"I actually have two of them."

"I've noticed." Her tone is dry and playful, and as much as I love the banter, I'm curious to know more about her.

"SAIC is one of the best art schools in the world. Why on earth are you working in property investment?" I know this is part of the conversation that we're meant to have on our own, but two things seem to happen when I'm with her: either I stare in a complete state of arousal, or I'm desperate to ask questions. Usually, those things are happening at the same time. Even with Holly sitting here, I want to know more. I don't want to wait.

She's quiet as she takes a sip and looks at the dancing bodies. Finally, she turns to me, and I almost regret asking the question. The heat is gone, replaced by the same sadness as when she mentioned her brother. "The agreement with my parents was that they'd let me go to art school if I got some real-world work experience after. In their company. I guess it just became easier to stay. Art was never a guarantee, and that was."

"But you're talented. They let you just throw that away?"

"You don't know that," she says quietly, turning her gaze back to the dance floor.

I'm about to answer that I do, but Holly's sitting there. She has the same expression that she did in the restaurant: confused, like she's watching a foreign movie without subtitles.

"Water, water, water!" Kat rushes toward the booth, waving her hands.

Part of me is annoyed that the moment is interrupted, barring me from asking Annie any more questions. But Holly is still watching us with the same confusion, and I'm thankful for the chance to move the attention onto my sister.

Following Kat are Lena and Juliet, who slide next to Holly. Juliet begins pouring water into glasses and handing it to a sweaty and very drunk Kat and Lena. Kat drinks the entire glass before refilling it. "I will not have my maids of honor sitting here all boring while we dance the night away," she says before taking another long sip. "Especially you, missy." She points at me.

I smile as the water ungracefully drips down her chin and onto her dress. "I thought we decided against the 'missy' nickname?"

"That was not a mutual decision. Now, come dance."

"I need a shot first." I reach for the bourbon.

"No shots. Just dancing," Kat whines.

"Yeah, Choo Choo. Just dancing," Annie says with a flirtatious smile.

I smile back and can't help my eyes flicking to her lips. I know Holly is still watching, but it's hard not to flirt. "Fine. But only if you come—"

"Annie, is this yours?" Holly's holding up a phone. "Ian's calling."

Annie takes it. She's handling it so gingerly, it's as if she's holding a bomb that's about to go off.

"Don't answer," Holly says. "This is a girls-only night. Ian can wait."

Annie simply stares at the phone. When it stops ringing, she looks like she's been slapped. She's the version of her that I met at my aunt and uncle's house: timid, scared, and unsure of herself. "I should call him back."

"Call him later," I reply in a low voice, not even caring that the table is watching us.

She looks at her phone again and shakes her head. "Will you move so I can get out?" she asks me, and it takes me a moment to realize what she means.

I give her one more look before moving. She doesn't make eye contact as she takes her phone and walks to the front of the club. It may have only been a phone call, but her decision to leave this moment to go call my brother is the reality check I need.

"Shot?" Holly asks, holding up a bottle.

"Let's dance," I mumble, needing to do something other than sit here and wallow over the woman who just walked away.

"Yes!" Kat grabs my hand and pulls me toward the dance floor.

CHAPTER THIRTEEN

I was telling Annie the truth earlier. I *can* dance, I just usually go to bars where it's unnecessary. I couldn't grow up in the Dawson household without learning to dance from my mom. She even made Ian learn ballroom when we were kids.

As soon as we hit the dance floor, Kat twirls me around, and I let the music flow through me, trying to forget about the fact that my heart feels like it's being clenched. After a few songs, Kat leaves to go to the bathroom, so I close my eyes and let myself become enveloped by the music. As the DJ smoothly transitions into the next song, I feel a pair of hands on my hips, and when I turn my head, Lily is pulling me into her.

This is the exact situation I tried to avoid all night, and even though a voice in the back of my head is telling me to move away, I don't. Maybe it's the alcohol. Or maybe it's the jealousy over Annie and Ian, but I don't have the energy to fight this anymore.

Lily seems enthusiastic about my consent because she pulls me closer and presses her body tightly against mine. Soon, we're moving seamlessly, and her hands are moving freely around my waist and front. When the music changes tempo, she turns me so that we're face-to-face.

As I look into her inviting gaze, it's obvious how much easier this would be. And if I do give in, it can snap me out of whatever Annie spell I seem to be under. Lily brings her hands from my hips to my waist before clasping them behind my neck. As we continue to move together, I can feel her breath on my lips, but I feel none of the urgency that I felt with Annie.

And yet, when Lily gives me a small smile, then leans in to kiss me, I do nothing to stop it. I'd do anything to get my mind off the woman talking to my brother outside.

The second our lips touch, everything feels wrong. Even if I can't have Annie, I can't turn off my feelings. And casual sex with Lily has no appeal. If I have to long for Annie from afar until I can get back to LA and move on from New York all over again, so be it. Continuing this kiss wouldn't be fair to Lily or me.

"I'm sorry, I can't." I take a small step back so we're no longer touching.

She looks at me thoughtfully, but her features are soft, and she doesn't seem upset. She simply gives me a small smile and nods. "Because of Annie?"

If I was expecting that, I may have been able to school my features in time, but I am not, and my mouth drops, giving me away in an instant.

"It's okay," she says quickly. "I won't say anything."

"Was I that obvious?"

She lets out a small but not unkind laugh. "No. Actually, she was the obvious one. It kind of felt like she was a dog marking her territory. She kept glaring at me in the limo."

I let out a small laugh; that sounds so much like something my sister would say. "Do all vets make animal references in every conversation?"

"Only the cool ones," she says, now fully smiling.

I feel an instant sense of relief that this isn't awkward. "I can see why Kat likes you."

"Your sister has good taste."

I catch a glimpse of Kat back on the dance floor, and my stomach tightens. I turn back to Lily. "Do you think she knows?"

"No, I don't think she noticed."

"It's just a crush." I don't know if I'm trying to convince her or myself.

"I can't blame you. She's very beautiful." She puts her hand out. "Friends?"

"Friends." Instead of shaking my hand, she pulls it to her lips and places a soft kiss there.

"If you ever change your mind, I'll be here," she says before smiling and winking. "Saving animal lives and looking amazing as I do it."

I laugh again. "Good to know. I'm going to go have a drink. I'll see you soon."

She gives a small nod before turning into the crowd and rejoining the others. I take one deep breath before heading back to the booth where Holly's sitting. Despite what's happening with Annie, the conversation with Lily went better than I could have hoped. But my relief is short-lived when I see Holly's expression. I assume it works well on her seventh graders. I'm about to be interrogated.

"What's going on, Charlie?"

"With what?" I answer in the most casual voice I can muster, even though I know what she's referring to.

"Annie left. She seemed upset."

"She left?" I look toward the front of the club, but I can't see her anywhere.

"It seemed to coincide with you kissing Lily."

I maintain eye contact, but I know she can see right through me. It doesn't help that I'm shaking. "She probably went to see Ian."

"Then you're telling me what I'm sensing is off?"

"I don't know what you're sensing."

"Don't bullshit me, Charlie. I know you too well. And I know when you're into someone. There's been a weird energy between you all night." She lowers her voice. With the music blaring, I can hardly hear. "Please tell me she's not the person you mentioned earlier."

I don't want to shout, so I slide next to her. "I can't tell you that."

"That's Ian's *girlfriend*."

"You don't think I know that?"

But she doesn't look judgmental like I thought she would. She looks concerned. "Does she have feelings for you, too?"

"No." I rub my hands across my face.

"Are you sure?"

"I know she's attracted to me. I don't know how much deeper it goes."

"But it goes deeper for you?"

I feel completely overwhelmed, and it's not just the line of questioning; it's everything hitting me all at once. Maybe talking to someone about it is what I need to show me just how crazy it is. I drop my head to the table and let out a long groan.

I feel Holly's hand on my back. "Hey. Take a breath, and talk to me."

When I lift my head, the concerned expression is gone, and she looks like she's trying to hold back a laugh. "Why are you smiling?"

"I'm not." She changes to an unconvincing scowl. "I just haven't seen you exude this much emotion in years. It's nice."

"This is *nice*?" I ask too loudly.

"No. This is a mess. But seeing you feeling something—whatever it is—is nice."

Now that everything's out in the open, I feel desperate to talk. I put my head in my hands and let out another groan. "Holly, what do I do?"

"Okay, back up. Is this just an attraction or has something happened?"

I look at the dance floor to make sure Kat is still there before I answer. "We met the night I arrived in New York. I didn't know she was with Ian. I didn't know until I saw her at your mom and dad's."

"The dinner that just keeps on giving. I really missed a good night. Where did you meet?"

"The Runaway."

"As in, the lesbian bar? Why was she at the Runaway?"

I give her a pointed look. Sure, sometimes straight women go with friends, but usually, there's only one reason to go there, and it's to meet women.

"Oh," she replies before a realization hits her. "*Oh.* And you two slept together?"

I nod slowly.

"And has it happened again?"

"No. It can't. And Kat can't know. It will ruin her wedding. Ian will think I was trying to sabotage his relationship."

"Then, you need to talk to Annie. Because I'll tell you one thing, that girl can't keep her eyes off you."

I hate how much her words make my stomach explode in tiny little butterflies, and I feel irrationally happy hearing from both Lily and Holly that Annie was obvious about her attraction tonight.

"And you're right. It will make things tricky with the wedding. Kat's sensitive about you and Ian. Maybe figure things out once it's over."

"I'll be in LA."

"Even easier, right? Isn't that what you want?" she asks, using her annoying teacher voice, as if she knows that it's not.

I don't answer because I don't have an answer. Going back to LA *should* be what I want. But the thought just makes me feel empty.

"Here," Holly says after a few minutes of silence. She reaches across the table, grabs my phone, and hands it to me. She then grabs her own and starts typing. A moment later, I have a text containing a contact card from her phone. "That's Annie's number. Go call her. Find her. Talk to her."

"Tonight?" I stare at the screen. Just seeing it makes my heart rate feel like it picked up.

"She looked pretty upset, Charlie. At least call her."

I look at the dance floor. "What about Kat? Won't she notice if I leave?"

"Kat has consumed sixty percent of the alcohol she'll drink all year in one night. I don't think she remembers that she's a vet, let alone who's still here. I'll get her back to the hotel. We'll see you for breakfast."

I nod as I continue to watch Kat. Holly's not wrong. Kat is *drunk*. In fact, I don't remember the last time I've seen her this drunk. As she and the others begin to do a sloppy conga line, I make my decision. I need to find Annie.

When I turn back to say good-bye, Holly has another grin that she can't seem to hide, despite her obvious effort.

"What now?"

"Nothing," she says with a shrug. "Just ironic that you and Ian fell for the same woman."

I narrow my eyes. "I feel like you're enjoying this too much."

"Just feels like old times," she says, her smile softening.

I pull her into a hug that I think surprises us both. Her hands come around my back, and she pulls me in tighter, just like her dad did. Even if I know I'll never be able to live this down, she's still here for me, like she always has been. It's only being back with this kind of support that I realize how much I've missed it.

"Thanks, Holly. For everything," I say, releasing her.

"Go get your girl. Or you know, Ian's girl," she says when I stand.

"I can't believe I was just thinking that I missed you."

"Aw, that's sweet. See you at breakfast tomorrow." She winks.

"See you at breakfast."

I look at my phone as I walk toward the front of the club. Now that I have Annie's number, I'm desperate to call her. I don't know what I'm going to say, but it's time we had the conversation we should have had days ago. My fingers are shaking, but as soon as I'm out onto the cold, quiet street, I click on the number.

"Hello?" Annie says on the other end. As soon as I hear her voice, it becomes clear that I don't need to see her for her to affect me. Just her voice does things to my body. "Charlie?" she asks when I don't say anything.

"Hi," I say quickly. "How'd you know it was me?"

She lets out a low laugh. "You have an LA area code. It was just a guess."

"Right," I say, mentally face-palming for my lack of cool. "Can we talk? Maybe find a diner or something?" She is quiet for so long that I look to make sure the call didn't drop. "Annie?"

"I'll send you an address. Buzz suite twelve once you're here."

A tornado of nerves flows through my body at the prospect of being alone with her, but I do my best to keep my voice steady. "On my way."

Chapter Fourteen

I thought Annie might take me to her apartment, but I'm here on the Lower East Side, looking at a slightly run-down building. I have a feeling this isn't where she lives, especially considering her family's background and money.

The building's keypad is next to the large steel door, but there are no names next to the numbers. I press twelve, and after only a moment, there's a loud buzzing noise, allowing me to open the door.

Annie's floor isn't any more inviting than the outside, and there's such a heavy draft flowing through the hallway that as I walk toward the door, I pull my jacket around myself to keep warm. Somehow, I can't picture Annie, always so clean and put together, in a building like this. It feels more like a warehouse than anything.

But when I knock and the door opens, the Annie standing in front of me is not the pristine version I'm used to. She's traded her dress for a pair of ripped, paint-stained jeans and a worn green T-shirt that says "School of the Art Institute of Chicago."

Her hair is still up, but it's messier than earlier, and she's barefoot. Every style I've seen on her works, but there's something special about casual Annie. As if I'm seeing a rare species that nobody ever gets to see. "You found it." She opens the door wider so I can see into one large room.

As adorably sexy as Annie looks in this outfit, this may be the first time she doesn't steal all my attention. For once, it's what's behind her that I can't stop staring at. "This place is yours?" I move in without an invitation. I can't help it. Not when I can see a large canvas against the far wall of the room showcasing a splattering of vibrant colors.

"Not just mine," she says, closing the heavy door and following me. "I share with two other artists. But nobody I know has ever been here. Or even knows I rent it."

"Ian doesn't know?" I ask, looking at the piece in front of me that is probably over eight feet tall.

She lets out a harsh laugh. "Of course not. He and I have become accustomed to keeping things from each other."

I glance over my shoulder. Annie's looking at the canvas as well. "Clearly," I say, causing her eyes to settle on my own.

She doesn't say anything before looking back up. "This one is by my friend Nick. He's brilliant. You know the Bowery Wall on Houston?" I nod. "One of his murals is currently holding that spot."

"It's beautiful." I turn and glance at some of the other work scattered about in what I assume is Nick's section. His use of color is consistent from piece to piece, and I can see how his style lends itself to murals. "You made it sound like you don't make art anymore."

"I don't tell strangers about this place. When I first met you, that's who you were." She moves to a curtain, pulls it aside, and tilts her head so I follow. "I don't tell anyone about it."

Behind the curtain is another piece, and this artist appears to be completely different and much less traditional than Nick. The space is full of scrap metal with a few tables featuring sculptures.

"This is Lucy's work. She does everything. Right now, she's really into metal." She points to a large structure that looks like a jungle gym.

I move around, looking at some of the larger sculptures. They're impressive but chaotic, and it's hard to know where to look. Even though I'm focused on Annie, I feel the familiar buzz I always feel when around new art, especially good art. Annie's friends are talented. "What changed tonight?" I ask as I wander through Lucy's work. I stop at a piece that looks like an abstract cube hovering in space.

Annie comes up beside me. Being in a room with new art may give me a certain kind of buzz, but it's nothing compared to what just standing next to her stirs in me. "I have trouble not being myself when I'm around you," she whispers.

"Why did you leave?"

"You know why."

"I stopped the kiss as soon as it happened."

"I know. I'm not mad." She lets out a small, cynical-sounding laugh, and I can feel her eyes on me. "I have no right to be. But it scared me how much it bothered me. And I didn't know how to pretend anymore. So I left. I'm glad you called."

We're both quiet as we study the piece, but it's clear neither of us are really focused on the art anymore. We're finally alone, and we know we need to talk. It feels as if we're on the edge of a cliff, and this conversation will push us over. One way or another.

But Annie was brave enough to bring me here. And before everything changes again, I want to see the part of her that nobody else gets to experience. If I walk away without her, I need to see this part of her.

"Will you show me your work?" I ask, knowing the weight of my request. Even if she brought me here, indicating that she's willing to open this side of herself, I know how vulnerable it can be to show someone your art.

She gently laces our fingers. "I'm nervous."

"To show me?"

"Yes. But not just that."

I pull her hand more fully into my own. "Then tell me why."

"Everything about you scares me."

"Show me your art. And then we can talk."

She takes a deep breath but pulls on my hand, leading me to the far side of the room. She pulls back a curtain, and we're in a new space filled with different canvases, all much more organized than Lucy's. Some are lined up against the wall, but many are displayed on different easels. Annie's hands are in her pockets, but she doesn't seem as timid as she did a moment ago. She seems proud.

As she stands there among her art, I have to take a few breaths to steady myself. The thought I had earlier tonight when I first saw

Annie is only solidified in this moment. The inevitability of our story is so obvious as I watch her study her own work, and I look away before I am completely overwhelmed with emotion.

For once, tearing my eyes away from her face isn't hard. Not when I'm surrounded by portraits, allowing me to confirm what I've known all along: Annie has a special talent.

I've never featured an artist who creates work solely using charcoal. Now I know why. Everything pales in comparison to this. I've seen the medium used for portraits, and I've seen works that are incredibly detailed and almost lifelike, one of the benefits of using charcoal or pencils. But Annie's work is fluid, as if the faces are changing expressions in the middle of the canvas. Each face has such a ghostlike quality, as if taken directly from someone's dream; they're almost real. But not.

"How did you get into charcoal?" I ask.

"In art school. We were using it as a preliminary method before delving into paint. I fell in love with it. I leave color to Nick. I prefer exploring shadows, the ethereal side of things."

"I can see that," I say, moving around and looking at all the different faces.

Besides the fact that they're all incredible, the most consistent feature is that each face belongs to a woman. After looking at a portrait of a young woman lying on a couch, I move to the next one, the profile of a tall, older woman.

Not all are pretty women. Annie's models are diverse and interesting. But the dreamlike quality of her work brings out something in each of them. Each piece shows a different side of what makes someone beautiful.

"They're all women," I say. "Beautiful women."

"Well, as the old prophets said, if you can't sleep with them, draw them."

I smile but continue my journey through the room. I don't know how long I'll have here, and I want to see it all. When I get to the canvas against the farthest wall, I stop because I recognize the face. "She's the woman on your phone. The one I saw that night in the hotel."

Annie walks over next to me and looks at the canvas. She lets out a hum and nods.

"She affected you."

"It's not the people," she says. "It's their features. Sometimes, it's one expression that captures me. When I see a face I want to draw, it's like my mind memorizes every line. And I can't stop seeing it until I get it on canvas. But some faces I don't forget. Hers is one of them. Yours is another. Maybe if I drew you, it would be easier to move on."

My stomach tightens. The idea of her moving on from me hurts, even though I know it's what we need to do. And now that we've gone through her entire studio, landing on this last piece, we need to have the conversation that's been looming over us. "Why do you keep all this hidden away?" I ask, dipping my toe into the ocean of questions I've had since first finding out who she is. "You could be showing anywhere."

She brings her eyes to mine and shakes her head. "I don't think that's true."

"Annie, I'm not some random person off the street. I'm an artist. I've owned multiple galleries. I understand this world, and I know talent. You said earlier that you didn't pursue art because it wasn't a guarantee." I point at the canvas. "This is a guarantee."

"Thank you." She's quiet as she stares at me. "Let's sit?" She points to a green couch pressed against one of the walls next to her area.

We keep a small space between us because it's hard to think about anything coherent when she's touching me or even close. We're both quiet for a few minutes.

"I don't know where to start," she says.

"Tell me about your family. It seems that's what everything relates back to."

Her expression goes from thoughtful to pained, and I can tell that this isn't going to be an easy conversation. It takes everything in me not to reach over and grab her hand. "Everything in my family revolves around my dad's company. It's always been like that." She takes a deep breath. "It was passed down to my dad from his.

Growing up, there was very little separation between family and Astor Properties. And family was everything. I grew up with that being pounded into my head. But what my dad really meant was that the company was everything."

"I can understand that to a certain extent."

"Yes, I know you can. But it sounds like your parents were a lot more open-minded than mine. The more money they earned, the more conservative and myopic mine became. If it looked bad for their image or their circle of snobby friends, it wasn't good."

"They let you go to art school. That's something."

"They're not bad people, per se. Just set in their ways. But as I told you, there was a contingency to all that. They paid for school as long as I came back to the company afterward. At the time, I thought I'd do it so they would pay for school. I'd stay at the company for a year or two, then leave."

"How many years has it been?"

"Five. Almost six."

"So why do you stay?"

"Families have a way of making us forget that we have a choice," she says, staring into space. "A couple of years after I left school, things in my family kind of fell apart."

"With your actual family or the company?"

"Both. First, my dad made a bad deal on a property downtown. I don't know the details, but we lost a lot of money. And quite a bit of clout. After that, it was expected that all hands were on deck. There was a lot of pressure to help in whatever way we could."

"You mean you and your siblings?" I ask, remembering what Holly had said about Annie's brother earlier.

"Not my sister, Zoe, she's thirteen years younger than me. But I have an older brother. Dylan."

"Why did Holly only think you had a sister?"

"My family doesn't talk about Dylan. Ian would never bring him up." She shifts so she can bring both her legs onto the couch. Her posture looks casual, almost as if we're just hanging out. But her face is anything but casual. I don't think I've ever seen her bright eyes so dim. "Dylan didn't want anything to do with the company. That was a disappointment for my dad but not the worst of it. Around that same time, Dylan came out as gay. And that pushed my dad over the edge. He conflated his flailing business with Dylan's coming out. That was almost four years ago. They still haven't talked."

"Do you talk to Dylan?"

"Pretty much every day. He lives in New Jersey with his boyfriend. But it hasn't been easy for him. My parents cut him off from everything, and he hasn't seen Zoe since. She's only sixteen."

"Do they know you talk to him?"

"Maybe. There's a lot that goes unsaid in my family."

"And that's why you haven't come out? Because of what happened to Dylan?"

She seems to gather her thoughts. She repositions again, and it's clear she's uncomfortable. "I was always fine dating men. I had a boyfriend in college, and we got along well. But I always knew I could feel more. During my last year at school, I slept with my female roommate. That opened my eyes, and I realized I might not be straight. But when everything fell apart at home, it seemed easier not to give in to that part of myself."

"Are you attracted to men?" I ask hesitantly. I have no issues with her being bisexual, but I absolutely don't want to think about her with Ian.

"Yes, but it's not the same as it is with women. I guess over the years, I let myself believe it was."

My stomach tightens as I roll my next question around in my head. The fact that Annie has stopped talking makes me think she knows what's coming. "So, Ian. How did that happen?"

"Things in my dad's company got worse over the years. There's still business, and the family name still holds weight, but it's been on a steady decline. But some of my dad's contacts and clients in other cities outside of New York are still strong. Cities that appeal to your brother."

The Dawson Hotel Group has hotels in other cities, so it's no surprise Ian is interested in expanding. But it makes me think back to the conversation my uncle and Ian were having over dinner about the hotel being franchised, a move I know my parents were against.

"Okay, so you met him through your dad's company. But how did you start dating?"

She wipes her hands over her face before leaning back into the couch. She shakes her head and looks at me. "I don't know what you think of me, but it can't be great. This isn't going to make it any better."

"Tell me." I don't want to hear about Annie and Ian, but ultimately, it's why I'm here and why we're in an impossible situation to begin with. "Unfortunately, it seems that nothing you can say makes me want you less."

"Until now." She looks away. The silence goes on for so long that I'm about to say something before she starts talking again. "My dad figured out a deal for Ian so he could franchise the Dawson Hotel line into specific markets across the Midwest. See, my dad's a good salesman. The fact is, Ian didn't really need him. He could have gotten the contract done with another company. But my dad needed Ian. And he needed the deal to go through, however that had to happen." She stares straight ahead.

"Did he set you up with Ian?"

"More or less. He introduced us at a party. Then, he started inviting him to family dinners and events. He even invited him to my sister's sweet sixteen. Soon, we just kind of fell into it. Kind of like my parents did when they were young. It wasn't romantic. It was convenient."

She looks around helplessly before she goes on. "By the time I met Ian, I had already set up this studio, and that felt like enough. Ian seemed to enjoy having someone with the Astor name on his arm at parties, and in turn, I helped the company. It's not like I don't know who he is. It just became easier to go with it. I told myself it was for my family, that eventually, I would end it and live my own life."

"Why didn't you?"

"I lost myself. I became a shell of who I was. I convinced myself that dating women wasn't worth losing them. Losing Zoe." Annie stops talking as if she realized something, and her eyes look bright and intense. "Until that night that I walked into the Runaway. And I woke up."

I've been so invested in her story that I let myself get comfortable. But as soon as those words are out of her mouth, I'm hyperaware of my body and how alive it feels.

"I don't even know what made me go there that night," she continues. "I guess I was curious and finally lost the battle with myself. I didn't expect to meet you, and I didn't expect to feel like this."

There are so many emotions rolling through me, but I still need more answers, and if I scoot over to her like I want to, I won't get those. "Do you love him?"

She looks taken aback, and her eyes get wider. "Charlie, no. I've never loved him. I did what I thought would make my dad happy. That's all. And I've always gotten the sense that Ian doesn't love me, either."

"Ian only loves himself," I say, not able to hold back the contempt I feel. "You're so different with him than you are with me."

"In my family, women are seen but not heard. I know, it's embarrassing. I forgot there's another way. I'm not like you. You know who you are. You're brave."

I let out a laugh at her misguided compliment. "Annie, I'm not brave at all. I left town. That's who I am. I leave when things are hard. You shouldn't be embarrassed for trying to make things work with your family. I'm embarrassed that I left mine."

"I understand why you would. Ian doesn't talk about it, but I can't imagine how hard that was. I am so sorry, Charlie."

I've heard every sympathetic phrase people throw at someone who lost their parents, and each one of them annoys me. But Annie's statement doesn't. Nor does the soft expression she's directing at me now. "I don't think my family understands."

"Your family loves you more than anything."

"Not your boyfriend."

"He won't be my boyfriend for much longer."

My eyes snap to hers again. "What are you going to do?"

"I don't know. I know I can't keep living like this." She looks around again with a thoughtful expression. "This is my only happy place. And it's a secret. Maybe it's time I start living for myself."

"I think that sounds like a good start."

"And you?" She smiles. The sight makes my stomach do a flip, and I can't help but smile back. "Back to LA?"

As fast as my smile appeared, that's how fast I can feel it drop. I don't want to think about leaving, not now that Annie has opened up to me. It's not that things aren't still messy, but it feels like there's a glimmer of hope. "I guess that's the plan." As I say it, her smile falls slightly. "I never expected to meet anyone that night either," I add, mirroring her words. "I never expected to feel like this."

"I find it hard to believe you don't have women lining up for you. Lily is just the start." She slides an inch closer.

"No other woman has ever affected me like this," I say, shifting slightly closer.

She lets out a mix of a gasp and a sigh. "I don't know how to go back to not feeling."

"So what do we do?" I don't even notice that we're right next to each other until her hand touches mine.

"What do you want, Charlie?" she murmurs.

I stare at our fingers as they lace together. Everything in the room changes in an instant, as if I've stepped into a sauna. "I can't have what I want. It's all so messy. You're still with my brother."

She moves even closer and brings our hands into her lap. I feel her breath against my face but I'm too nervous to turn my head. I'm too scared to look into the eyes I have no power against. "And if I wasn't?" She pushes my fallen hair behind my ear. Her breath hits my cheek, and it ripples down my spine as if she is caressing me.

"We shouldn't do this," I whisper, but I'm not even convinced by my own voice, so I doubt she is.

"I know." But her actions don't match her words because she brings one finger from my hair down my jawline.

"*Annie.*"

"Do you want me to move my hand?"

I turn my head to her, which causes her hand to drop. She's so close that I can see every speck that makes up her eyes, every freckle across her nose. If there was ever an excuse for lacking self-control, it's her face. We both know that I'd never tell her to move away.

As she looks at my lips and licks her own, I make my decision. There are still so many things we should talk about. And things Annie should work out on her own. But right now, the only thing I can think about is kissing her again.

"I want you. Right now. On this couch," I whisper, lightly pinching her bottom lip. My mind has been consumed by this mouth since I met her, and I feel a desperate need to feel her lips, even if it's not with my own yet.

Her chest is rising and falling so that I can tell that her breathing has picked up. Instead of saying anything, she grabs my wrist and takes my fingers into her mouth. My eyes slam shut at the feeling of her tongue swirling around my fingers, and a soft moan escapes my lips. The move is so hot that it feels like there's a direct current from her mouth to my pussy.

"*Fuck*," I groan as she takes my fingers out.

"Might I suggest you stop playing with my lips and kiss me already?"

I may not usually submit to women, but with Annie, I don't need to be asked twice. I put my hand behind her neck and pull her into me until our lips connect. It isn't graceful or romantic, but she doesn't seem to need that. Because she lets out her own series of moans as her hands come around my back, and she opens her mouth.

Our lips don't have time to get reacquainted before our tongues are fighting for dominance. They move in an erotic rhythm, and the way hers pushes in and out of my mouth has my pussy aching for the same. We kiss for so long that I lose track of time, but when my hands wander down her back, I need to feel her bare skin.

I break my mouth away and laugh when she lets out a cute little sound of protest. "This shirt looks adorable on you. But it has to go." I move my hands to the hem.

She lifts her hands above her head and allows me to pull it over. As I'm throwing it to the side of the couch, she wastes no time taking her bra off. It's only been a handful of days since I've seen her naked, so I don't know how I could forget just how perfect her body is. And there's something even more beautiful about the fact that we're here. Not in a sterile hotel room but an art studio. Full of things that she created.

Every inch of her deserves to be touched and pleasured, and if I have my way, devoured. It's a battle between my mouth and hands as to which gets to touch her tits first, and my mouth wins.

I take one of her hard nipples in my mouth. She grabs the back of my head and pulls me into her as she lets out a loud groan. I swirl my tongue messily around her nipple before she tugs my hair, bringing my head to her other nipple. I bring my hands up so I can cup her as I lick, every now and then bringing my finger roughly over each nipple. I increase my pace, moving my head back and forth between her tits, and soon, our mutual moans are filling the room. When I feel her jerk in pleasure, I know she needs more. I move between her legs.

We're both breathing heavily as I get situated. Annie leans back, and the sight of her drowsy eyes and soaked tits is so sexy that I don't rush my next move. I need to take a moment to appreciate the sight. She gives me a small smile before she sits up, leans down, and cups my face. Everything so far has felt urgent, but when she leans in to kiss me, it all slows down. Our lips move together slowly before our tongues flick against each other.

Annie brings her head back from mine but only by an inch. "Fuck the art studio. I think your lips may be my new happy place," she says, grazing one finger over them.

I take her hand and kiss the tip of her fingers before she leans back, ready for whatever is coming next. "Let me show you a world where you can have both."

CHAPTER FIFTEEN

As I sit between Annie's legs, I bring my hands up her thighs until I reach the top of her jeans. I let my fingers play with the button, watching her as she closes her eyes and drops her head back against the couch.

Everything about this moment feels different to our first time. That night in the hotel might have been sexy and mysterious, but it was also fast. I feel like I'm seeing a whole new Annie tonight. The real her. I want to savor every minute of having her like this. I want to relish the fact that she won't be running the moment we're done.

An overwhelming number of emotions flows through me, causing my hands to pause. The second I stop unbuttoning, her head lifts, and she looks at me. All I've thought about this week is being with her again, but as many times as I've repeated this moment in my head, I don't feel rushed. The reality of where we're doing this isn't lost on me, and I need her to know that. "Thank you for showing me this place."

She smiles as she puts her hands over mine. She moves my fingers aside and unbuttons her pants before sliding them down her legs and off her body. Her underwear quickly follows. "Charlie," she says, flinging her clothes aside. "How about you thank me later and fuck me now?"

I'd laugh at how direct and demanding she is, but her pussy, clearly wet, is now in front of me, and the slow pace seems futile. "Yes, ma'am," I say, my voice thick with desire.

I graze my hands up her thighs, but this time, I feel a trail of goose bumps in their wake. Her head drops back again, and she lets out a small sigh, as if she can finally breathe now that I'm touching her. Seeing her so turned on has my pussy clenching. As sexy as she looks leaning back, so open and ready for me, I need to taste all of her, and I can't do that from this angle.

I slide my hands under her body, grab her ass, and pull her forward until she's on the edge of the couch, and I have better access to her entire pussy. Her breathing is now audible, and a sense of urgency is starting to settle in. I want to taste her again, devour her for as long as she'll let me, and I'm done wasting time.

But before my mouth can touch her, she puts a hand on my shoulder, stopping me. "Wait," she pants. "I want to see you as you have me. All of you. Take that jumpsuit off."

"You're very demanding." I rest my head on her bare thigh. I'm so close to her pussy that I can smell how turned on she is, and it would take nothing to lean in and capture her wet folds in my mouth. But I know she likes control, and I don't think I can deny her anything when I want her this bad.

"Is that a problem for you, Choo Choo?" She strokes the top of my hair.

I'm glad I'm still wearing underwear because the challenging, heated expression she's directing at me causes my pussy to become so wet, it would be dripping down my legs if I wasn't. "With you, it's weirdly not," I reply honestly. I don't waste more time and quickly take off my outfit. Once all my clothes are thrown into a pile with hers, I kneel in front of her. "Better?"

"Much," she says, playing with a strand of hair that's come out of my pins. "You looked gorgeous tonight. But I prefer you like this."

I let out a small laugh. "Good to know. Any more requests, madam, or may I proceed?"

She simply puts her hand on the top of my head. She doesn't push, but that's all I need. As soon as my mouth touches her pussy, I lose all sense of anything else. She wants this as much as I do, and that only fuels my desire. She's so wet that I have to spend some time purely licking up and down her length just to clean up some.

She pushes gently on my head, and I take her cue, giving her more of my tongue. I put my hands under her ass so I can bring her closer to my face and keep them there, squeezing as I flick my tongue against her clit.

The memory of how good she tastes has been on constant repeat in my mind since last week, but my memory must have faded because she tastes better than I ever remembered. Needing to taste and feel it all, I slide my tongue down her length until I'm at her opening. I circle the spot with my tongue, but when she grabs my hair and squeezes, I push my tongue all the way in.

I push in and out before bringing my tongue back to her clit. I repeat the motion over and over until she's letting out a series of gasps and moans. With each flick, I can feel her clit getting harder. She begins to thrust her hips, causing me to bring my hands back to her thighs so I can hold her down.

"Charlie," she gasps after bucking up again.

"Yes, baby? Tell me what you want," I say before resuming my attack on her clit.

"Let me fuck your tongue."

"It's yours." I slide my tongue as far into her pussy as I can. Just like the first time we were together, she is taking control, and I love her like this. Her commanding tone is so sexy that I find myself consenting without a challenge. I moan into her pussy as she grabs the sides of my head and directs my tongue where she wants it.

"Fuck, Charlie," she moans. "You feel so good."

Keeping her hands where they are, she changes the pace with which she's fucking my face, now moving in a slow, upward thrust, making sure to get my entire tongue inside.

I can tell my face is wet, but I have no interest in fixing that. I'll do anything to make sure that her pussy continues to drip on me. I can feel her walls clench around my tongue every time it slides in, and I know she's close.

"Fuck me," she says, releasing my head. I push her back onto the couch and slide two fingers inside as my tongue latches back on to her. She's so wet that my fingers slide too easily so I add another and begin to fuck her like she asked. "Yes, yes, baby. Like that. I'm so close." Her voice is low and almost guttural, as if her orgasm is coming from somewhere deep within her body. "More." She pants, throwing her head back onto the couch. "Just your fingers."

As good as she tastes, my fingers would agree that it's their turn to shine. I lift up so I can put one hand behind her neck as my other continues to pump into her. I anchor my hand in her hair as I pull her closer.

There's nothing in this world that feels better than Annie does at the height of passion. I knew it our first night, and I know it now. And even as I fuck her, a huge realization hits me: I keep trying to find a home in a city when nothing in my life has ever felt like home as much as this does.

My overwhelming thoughts are interrupted when her fingers dig into my back, and she lets out something that sounds more like a cry than a moan. "I'm coming. I'm coming. Yes, fuck. Keep going."

I almost laugh. The only thing that could get me to stop is if she told me to. Otherwise, I could do this all day; food, water, and sleep be damned.

She grabs my hand as she moans and pushes it even farther into her. I'm wet everywhere, from my fingers to my wrist. Everything I feel is her. After a few more thrusts, she lets go and sinks into the couch. The only sounds are our heavy breathing, and I let her enjoy the feeling as I sink to the floor and rest my head against her thigh.

Her eyes are closed, and her lips are parted slightly. It's been a while since my fingers itched to sketch something, but as I watch her post-orgasmic glow, I wish I could. In lieu, I memorize every feature and line of her face. I want to remember how beautiful she looks in this moment: relaxed and raw and *happy*.

She lifts her head, and the relaxed expression is replaced by something much hungrier. A slow, confident smile grows on her lips as she looks at me. "There's something about controlling someone who's so in control," she says. "It's so damn sexy."

"I'm not in control around you." I lift my head from her thigh. "And you know that."

"Good. Now lie down. On the ground."

"Are you sure you're done?" I give her a challenging look.

She smiles before she leans forward and puts one finger under my chin. "I am not by any means done, baby girl. But right now, I want to feel you. Lie down."

I can't imagine a world in which she would ever need to ask me to do something twice, and as she gives me a stern look, I do as she commands. She moves onto the floor with me. She lifts her leg over my body so she can straddle me. As soon as I feel her pussy hit my stomach, I let out a long moan.

"Fuck. You feel good right there," I say as she grinds on me, my stomach and chest getting wet.

"I may have lied earlier." She waits until my eyes are open and focused on her before she continues. "Your lips *are* my happy place. But they have competition."

"They do? With what?"

"These," she replies as she trails a finger over one of my nipples, hardening it immediately. "And this." She grabs as much of my ass as she can while I'm on my back. "But mostly, this." She trails a finger down to my pussy. The feeling sends a bolt of electricity through my body, and I can't control the way it arches into her, which only causes her to let out a low laugh. "Is there something you need?" she asks in a playful tone.

"Yes."

She leans forward until both of her hands are on either side of my head, and her face is above my own. "Yes, what?"

"Yes, please."

"As much as I appreciate your manners," she says before licking my lips quickly, "I'd like to know more specifically what you need."

"I need you to fuck me," I reply in a throaty voice I hardly even recognize as my own. "Fingers, mouth, I don't care. Just fuck me. *Please.*"

I put my hands above my head and gaze up at her, knowing she'll enjoy such a submissive move. When she smiles like she's won some prize, I know that I'm right. "You are the sexiest thing I've ever seen in my whole life," she says quietly, pushing her hands into mine above my head. "And right now, you're mine."

When I nod, she moves so she's no longer straddling me and can trail one hand down my front. I do my best not to squirm, but her slow tortuous journey down my body is sending me into a frenzy. I need her fingers on my pussy soon, or I may combust.

I'm about to beg her for her touch but before I need to, her fingers reach my pussy. I let out a long groan and feel a sense of relief that she's finally made contact.

"My poor baby," she says, sliding a finger up my folds and onto my clit. "So patient. Let me make it up to you." She moves her fingers down and without teasing, she pushes what feels like two of them inside. Her eyes are glassy, and she looks incredibly turned on.

Every moment I've ever had with Annie seems to get more unbelievable than the last. And right now seems to top them all. The last thing I would have ever predicted was that she would be on top of me, looking at me like I'm the most delicious thing she's ever seen, as we fuck in an art studio. *Her* art studio.

My eyes slam shut again at the sensation, but as soon as they do, I hear her voice. "Look at me," she commands.

I open my eyes again and lock them on hers. She's moving her body up every time she thrusts, and soon, we're in a horizontal dance that's so seamless, it's like she's been fucking me like this for years.

I've been told that when I'm really turned on, my eyes become almost black, but Annie's eyes never stray from their true color. They always look clear and intense, as if they could drown me in their perfection.

As she continues to stare, she adds another finger. At the same time, she anchors her other hand into my hair and holds me there so I'm forced to look at her as she fucks me. The move is so hot that I can't stop the breathy moans spilling out of my mouth.

"Does that feel good, baby girl?" she asks, pushing in even deeper and pressing her lips against my neck. Her heavy breathing is a giveaway for how turned on she is as well. Her fingers stay inside, but I can feel her thumb pressing against my clit, eliciting another long moan from me. "Answer me," she says, not slowing.

"Yes," I reply, not able to say much more. "Fuck. Yes."

She picks up the pace and is now pushing into me with her full weight. With her on top like this, I won't last long, and soon, I feel myself getting closer and closer to an orgasm. I grab her back, pulling her into me so I can feel her tits press against me.

"Baby, fuck. I'm going to come."

"Come for me, baby girl," she whispers into my neck, and her command is all I need to let go.

"I am," I cry out. "I'm coming." My nails dig into her back. She lets out a groan and pushes her fingers even harder.

I don't know what I say or what sounds I make. As my eyes slam shut, I feel a high that takes me to another plane. All I can see behind my closed eyes is Annie, as if I'm engulfed by her presence. When I open my eyes, she's hovering over me, her fingers still inside my pussy, and we're both breathing heavily.

"I think I just blacked out. I don't remember anything. I don't even know my name."

"It's Choo Choo," she replies. "And I'll take that as a compliment."

I roll my eyes, but I know my smile gives me away. "You're really fucking sexy. And really good at that."

"I'd say it all comes from experience, but some rookies are just gifted," she replies, slowly removing her fingers. She puts them in her mouth and sucks before bringing them back out and smiling at me. "You are also very, *very* sexy and good at that."

"Well, you know. I read a how-to manual once."

"Oh yes, I'm sure that's how you figured it out."

I give her as innocent a smile as I can muster. "Being with you is like my first time because nobody else compares."

She lets out an exaggerated snort. "That was a terrible line. Good thing you already got laid."

I laugh as she moves next to me on the floor. "I've been in a lot of art studios before," I say, glancing at the less-than-clean floor. "Am I going to need a tetanus shot after this?"

"I didn't take you for the prissy sort."

"I'm just health conscious."

"And if you did happen to catch Art Studio Floor Disease, would it be worth it?"

"Every moment with you is worth it." I keep my tone light, but my words are genuine. As crazy as this entire situation is, there is nowhere else I want to be than right here.

Her eyes are soft, and it seems that despite our teasing, we both feel something significant. "Would you like me to get you a blanket, princess?" she asks.

"Don't you dare go anywhere." I slide my arms around her.

"Then let me show you just how worth it I can be."

Annie's studio is *bright*. That may be good for art but not for attempting to sleep. And though I love the feeling of her arms around me, her front pressing firmly against my back, the light is too intense for whatever hour it is.

I turn so I'm not facing the window and see that Annie's eyes are open. Her hair is wild, but it makes her look even more beautiful. She gives me a small smile as she puts her arm around my back and grazes her fingers up and down.

I close my eyes as my skin erupts in goose bumps. Even after spending an entire night with her, her touch is still electrifying. "I don't remember the last time I slept on a couch. I feel like I'm in college." I smile at her.

"How is that possible? I sleep on this couch all the time."

"I prefer beds. But I suppose this isn't so bad."

"No?"

I shake my head. "In fact, I think I could get used to couches."

Her smile widens before she looks toward the window over my shoulder. "It looks like it's still early. Only seven."

"Can you tell time by the sun?"

"Yes, Charlie," she replies, her face becoming serious. "I didn't know how to tell you, but I'm actually a pirate."

"That's suspect. You don't have an eye patch *or* a parrot."

"It's rude to stereotype us," she replies with an exaggerated eye roll. She points to the window, and when I turn, I see that there's a clock on the wall next to it.

"I'm slightly disappointed," I say, turning back. "The pirate thing was kind of hot."

"Then, let me fix that disappointment." She captures my mouth in a soft kiss.

Despite how early it is, and despite how recently we did this exact thing, my body takes no time to respond, and I push into her so I can deepen the kiss. When we break apart, we're both breathing heavily.

"Better?" she asks.

"Aye, matey."

She laughs before leaning in and kissing me again. This time, the kiss is cut short when she pulls away. "You're vibrating."

"You think you're that good, huh?" I smirk.

"Well, yes. But that's not what I meant. You're *vibrating*. Your phone. I hear it."

Once it's quiet, I can hear what she hears and turn so I can reach into my jacket and grab the interrupting device.

I have a text from Holly. My stomach tightens: *Morning, Sunshine. Came down to see you. Unless you're out for an early morning run, which I know you're not because you're lazy, I assume you're not here. I'd maybe say bye to Annie and get your ass back to the hotel before Kat wakes up. Pancakes at nine.*

"Everything okay?" Annie asks.

"It's Holly." I turn my head and notice that her face is so much more relaxed than I've ever seen it, and I hate that I'm about to ruin that. "She's the one who gave me your number last night."

She is quiet for a moment, but her face doesn't change. "Does that mean she knows?"

"She could tell."

"I guess I didn't leave the club very subtly."

"You don't need to worry about her. She won't say anything."

"I'm not worried."

"What are you going to do?"

Her eyes close and she takes a deep breath before she speaks. "I have no idea," she whispers, putting her forehead against mine. "Last night was so incredible."

"It feels like there's a 'but' coming."

"No. There's not. I'm just confused."

I pull my head back. Now she looks the opposite of relaxed. "About Ian?"

"No, not about him. I know what I need to do, and it should have happened ages ago. With my family." She is quiet for a moment as she starts playing with a strand of my hair. "I'm scared."

"Of what?"

"Losing them."

"I understand. More than most. But you don't seem happy in that life. It's all a lie."

"They're still my family."

"And what about us?" I ask in a quiet voice. I brace myself for whatever she has to say. Last night *was* incredible. It was one of the best nights I've ever shared with a woman, and I don't know how I can walk away now. Not from Annie. Not ever.

"You're leaving, Charlie. You've said so yourself."

"And if I wasn't?"

"I don't know."

"Why don't we start with a date?"

"A date?"

"Without sex. Since we already know how we are in that department. And we see how things go."

"Wait, a no-sex date?" she asks playfully, pulling me into her.

"A no-sex-until-the-end-of-the-date...date."

"That may be hard for me. Have you seen yourself?"

"I have. And I've seen you. But I think we can do it."

"And you think going on a date will cure my mess of a life?"

"No. But it might show you that living the life you want is worth making it a little bit messier."

"Who are you, Charlie Dawson, and what have you done to me?"

"Is that a yes?"

"That's a yes."

We're both smiling now, and we probably look ridiculous, but I don't care. Nothing has been resolved yet, and she's still technically with my brother, but I can't erase the significance of what last night meant to me. And seemingly what it meant to her.

Taking her out on a date is the last thing I should be doing this week, but our time is limited. And if I'm going to be thinking about her nonstop anyway, I may as well see her.

"What are you thinking right now?" she asks.

"That you're really beautiful."

"Very smooth."

"I try."

"What time do you need to be back at the hotel?"

"Nine."

Her eyes flick to the clock on the wall behind me again. "That gives us an hour or so. Any ideas on what we could do in an hour?"

I smile, knowing exactly where her head is at. "Well, I guess we could look at some more art." I point at her canvases.

"I already am." She moves over me.

"Very smooth."

"I try."

Our banter is cut short when her lips find mine again, and I'm not complaining. We'll have plenty of time to talk on our date. Right now, my mouth has other plans.

CHAPTER SIXTEEN

There are places in this city that I know so well, I could sketch them with my eyes closed. Places that are as nostalgic as my childhood bedroom. Rosie's Diner is one of those.

The place itself is unremarkable, just your standard Manhattan diner featuring a handful of old, worn booths with décor that hasn't changed since it opened. It's not the food or ambience that has me so sentimental about the place. Rosie's Diner was a core part of my childhood.

One of the things I always appreciated about my parents was that no matter how much money they earned or how many hotels they opened, they were always grounded. While other private school kids spent their weekends being waited on by chefs and staff, my family spent our Sunday mornings at Rosie's, ordering greasy food and arguing about who got which side of the booth.

We might not have always had a lot of my parents' attention, but they always made time for Rosie's. I don't even remember fighting with Ian on those Sunday mornings. It was as if there was a truce in Rosie's that we both stuck to, and looking back, those breakfasts are some of my happiest family memories.

When my uncle asked to get lunch, this is the first place I thought of. Rosie's reminds me so much of my parents that before I came back to Manhattan, I had planned to stay away for the rest of my life if I could help it. But something seems to be happening to me on this trip. The pain I've held on to for so long isn't as easy to grip anymore, and for the first time, I want to let go. For once, I feel like being closer to my parents. I don't want to push the memories away. Everything about being back has made me feel closer to them, and I don't know if it's just time that's helped to heal my pain or something else. Perhaps it's *someone* else.

As I sit waiting for my uncle, I can't help but smile thinking about that someone. It's only been a day since I've seen Annie, and yet, my mind seems to be on one constant loop of her. There's no way I can deny the impact she's had on my trip.

It's not as if our situation has miraculously fixed itself; not even sex as good as ours has that power. But I've been riding a high since leaving her studio that I'm not willing to spoil with reality. Or at least not yet. She makes me feel like myself again, like the person I thought I lost the night of my parents' accident. She makes me long for the next moment, and for a long time, I've been stuck in the past.

Considering she's still with Ian, I should regret what happened Saturday night. But the only thing I regret is that I had to leave so early the next day. Luckily, Kat was still passed out by the time I got back to the hotel, and our group breakfast became a lunch with nobody even noticing that I was gone all night. Nobody except Holly, who kept giving me meaningful looks.

I was thankful when Aunt Sandra gave us time off from wedding duties. Now I won't have to face my nosy cousin again until tomorrow, when we're doing a movie night at Kat's. Hopefully, Holly will be distracted and won't focus on me. Not that she hasn't been texting incessantly. Those are just easier to ignore than her face.

I don't know how to answer her, and I don't need to confirm what she already knows. Sex is one thing, but the last thing I need is for Holly to know that I asked Annie out on a date. While I do trust her, she tends to let things slip when she drinks, and she *loves* to drink at family events.

My stomach does a flip as I think about that date. Annie and I haven't spoken since yesterday morning, and I've stopped myself from texting her numerous times. I haven't heard anything from the family about a breakup with Ian, but she never told me when that was going to happen. Considering how we spent Saturday night, part of me assumed she'd do it right away, but the timing isn't great with Kat's wedding coming up.

I check my phone and see that my uncle is ten minutes late. Usually, he's as punctual as his daughter, but it is the middle of a workday, and he gets busy at the Dawson offices. I turn my phone around as I think about Annie again. I have no idea what the etiquette is for texting your brother's girlfriend, or possible ex-girlfriend. But I can't exactly play it cool considering I head back to LA in a week.

I open a new message and send her a text. *Hello, Annie.*

As soon as I hit send, I regret my decision. Or at least, I regret my decision to say *that*. But just as I'm about to follow it up with something a little more charming, I see the three chat bubbles that indicate she's responding. It's ridiculous that the sight of her texting can make my entire body heat up, but there's no use telling my body that. I feel a rush of excitement, and she's not even here.

Um, hello. Who is this?

I smile. She already gave herself away with her little area code trick on Saturday, but if she wants to play, we can play. *Charlie...I think you may remember me?*

Hmm. I'm trying to place you.

Sexy blonde. Unbelievable tits. Charming. Gives the new meaning to "dream girl."

Okay, that helps a bit. Did we meet at the club on Saturday?

Yes, I was the one giving you orgasms. I worry that was too forward, but the feeling is erased as soon as Annie's quick response comes in.

*Oh! Right. That Charlie. I was confused because *that* Charlie asked me out but never followed up about it.*

It's only been a day. You must miss me a lot.

A day is a long time to be as wet as I am.

I almost drop my phone. The bravado I felt a moment before is replaced by arousal, and once again, Annie has taken control of the situation. I'm so turned on, I have to cross my legs to temper the throbbing. I look at the diner door and am relieved to see that Uncle Neil isn't here yet. I don't want this conversation to end, and I *really* don't want to explain why my face looks three shades redder than normal.

I look back to my phone, but before I can think of a response, it's buzzing, and there's a new text from Annie: *Did I get you flustered, baby girl?*

The throb within my center only intensifies with that pet name. I would never have imagined getting turned on by such a submissive term, but with Annie, everything is different, and when I think about our Saturday night, it's one of the things I fixate on the most.

I take a few breaths. I can't let Annie think she can fluster me this easily, even if it's true. As I type my response, I try to remind myself that I do have *some* game: *An entire day is a long time to be perpetually wet. You should do something about that.*

Agreed. Know any good doctors?

Unfortunately, no. I prefer holistic methods, myself.

Sounds intriguing. Care to share?

I'm always willing to lend a hand. Or anything else that will help.

How kind.

I wait to see if she says anything else, but my phone goes quiet. I don't want our sexy banter to end, but I'm running out of time, and I did text her for a reason, one we're dancing around. If I wasn't afraid of how it would look, I'd ask to see her tonight. But I don't want to rush her. For the first time in a long time, I want to do this right. I send another, much tamer text: *How about we discuss it more in person. Wednesday? 6:00?*

Wednesday marks our one-week anniversary. How romantic. She sends a winking emoji, and warmth moves through me that has nothing to do with arousal. She has the unique ability to make me feel like I'm on fire one moment and a puddle of mush the next.

I attempt to suppress my smile as I respond, but I'm pretty sure I'm unsuccessful. *I have my moments. Is that a yes?*

Yes. She had already agreed to this date, so I don't know why her simple answer makes me feel so giddy, but it does. *And what will we be doing, Casanova?*

Ha. My sister calls me that.

Do I want to know why? This time, the emoji is of an angry face, and the small show of jealousy just makes my smile grow.

Maybe because I like Italian food.

Choo Choo fits you better.

Noted. Now, for Wednesday, can the Astor Princess get herself to Harlem, or does she need an escort?

*I'm just going to move past the Dawson Heiress calling *me* a princess. And, yes, I can get myself to Harlem just fine. My crown is waterproof.*

I laugh and am about to keep the teasing going, but I see my uncle crossing the street, and I need to put my phone down. *Elegant and practical. I'm about to have lunch with my uncle. But I'll send you the address. And I'll see you on Wednesday?*

I see her text bubbles appear before they disappear again. My uncle is opening the door by the time she responds, and I have to hold in a gasp. *I'll be the one with the soaked undies. See you on Wednesday.* Her text is accompanied by a train emoji, and I'm again confused as to how she can have me turned on and amused at the same time.

"Hey, kiddo. Sorry I'm late. I had a meeting run over." My uncle rushes to my booth and pulls me up into a quick hug before moving into the spot across from me. His tie is loose around his neck, and his jacket is open. He appears more disheveled and distracted than usual, but that gives me a moment to compose myself.

I'm still vibrating from my final exchange with Annie, so I take a sip of water before I respond. "No problem," I say, moving a menu over to him. "The menu hasn't changed so I already know what I want."

He smiles as he looks at the crinkled, laminated menu in front of him. "I'm pretty sure the menu hasn't changed since 1979."

"Dad always did like consistency."

"That he did." He gives me a soft look before turning his attention to the menu. "He always got the Rueben."

"Even when it was breakfast. They'd make an exception and serve him from the lunch menu early."

"I suppose I'll do the same in his memory." He sets his menu aside and looks around the diner. "I haven't been here in years. I'm surprised this is where you wanted to meet."

"I'm trying something new."

"Oh? And what is that?"

"Feeling."

He nods quietly. He has always been good at knowing when to push and when not to, and I'm grateful he lets my comment go without overanalyzing it. "And how was the bachelorette party? Holly says that everyone had a good time. I think she is still hungover."

"It's nothing compared to Kat. Jake already texted me a lecture about letting her get that drunk."

"Your sister is an adult and made her own choices."

"Can you text that to Jake? And while you're at it, tell his mom that I'm a lovely human."

He laughs, and it reminds me so much of my dad that I have an immediate craving to hear it again. But before I can continue joking, a familiar gray-haired woman is beside our booth. "What can I get for you?" she asks.

Apparently, Rosie's hasn't changed their staff in decades, either; I'm pretty sure this is the same woman who used to wait on us all those years ago. "Waffles, please," I say.

"It's noon," my uncle says in a fatherly tone.

"There is no unacceptable time to have waffles. Waffles transcend time."

He gives me a judgmental look before turning his attention to the server. "I'll have the Reuben and a Diet Coke, please."

She rolls her eyes as if we somehow inconvenienced her, but her attitude only makes me smile. Getting bad service at Rosie's is part of the experience.

"So you wanted to get lunch," I say, once she's left. "As much as I love seeing you, I know this isn't simply quality time."

He takes off his jacket and rolls up his sleeves. "I'll take all the time I can get with you before you disappear again. Unless you're thinking about staying."

My stomach tightens. I have a business to run in LA, and I have a life there now. But verbalizing that is another matter. Because leaving New York means leaving Annie. "Why would you think I'm staying?"

"Wishful thinking," he responds with a smile. "But you're right. I didn't ask you here just for quality time. I want to talk about the Dawson Hotel Group."

I already knew why. Maybe I've been able to face more of my past throughout this trip, and even if thinking about my parents doesn't hurt quite as much as it did, I'm still not interested in the business. That's Ian's domain now. "We're at a New York diner talking about the family business," I say with a smile, trying to delay the inevitable. "I kind of feel like we're in the Mafia."

He lets out a quick laugh. "You certainly are in a better mood than the last time I saw you."

I smile before growing more serious. As much as I'd love to keep this light, it's hard when I know he wants something I can't give him. "That doesn't mean I can help you, Uncle Neil."

"We need to talk about it."

"There's nothing to talk about."

"Charlie, the will—"

"I made it clear to Mom and Dad that I never wanted anything to do with the company. Years ago. So who cares what the will says?"

"You should care that their legacy is being destroyed. And you should care about your future. And what has been financially withheld from you."

"I don't need my parents' money. Kat was taken care of, and I know Ian didn't mess with that. That's all I care about."

He leans back and shakes his head. We've talked about this before, but this is the first time he has looked truly upset with me. "I'm surprised by you."

"Why?"

"You seem so precious about their memory. You left here because you were so broken." His voice is harder than I can ever remember. "But you don't care about the thing they cared about most. Outside of their children, that is. The Dawson Hotel Group meant something very important to them. And to me. You don't have to be CEO, you just have to *care*, Charlie."

I turn my water cup around in my hands as I let his words sink in. His hard expression is gone, and he seems more tired and defeated than I've ever seen him. "Tell me what's going on." Even if I don't want to be involved, he is right about one thing: my parents would want me to at least care.

"Ian is making a deal. A bad deal. Phillip Astor has been in his ear for too long."

My stomach does a flip at the mention of Annie's dad, but I move past it so I can focus. "The franchise deal? He's moving Dawson into the Midwest."

Our conversation is paused as the server sets our food down. My uncle stares at his sandwich. "How do you know that?" He brings his gaze back to me.

My mind races as I try to think of a way out of what I just revealed since Ian would never tell me anything about the company. I quickly decide that a version of the truth is probably safest. "Annie mentioned something while we were all out on Saturday," I say, cutting my waffles up even though I'm not hungry now.

"Right. I forgot she went out with you." He plays with his napkin. "That's only part of it. From what I've been able to gather, one of the companies that Astor Properties is working with is an investment fund."

He's acting like I should know what he's talking about, but I don't. I take a bite and wait for him to go on.

When he continues to stare, I swallow and point at myself. "Artist, remember? I may have grown up in a Dawson house, but I don't really know what any of that means."

"Franchising is one thing if the Dawson Hotel Group maintains ownership. But I've seen the proposal. Your brother is selling the company, and our family will lose sole ownership."

"Can he do that?"

"He runs the company."

"Why would he do that?"

"Your brother knows as much about the hotel business as you do. He may have more interest in it, but he has no real experience besides a few summers when he worked for your dad and me. He's taking advice from the wrong people. People who see a very large dollar sign attached to the Dawson Hotel Group portfolio."

"You mean the Astors."

"Phillip Astor, specifically." He looks like he swallowed something toxic, just the opposite of how I feel anytime I hear the name Astor. But he also seems even more worn down than when he came in. He hasn't touched his food, and his entire body is slouched.

"I don't know what I can do." I push my plate aside. "Why didn't you stop him?"

"Ian doesn't listen to me. He doesn't listen to anyone in the company. The only people who can do something are you and your sister."

"How? You just said it. He runs the company."

"It's not his to run."

"How do you know that?"

"Because I've seen the will."

"Is everything okay?" the gray-haired server asks as she comes back, oblivious to the cliffhanger she just interrupted and seemingly annoyed that we've hardly touched our food.

"Perfect," my uncle says. His tone is polite, but I can tell that he wants her to leave. I just shake my head, and she walks away, mumbling something about wasted food.

"How have you seen it?" I ask once we're alone again.

"It's public record, Charlie. I've known what it's said for years. You've never been willing to talk about it."

"You never told me you saw it."

"Would that have mattered? Do you want to know what it said?"

"No."

We're both quiet for a few minutes, and I avoid his gaze. I know I look like a child refusing to face the real world, but it's only this week that I've even been able to face my parents' death. Whatever my uncle is about to tell me feels like it will bring that precarious progress tumbling down.

"When your parents died, I just wanted you three to be okay," he says quietly, breaking our prolonged silence. "Kat has her clinic, and you disappeared. Fighting over the will seemed like it would just destroy the family. I don't want to do that. As much as your parents loved that company, they loved you three more. They'd tell me to let him destroy it."

"So why don't you?"

"Because what he is doing isn't right." His eyes move around the diner again, but this time, the nostalgic expression is replaced by a deep sadness. "I understand why you wanted to come here. To feel closer to them." His voice breaks. "That's what the Dawson Hotel Group is for me. It's my life. It was his life. The three of us built it together. I can't lose my brother *and* this. Please, Charlie. Help me." When I don't say anything, he reaches across the table and grabs my hand. "When you wanted to leave, we let you. I made it clear I wanted you to stay, but we didn't fight it. Because I knew you needed to get away. For you. But it's been four years, and now I'm asking something of you."

"I don't know what I can do," I reply, looking at our joined hands.

"Most of your parents' assets are in the trust, which as you know, Ian also has control over." He moves his hand off mine. "I can't see what's in there or what he's withheld from you. But the company was handled in their will." He pulls over his briefcase and opens it, bringing out a file. He slides it over in front of me, but I don't make a move to open it.

"Now I really feel like we're in the Mafia," I say.

"I don't think the Mafia operates on the upper west side," he replies, but his tone is still serious. He points to the file. "That's the will that Ian filed with the court. But I have a feeling you won't open it. So let me tell you what's in there. Your parents left the company to the three of you. Evenly."

His words hang heavy between us, but they don't surprise me. I think I've always known my parents did that. To them, the company was a legacy that belonged to all of us. But they always put too much trust in Ian, and their hope that one day, we'd all put our differences aside was unrealistic.

"You two can stop him," my uncle continues.

"If I bring this up, you know what will happen. He'll just tell me to fuck off. So what am I supposed to do? Take him to court?"

"That's one option."

"Any others?"

"Kat. She's the only person he listens to. She can make him see reason."

"Kat's getting married in five days. I can't bring this up to her now."

He lets out another deep sigh. "I know." He rubs a hand over his face. "But this Astor deal is getting close. As soon as the wedding is over, you need to talk to her."

My mind is racing. Between Annie breaking up with Ian and this mess, I'm going to be putting a lot on my sister right after the happiest day of her life. My plan to come quickly into New York before slipping back out is proving impossible. I'm like a bulldozer that's come to ruin my sister's life. A life she's worked hard to come by.

"Eat," he says, pointing to my food and moving his sandwich in front of him. No matter what tension is happening at the moment, a Dawson never wastes food. "Take a look at it. We'll talk in a few days at the rehearsal dinner."

"Okay," I mumble, still thinking about Kat and how much all of this will devastate her.

I watch my uncle eat, but I have a very different feeling in my stomach than when he walked in, and I've lost my appetite. All the sexy excitement I was feeling earlier is now dimmed in light of what he just asked of me.

I suppose I was naive to think I could just slip in and out of New York like it was nothing. This city has a way of moving and shaking even when I'm trying desperately to stand still.

CHAPTER SEVENTEEN

*A*n *address? You just sent me an address? That's kind of creepy.*

I tip my phone away from Kat and Holly, but I know I'm not able to hide my smile the moment I see Annie's name come across my phone screen.

"I said no phones during the movie, Charlie," Kat says from the couch where she's sitting with Holly.

"You've been on your phone the entire night," I argue.

"Talking to my fiancé. About wedding planning. Because my wedding is this week."

"It's bad enough you have us doing a bridal movie marathon. Are you going to continue mentioning your wedding every sentence?"

She sticks her tongue out at me but smiles right after. She knows I'm not serious and that she's welcome to talk about her wedding as much as she wants. But I'm not going to pretend that I'm paying attention to the horrible movies she's put us through for the past six hours. She claims she's still hungover from Saturday and needs a movie night to recharge while Jake is hanging out with his parents. I don't mind since it gives me a chance to hang out with her without Holly being able to corner and interrogate me. Not that I can't tell she wants to, with the glances she keeps directing my way. I've also ignored about fifteen texts from her about the situation since the weekend.

"What next?" Holly asks when the credits roll for whatever movie we were just watching.

"Can we please watch something that's not a Hallmark movie?" I ask, hoping it will launch the two of them into another half hour debate so I can text Annie back in peace.

"*Father of the Bride* is not a Hallmark movie," Kat says. "It's a classic."

"I'm with Charlie. I'm beginning to hate weddings. And movies. And love." Holly throws her head back against the couch. "*Please* put on something else. Or we can go out. I feel like I've melted into this couch."

Kat shakes her head. "I know what going out with you means. And I'm still recovering from the last time."

"You're so dramatic." Holly rolls her eyes. "That was three days ago. I think you're fine."

"Yes, but I drank almost every drink available on the lower east side. I think I'll need at least two more days to fully recover."

"Or maybe you're just trying to avoid hanging out with Jake's parents," I say.

"There is no avoiding his mother, believe me. She's everywhere. I'm surprised she lets me pee alone. I can't lie, I am quite enjoying this relaxing reprieve from her."

"I think that's the first time I've ever heard you say something negative about someone," Holly says with a fake gasp.

"That's not true. I say mean stuff about Charlie's ex all the time."

"She does. All the time," I respond.

"Oh, well that's warranted," Holly says. "Jen sucks."

"I still think you're crazy for not going for Lily," Kat says as she grabs the remote and hands it to Holly.

"They don't even live in the same city." Holly gives me a quick glance. I'm thankful that she easily smoothed over that topic. I don't want to have a repeat conversation about why Lily isn't right for me. "Does this mean I get to choose what we're watching?"

"Only because you're being annoying about it," Kat responds. "Anyway, if Charlie fell in love with someone here, maybe she'd stay. You can't blame a sister for trying."

"There's still time," Holly says, giving me another significant look. "Maybe she will."

"I won't hold my breath," Kat says.

"Since you two don't seem to need me for a conversation *about* me, I'm going to go find more snacks," I say, coming up with any excuse to be alone with my phone.

"There are chips in the top cabinet," Kat says as I pass the couch, causing me to stop.

"There are chips in this apartment, and you've been making me eat paper?"

Kat rolls her eyes. "It's not paper. They're quinoa chips. They're healthy."

"Those are not chips, Kat. They taste like the arts and crafts I give my students." Holly pushes the bag on the coffee table aside with her foot. "Get me some real chips."

"Only one of us has to fit into a wedding dress this weekend, so hush," Kat says.

I look at her fondly as she shoves a "chip" into her mouth and gives us an overexaggerated hum of approval. Kat is just one of those people who can easily make others smile, and I've missed her personal brand of silly.

"Stop. You're going to be the most beautiful bride anyone has ever seen," I say, then nod to the offending bag of chips. "Even if you have a Dorito."

She smiles at me. "Thanks, sis. But sorry, we don't have Doritos."

"Well, I'm going to go see what you do have."

I wait until I'm all the way out of the room before I pull my phone out. A smile grows as I read Annie's last text again. If I take too long, Kat or Holly will come find me, so before I respond, I look through Kat's top cupboard to see if I can find some popcorn.

Luckily, there's a box in there, and I'm grateful that it's butter and not infused with something gross like kale or sunflower dust. You never really know with Kat, and I'm guessing this box is Jake's.

As the popcorn begins to cook in the microwave, I open Annie's text so I can respond:

Sending you an address is creepy? I seem to remember you doing the same thing to me Saturday night.

I have a feeling that she was waiting because only a second later, I can see three bubbles: *That was different. I was sending you to my art studio.*

And where am I sending you? A dungeon?

I thought this was a 'no sex' date? Now we're talking about dungeons?

Her text makes me laugh out loud so I pretend to cough to cover the sound. I send her a response just as the microwave beeps. *Maybe your mind is just in the gutter, Ms. Astor.*

If she is in the mood to text, I don't want to stop that. I'll just have to be subtle about it in front of Holly and Kat. As I come back into the living room with the popcorn, Holly and Kat hardly even notice. Holly is staring intently at the TV, and Kat is hiding behind a pillow.

I'm not surprised to see that Holly chose some horror movie to make Kat suffer through; Kat, who used to get scared by animated musicals. And according to Jake, she still sleeps with a nightlight on.

"I made popcorn," I whisper as I set the bowl on the coffee table. Kat stays behind her pillow, but Holly grabs a handful as she continues to stare at the screen.

I move back to my chair. I don't even need to be subtle at this point. Holly's choice created the perfect distraction. When I pick up my phone, there's a new text waiting for me:

That's entirely possible. When it comes to you, my mind seems to always be in the gutter.

As much as I'd love for this conversation to go the way it seems to be going, I'm hyperaware that my sister and Holly are sitting only feet away, so I send a safer text: *You could just google the address, Modern technology is incredible.* I include a winking emoji so she knows I'm just teasing and put all my power into not smiling in case Holly looks over.

I did google it, sassy pants. It's just a building.

Then I don't know what the problem is. You can see it's not a dungeon.

The problem is attire. How am I supposed to know if what I chose to wear is appropriate for this secretive date?

Just dress like you usually do. You always look beautiful. We aren't going anywhere fancy. I can't stop the rush of butterflies through my stomach. The fact that Annie is stressing about what to wear indicates she's as excited about Wednesday night as I am, and I can't believe I have to wait another day.

The text bubbles keep appearing and disappearing, and it's adorable that she's overthinking what she wants to say. As her next text comes, I feel an instant rush of heat. *...would you like to see if what I chose is appropriate?*

I type so quickly, I almost drop my phone. *Yes.*

Are you sure? That doesn't seem very enthusiastic.

I can't seem to type as fast as I want, and I should probably be embarrassed at how eager I sound, but I'm too curious to know where this is going. *Yes. Please. Show me. Please.*

That's better. And I like your manners, baby girl.

I wait, but nothing comes in for a couple of minutes. The movie has gotten gorier and more intense. When my phone lights up, I open the new text, and this time, I actually do drop it.

"Whoa there, sparky," Holly says, glancing over before her eyes dart right back to the movie. "Is the movie scaring you?"

"Here," Kat says, throwing a pillow to me. "Put this over your face. It helps."

"Thanks," I murmur as I pick up my phone. I position the pillow on the side of the chair, giving me extra coverage that is now essential as I look at an image of Annie on her bed wearing nothing but a black bra.

She's lying down and staring up at the camera with a mischievous expression, and all I can seem to do is stare with my mouth hanging open.

You can answer now. Her text causes my mouth to close, but my whole body is shaking, and my fingers don't seem to want to cooperate.

Over the years, I've received sexy photos from women. But nothing has paralyzed me quite like this. Artists around the world would sell their fortunes for one glimpse of such a perfect model. Each curve and angle was meant to be painted. Not for the first time, my fingers ache for a brush. But I know that would be futile. Annie *is* the art. And live art can't be replicated.

I take a few deep breaths so I can respond. *Well, that's not fair. What's not?*

I didn't realize you weren't dressed.

How is that unfair?

Because you're really hot, and I'm here and not there.

You could always remedy that by leaving wherever you are to come here.

I feel another shot go straight to my pussy. *Don't say 'come.' This is hard enough.*

Poor baby. But you still haven't given me any feedback on my outfit.

I'm a fan. To say the least. But you might get cold? It's December.

Hmm. Very logical. I'll have to rethink my choice.

Maybe just throw a scarf over it?

You're really not going to tell me where we're going?

I take it you're not very good with surprises.

I'm just impatient to see you.

I wasn't expecting an honest response, and my body warms in an entirely different way. She has a way of disarming me with just a simple word or look, and her text doesn't fail to do the same. I take another deep breath and slowly type. My finger hovers over the send button, but if she can show some vulnerability, I should reward her with the same. Finally, I hit send. *Seeing you is all I've thought about since Saturday.*

So you're saying you like me, then?

I more than like you, Annie. I stare at the text. I didn't even think before I sent it, as if my fingers had their own agenda.

When I see the text bubbles appear and disappear again, I regret being so honest. That was something I should have said in person, and I probably just freaked her out. I don't even know what's happening with Ian, and I should probably hold off on spewing romantic statements until I do.

I've almost resigned to watch the movie when a new text appears: *I more than like you, too. And it scares me. I wasn't expecting this. Or you.* Before I can respond, she sends another: *I don't know what to do.*

I don't know if she is talking about her feelings or her situation with Ian or both. I chew my lip. This is the Annie I want. Open and free and raw. But right as a woman screams for someone not to kill her on the screen, I decide that maybe this conversation would be better face-to-face: *Let's start with our date. And then, we can figure things out. I'm taking you somewhere that means a lot to me—not a dungeon.*

I'm relieved when she sends a laughing emoji and then a lighter text. *I look forward to it. And on that note, this grandma is taking herself to bed. We're not all on a two-week vacation. Some of us have work in the morning.* Her text is accompanied with a winking face, and I feel a sense of relief and regret.

I still don't think we should process all these intense emotions over text, but I'm also disappointed that our conversation is coming to an end. *I'll think about you when I'm sleeping in tomorrow and lounging around until our date.*

Well now you're just being mean. Careful, Choo Choo.

Careful? What are you going to do from over there, darling?

Hmm, I guess nothing. By the way, I thought you might want to see my updated date outfit. I think the scarf works.

She sends another photo along with her text, but this time, she's lost the bra and a bright red scarf is loosely covering her bare tits.

"Fuck," I say aloud.

"I know," Kat says, her voice muffled behind her pillow. "I hate this movie."

I'm grateful she thought I was talking about the movie and not our brother's half-naked girlfriend. I've never met a woman so naturally confident. She knows the effect she has on me, and I feel frozen to do anything but stare.

Not a fan of red? Her follow-up makes me smile, and I type out a response, even though I feel more turned on than I should be in my current predicament.

Big fan. And touché. You win. Skip work and come sleep in with me.

I thought we agreed not to use the word 'come'?

I broke the rule.

Good to know you're willing to break rules. I'll have to keep that in mind tomorrow. Good night, Choo Choo.

Good night, Annie. Looking forward to tomorrow. I set my phone down, but there's nothing I can do about the smile that seems to be stuck on my face.

Thankfully, I don't have to school my features for long because Kat pauses the movie and throws her pillow at the screen. "Holly, you're never choosing a movie on wedding movie night again."

"I think you just made that up. And you paused at the best part. You have to see what she does."

Wait," Kat says, holding up her hand. "You've already seen this horrible thing you're making me sit through?"

"We've only seen like thirty minutes of it, but yes. I've seen it. And technically, it is a wedding movie."

"The groom was trying to hunt down and kill the bride," Kat responds.

"Exactly. Bride. Groom. Just slightly more blood."

Kat gets up and throws Holly the remote. "You two finish it. I have a facial in the morning, so I'm going to bed."

"It is past ten. I'm surprised you're still awake," I say as I stand to give her a hug.

"I know." She pulls me into her. "You guys broke me. I'm a party animal now."

"You should change your clinic name to that. Specialize in hamsters," Holly says.

"Why hamsters?" I ask.

Holly looks at me like I'm an idiot. "Because they have little parties in their cages at night. My college roommate had one."

"Well actually, many animals that are nocturnal—" Kat begins before Holly cuts her off.

"Weren't you heading to bed?"

"Fine. Remain ignorant," Kat says playfully. She pulls Holly in for a quick hug. "And anyway, I'd have to pass this new clinic idea by Jake. He hates hamsters."

"And the patriarchy wins again," Holly says, releasing her.

Usually, I'd join in the banter, but I'm still so distracted by Annie's texts that I'm relieved the night is coming to an end. I want alone time so I can read our conversation again.

Kat moves to the door but turns as soon as she gets there. "Charlie, you can stay on the couch if you don't feel like going back to the hotel."

I shake my head but smile. "Thanks, but I'm going to head back. All my stuff is there, and I'm sure you and Jake want some alone time."

"If his mom ever releases him to me." She leans her head against the door and lets out a small sigh. "Thank God, Ohio is states away from Manhattan. I'll see you guys on Thursday. Thanks for watching trashy romance with me." She makes a kissing face and opens the door to head down the hall to her bedroom.

The room is silent, and I don't remember another time that I felt this awkward with Holly. "What's happening on Thursday?" I ask, doing anything I can to sound casual, even though I know this is exactly what Holly has been waiting for.

She lets out a loud laugh. "You truly are the worst maid of honor ever."

"We always knew I was going to be bad at this. Mom and Dad missed my graduation because I gave them the wrong day. Kat knew better than to do this to me."

She playfully rolls her eyes. "How do you run a gallery?"

"With help. So what's on Thursday?"

"The bridal lunch with the bridesmaids. It's all in the packet my mom sent you. And we have our final fitting before that."

"Right. The packet. I totally read that. And the lunch is where we take the bride to lunch?"

"No. She takes *us* to lunch as a thank-you for being helpful with the wedding."

"Do I have to go?" I ask with a smirk. "I haven't been helpful."

She directs an expression my way I'm sure her students have seen once or twice. "And Friday is the rehearsal dinner," I add proudly, finally remembering one of the events.

"Bingo. See? I am a good teacher."

"And an asshole."

"Only you think that. Anyway, are we finishing the movie?"

"No, it's terrible. I'm going back to the hotel."

"How would you know it's terrible? You were texting the whole time. And how is Annie?"

I narrow my eyes, trying to decide if I should be truthful or not. But ultimately, this is Holly, and I know I can't lie. So I decide not to answer at all. I busy myself by going over to the chair and grabbing my coat.

She lets out a harsh laugh. "It's as if you think four years away could erase an entire life together. I know you. And I can tell when you're texting someone you like. That's how you looked when you met Jen."

I stop myself from telling her that what I felt for Jen pales in comparison to what I feel for Annie. "She's fine." I head toward the hallway that will take me out of the apartment.

She follows me. "That's all you're going to tell me?"

"There's nothing to tell. And keep your voice down. I don't want Kat to hear."

"Well, you still haven't told me what happened after the bar on Saturday."

I turn at the door and lean against the wall. It's not like I can just walk out in the middle of Holly's interrogation, so I resign myself to finishing this conversation. "Nothing. We talked."

"That's all?"

I take a deep breath and close my eyes as my head falls against the wall. I let out the breath before leveling a gaze at Holly. "No, Holls. We didn't just talk."

"And have you seen her again?"

"No."

"Are you going to?"

"Well, I suppose she'll be at the wedding." I decide not to tell her about our date. She'll find out eventually, but this is probably the worst place to discuss that.

She stares for an uncomfortable amount of time before she speaks in a steady, quiet voice that I'm not used to hearing from her.

"Shit happens, Charlie. If you like her, the family will get over it—"
I start to interrupt her, but she puts a hand up. "Even Kat. She loves you, and I don't think she's under some assumption that those two are right for each other. If you like her, tell her. This family deserves some happiness, and if she makes you happy, don't let that go."

Her words almost take my breath away. A tear stings the corner of my eye, and while it doesn't fall, something in me wants to let go and just confide in her. "I'm seeing her tomorrow night."

She doesn't seem as surprised as I thought she would. She leans against the wall opposite me. "I assume she hasn't ended things with Ian?"

My stomach tightens. "I don't think so. Not yet, at least. This has all happened really fast."

"Why are you seeing her tomorrow?" Her voice isn't judgmental; if anything, it's gentle.

I let out a long sigh. "Because I'm an idiot who wants to see her again. Because I always want to see her. Because I want her to experience life outside of her parents' clutches. Because she deserves so much better than Ian. And probably because I've fallen in love with the girl." I say the last part way too loudly and look down the hall to make sure it's still dark and quiet.

Holly puts her hands up in the "time-out" position, and sometimes, it seems like she really can't help but be a teacher. "Let's deal with one 'because' at a time. She hasn't broken things off with Ian." She waits for me to nod. "That makes sense, considering how fast all this has happened. And the wedding is coming up, and I'm sure she doesn't want to ruin things for Kat. On to the next one. You want to see her. So what? Charlie, maybe it's not the worst thing that you feel something for someone again."

"I feel things for people," I say, but even I can hear how defensive I sound.

"Outside of family? Annie excites you. You know how long it's been since I've seen you look like anything but a bored sloth?"

"Uh, thanks?"

"The point is that, yes, this is messy. And Ian will be mad. But everyone could get over it if she's your person."

"I live in LA, Holls."

"Yeah, why, exactly?"

This time I let out an even louder, more exaggerated sigh. "I have a life there. I own a gallery."

"Oh, and we have no art here in New York," she responds sarcastically. "If nobody else will say it, I will. And I only am because of what's happened with Annie. You're in LA because you ran. Because you can't handle the hurt of being here. For fuck's sake, you owned a gallery here. You could have owned dozens with our name."

I push off the wall and take a step closer so I don't have to shout. "You don't think I know why I left? I know I'm a coward. But I can't handle being here. I had to leave."

"And what about leaving Annie? How will that feel?"

The anger dissipates in an instant. I rub my face and take a step back. "I hardly know her, Holls."

She gives me a small smile before she shakes her head. "Charlie, I've known you through every gay phase you've ever had. Like that time you only dated vegans, even though you hate most vegetables." We both let out a small laugh. "But one thing I've always admired about you is your ease. You're so smooth and confident. I've always wanted your blasé attitude with women. But I've never seen you like this. You're like a puddle. Annie has affected you, and even from the small exposure I had, I can see that. You really think you can just walk away?"

"It's so much more complicated than that."

"Everything in life is fucking complicated. Let me ask you this, how has it felt being back?"

I know what she's asking, and I take a moment to really process the question. Parts of being back in this city have still felt heartbreaking. But more than I could have ever imagined, it's also felt good. Like I'm back in a home that doesn't continuously remind me of what was lost. "It's not as hard as I thought it would be."

"Then see her tomorrow. With an open mind. And see how you feel. No location is permanent. No decision is permanent."

"What about Kat?" I ask after a long pause.

"You mean about Ian and Annie?"

I nod.

"She'll be upset. She loves Ian, too. But she wants you to be happy. And she'd give just about anything to have you back in Manhattan. Just wait before you tell her. Because if you ruin her wedding, the dinner menu will be updated to offer fish, chicken, or Charlie."

"That's disgusting."

"You're right. There is in no way enough of you to feed one hundred and fifty guests."

I roll my eyes as I pull her into a hug. "I'm going to head out. Thanks for talking."

"I love you. But that wasn't talking. That was me prying things out of you with pliers"

"Whatever works." I wink before grabbing the door. "See you Thursday for the bridal brunch."

"Bridal lunch."

"Bridal brunch has a better ring to it," I say as I walk out.

"I'll be sure to bring it up to the official wedding association," she shouts after me.

I wave back to her, shaking my head. As I walk down Kat's street, waiting for a cab to pass, I shiver. I have a coat on, but my shaking has nothing to do with the temperature and everything to do with what I just told Holly. My own words keep rolling around in my head as I walk.

Because I've fallen in love with the girl.

I didn't need Holly to tell me what I already know. I've never felt for anyone what I do for Annie. But what to do with those feelings is what is causing my stomach to tighten. Beyond the hurt I'd cause Kat, can I really come back to this city? For a woman I just met?

CHAPTER EIGHTEEN

A nnie." I opened my hotel room door without checking to see who was on the other side. I'm so used to Dawson hotel employees dropping off random things at all hours that I didn't even think to look through the peephole. If I had known it was Annie, I would have at least combed my hair. Or changed my shirt. But it's two hours before we're meant to meet, and I wasn't expecting to see her.

And yet, here she is, looking stunning in a long red peacoat and tight black pants. Her hair is falling over her shoulders, and it's clear it's cold outside because she has an adorable flush to her cheeks. Her lips slide into a slow smile as she stands there confidently, as if she's pleased with herself for catching me so off guard. "I like the way you say my name," she says, leaning against the door.

"How do I say it?"

"Like it's the most delicious thing that's ever rolled off your tongue."

I open my mouth, but nothing comes out, so I close it again. Her sudden presence here and her easy swagger has disarmed me unusually fast.

Her smile grows right before she leans in and speaks in a much quieter voice. "It's probably safer for me to come in. Unless you'd prefer to keep standing here staring."

Her confidence seems to increase every time I see her, and all it does is cause my attraction to grow. "No, it's not safe," I manage to get out in a hoarse voice.

"Which is why you should maybe let me in?"

I can't trust my voice right now, so I open the door. Before she moves in, she stops and looks at my hair. She pushes some of it aside before dragging one finger down my cheek. "You look so sexy when your hair is a mess," she says before moving past.

My legs feel unstable, but the main thing I feel is regret as I see where her gaze has landed. If I had known she was coming, I would have made my bed, but it's a complete mess, with clothes thrown all over it. "Sorry, I wasn't expecting you," I mumble.

She turns to me with a look of amusement. "I'll forgive you for not making your bed. You're in a hotel, after all."

"Maybe I should tell you now that I rarely make it at home, too." I hear my voice becoming steadier than when she first arrived. Maybe I can talk if I'm not right next to her.

"We can work on that."

"We can?"

She gives me a small smile before walking to a chair on the other side of the room and setting down her purse. She stands there as if she owns the room. As if I'm in her space now. "I know we didn't agree to meet here."

"I'm not complaining." I look at my old T-shirt and ripped jeans. "Though, if I had known you were coming, I would have made myself look a little less like a teenage boy."

She lets out a quick laugh before her face becomes serious, and she walks slowly over to me and plays with the hem of my worn shirt. "That's not exactly how I would describe you," she says, focusing on my lips.

"How would you describe me?"

"Are you okay, Choo Choo?" she asks. "Your voice just got very raspy. Do you need some water?"

This version of Annie will always have me wrapped around her finger, and by her expression, she knows it. I shake my head, not trusting my voice again.

She pushes some hair behind my ear. Not that it will stay there. "Do you know why I like your hair so messy?" I shake my head, too mesmerized by the glint in her eyes to speak. "It reminds me of you on your back. How you look after I fuck you." She moves her hand down my neck to my collarbone. "And I like this outfit. Don't get me wrong, you looked beautiful at the club. But you look even better like this. It reminds me of the first night we met." She moves both hands around my back and trails her fingers to my waist. "To answer your question, I guess I would describe you as my perfect brand of sexy."

"Does that mean I don't have to change?"

Her face is so close that it's becoming almost impossible to keep the conversation going without kissing her. "Considering I don't even know where we're going, I can't answer that. I'm here for a different reason."

"Which is?"

"To discuss loopholes."

"Should we move our mouths farther apart?"

"Not necessary," she replies before swiping her tongue against my mouth and sending a shiver down my spine. "Be strong, baby girl."

"And what are these loopholes?" I ask, doing my best not to shake from the extreme arousal growing with every breath that hits my lips.

"I'm sure it's not lost on you that I'm early. And I'm not in the location you sent me."

"This has not been lost on me."

"Then technically, our date has not yet begun."

"This is true. We are outside of technical date time."

"And if I remember correctly, the 'no sex' rule only applied to the date." She pushes my waist until I'm moving backward toward the door.

I allow her to move me easily, too turned on by this little game to stop it. "Also true." My back hits the door, and she leans in, and her lips brush my ear, sending another shiver down my body that I know she can feel.

"I guess that means I can fuck you right here, and we're not breaking any rules." Her lips latch on to my ear right before she drags her tongue down my neck.

I close my eyes and let my head fall back against the door. Her lips feel so good that I don't even remember why I made the stupid rule to begin with. "I've always been a rule breaker anyway," I say, opening my eyes when her lips leave my neck.

Her eyes are cloudy, and she looks ready to devour me. "I had a feeling that might be the case. But just to make sure we're at least *trying* to follow the rules, I'll just fuck you against this door. Not in bed."

"You may be the smartest woman I've ever been with." I pant as my head hits the door again.

Annie pushes off my waist so there's more space between us. "Shall we continue to talk about your past women, or would you like me to fuck you so hard you forget about them forever?"

I've never been one for possessiveness, but this show of jealousy, still dripping with confidence, has me even more turned on. "What women?"

"Good girl," she says and captures my mouth in a kiss.

❖

I feel soft kisses down my jawline, and this has to be my new favorite way to be woken up.

When I finally open my eyes, she's staring at me as if she's been watching me sleep. But her face isn't as happy or serene as I thought it would be after the hours we just shared. I can't decipher the expression, but I wouldn't describe it as relaxed.

I check the clock on the bedside table and realize I've been sleeping for two hours. "I'm sorry. I didn't mean to sleep for so long," I say. "I guess sex makes me sleepy."

"All sex?" She smiles, and it lightens up her face a bit.

"No, just sex with you." Her hair looks disheveled, so I push some behind her shoulder. That same concerned expression settles back on her face. "What's up?" I ask, continuing to play with the ends of her hair.

She's quiet for a while, her eyes moving over my face as if she's etching each part. As if she's trying to memorize something. I wonder if it's the artist in her or if it's just my face that affects her like this. "I don't want to scare you." Her voice is so quiet and strained that it's almost jarring. Her presence has felt so large tonight, but right now, she feels fragile.

I push up against the pillows so I'm in a better position to talk. She sits up to face me. I'm grateful that she pulls the sheet up so I'm not distracted. We're obviously about to talk about something heavy, and I don't think I can do that while her bare body is so close. "Annie, how could you scare me?"

She seems so small but not the way she is with Ian. I've never seen her so vulnerable, even at her art studio telling me about her family. "I've never felt like this," she continues in the same quiet voice. "For any man or any woman or any person at all. When I'm with you, I just feel like me. A me that I didn't even know existed. Like I was this shell that could eat and breathe and sleep. But that's it. I've been sleepwalking."

I pull her hands into mine, trying to do what I can to reassure her. "I feel the same way. And it scares me, too. I've never had something I've felt so strongly about. Or someone."

"But you had that ex—"

I cut her off with a harsh laugh. "You mean Jen? That wasn't the same."

"How? Ian said you proposed to her."

I sigh and feel the same annoyance I feel every time I think about my ex. But if Annie and I are really going to get to know each other, I suppose this is important information in understanding why I'm so reticent about relationships. "Jen and I met at Pratt. She's a sculptor. Or she was when we met. She was a year ahead of me at school, and everyone seemed to know her. She wasn't a brilliant artist, but she was engaging. And she had a way of surrounding herself with talented people. I guess you could say she was charming. And beautiful."

"Okay, okay. Moving on," Annie says in a cute, jealous voice that makes me smile for a moment. "And you were one of the people she brought into this circle?"

"No. I wasn't nearly as talented as her snobby Pratt friends."

"I bet that's not true."

"I did well at Pratt. But not like the people she surrounded herself with. I was enamored with her. And she was enamored with my family's resources. I didn't see that at the time. Soon, I was helping finance art shows for her friends. I thought it was romantic that we were creating things together. But once I graduated, she started pressuring me to give up art and become more involved in the family business. She said it would give us more opportunities to do what we wanted, and she made it clear I wasn't talented enough to do it on my own. She hated it when I opened the gallery. She thought it was a waste of time."

"You must have felt strongly about her, though. Were you in love?" Her voice doesn't hold any jealousy. It's soft and understanding, and in four years, nobody has made me feel so open about talking about any of this.

"I thought I was." Playing with her hand seems to relax me, so I turn it over and begin to trace lines down her palm. "Jen has this big, enigmatic personality, and it took me too long to realize that her personality changed based on what she wanted. She was my first real girlfriend. She was very good at making it seem like I was lucky to be with her. And I felt like I was at the time. Now, I can see we weren't right for each other at all. Anyway, after I graduated, and we moved in together, I proposed. My parents died shortly after."

"Ian told me it was a car accident, but he doesn't talk about it. We don't really talk about anything," she says, and it seems like she didn't want to mention his name, but in this instance, it doesn't bother me. I'm not surprised Ian doesn't talk about it. None of us do.

I pull the covers up as if trying to create some sort of protective blanket. I know where this conversation is going, and it's so much bigger than Jen. But it's also something I haven't talked about in four years, not even to Kat or Holly. "It was an accident," I repeat in a strained voice. "They were running late, and their driver went through a red light." My throat tightens, but the tears that usually sting my eyes don't fall. Maybe it's the way Annie's scooted closer so our knees are touching, and I feel her warm body against mine. "Anyway, my parents left Ian as the executor of the will. He didn't give me a dime from the trust. I didn't care. I wasn't interested in their money. But Jen flipped out over it. She wanted me to fight. And that's when it became clear what her real interest was. My parents had just died, and all she cared about was the money. When she realized I wasn't going to do anything about it, she moved out."

Annie is quiet for a moment. "That's horrible. And she obviously never deserved you." She opens her mouth before she closes it again. "But why *didn't* you fight him? I didn't know he did that."

"He's not going to tell his girlfriend that he did something illegal. And I didn't want the money. I wanted my parents back."

"Is that why you two hate each other? He's never spoken kindly of you, but he's never mentioned a reason."

The elephant in our sibling relationship has stampeded into this room, and I know there are things Annie and I need to talk about. Things we didn't get to the other night in her art studio. This isn't exactly how I thought our first date would go, but I never thought I'd fall for my brother's girlfriend, either. "We've never gotten along. We're just too different. He's always cared about status and money, and he's always been a bit of a misogynist. I think my parents wondered how he got like that. My dad even sent him to boarding school in upstate New York, which I don't think helped."

"He talks fondly of that time."

I laugh. "I'm sure he does. It's where he met all his asshole conservative friends. But he's always had different values than the rest of us. And yet, he tried so hard to get our parents' approval. He just did it in all the wrong ways. When I was sixteen and he was eleven, he found a note in my room that a girl had written to me, and he made a big deal of showing it to my parents, as if he could out me. Too bad they'd known since I was six."

She lets out a genuine laugh, and it's nice to hear something lighter as we talk about all this.

"He's always tried to undermine me," I continue. "He used to lie to our parents about things I did to get me into trouble. And that's followed him through his whole life. He can't be honest."

"But Kat doesn't have the same relationship with him?"

I take a deep breath as I try to decipher the situation as well as something that's always bothered me, even though I understand it: Kat's loyalty to Ian. "They're twins. They have a bond, I guess. And he has always been sweet and protective of Kat. Even if it's usually in a sexist, controlling way, like trying to decide who she could and couldn't date in high school. She knows who he is. But they'll always be twins."

Annie pulls her hands away before she shakes her head. She continues to stare at the bed until I put a hand under her chin and gently lift it.

"What just went through that beautiful head of yours?"

"I can't imagine what you think of me. For being with him."

I grab her hands again. "I understand family dynamics. And the pressure that can bring."

She shakes her head again. "But you didn't give in to it. I've done everything my parents wanted for so long that I don't know what the difference is between what they want and who I am. And I don't know how to stop it." My heart clenches at the tears pooling in her eyes. "Until I met you. And I know we just met, but you make me feel at ease. For once in my life."

I push up on my knees and take her face in my hands. "I feel the same," I say, swiping away the tears. "I haven't felt like myself since my parents died. Until I saw you walk into that bar, and you completely dismissed my presence for an hour."

She laughs, and I wish I could record it. It comes out so easy and sharp, and I could listen to it all day. "I was playing a game. I couldn't give in to that swagger too easily."

"Swagger, huh?"

"Don't let that go to your head. Your nickname is still Choo Choo." She smiles softly. "I thought you'd be mad that I haven't ended it with him yet." Her voice is so quiet that I can barely hear. "I haven't even seen him since our night together at the art studio. I'm going to do it."

I drop my hands but stay where I am. I'm not mad that she hasn't broken it off with Ian yet. In fact, I was so surprised by her arriving here and the subsequent activities that I haven't even thought about him. But now, my stomach tightens. I meant everything I said about how I feel, but I'm hyperaware of how all this could affect my family. Affect Kat. "When are you going to end it?"

"As soon as I see him next."

"How do you think he'll take it?"

"From the way he talks, nobody has ever broken up with him. Maybe his ego will be hurt. But he won't be heartbroken. He's only with me for public appearances. I've been with him a year, and he's seen my apartment once."

My entire body tenses. Talking about this is one thing, but the last thing I want to think about is Ian in Annie's apartment. Where her bedroom is.

She seems to notice because she quickly continues. "Sorry. I didn't mean it like that."

"Let's not talk about that," I say, trying to relax.

"If it helps, we were never a real couple. It was all for show. And honestly, my dad will probably be the most devastated. Not only does he like Ian, he thinks we're a 'proper match,' as he puts it."

I remain tense. Everything my uncle told me at lunch about his part in the decimation of my parents' company is rolling through my head. But this isn't the time or place to bring that up, and I doubt my uncle would want me to. This conversation is about Annie and me.

"It's pretty brave," I say. "What you're about to do."

"Breaking up with a man I don't love, never did, and was only with to appease my parents? How is that brave?"

"For finally making a decision for *you*. Some people spend their whole lives trying to make others happy. You've followed their plan for a while. It's brave to deviate from that."

"What would be brave is to tell them that I'm gay. But I'm still so scared."

"Because of your sister?"

More tears fall down her face, but before they can go far, I catch them. "I don't want to lose her," she whispers. "Not like Dylan did."

"She's only a couple years from being an adult. And there are other ways of staying in touch. Your parents don't need to know everything. Who you're dating isn't really their business if you don't want it to be."

"I would never hide the person I love. I couldn't do that to you." Her eyes widen the second the words come out.

My heart begins to pound, but neither of us is ready for that kind of declaration, so I move the conversation along. "Maybe just one thing at a time, then."

She takes a deep breath and rubs her face before letting out a small laugh. "I promise, I'm not usually the cry-after-sex type."

"I don't think it counts if its two hours after." I smile and rub her hand.

We're both quiet for a minute before she says, "You're going back to LA."

The statement has my stomach tightening all over again. "I have my gallery." I don't know what else to say.

"And here?"

"I don't know what I have here yet."

"Because I haven't ended it with Ian?"

"No. Because being back here is more complicated than that. It hurts."

She puts one hand on my cheek, bringing my eyes to hers. "Does this hurt, Charlie? Has any of this hurt? Because I've felt more alive with you than I've ever felt. Are you telling me I'm alone in that?"

"No. You're not alone."

"So I'll end it. And we'll figure out what's next."

I wish I could kiss her and tell her that we can have some happily ever after once the wedding is done. But I know this is more complicated than that, and this will cause a tidal wave of drama with my family. "Not until after the wedding."

"What do you mean?"

"Don't break up with him until after the wedding. When my parents died, I left. I left Kat alone. It's not like Ian would talk about it, and Holly and Logan didn't get it in the same way. Now that I'm back, I want to do right by her. She deserves this week to be about her, not Ian going through a breakup."

She nods. "I can wait. As long as you know where my heart is." She's looking at me so softly that I want to wrap her in my arms and never let go. Her expression is so soft, in fact, that her next words cause my eyes to widen. "And as long as you also know that my pussy won't stop throbbing until I can really be with you."

My mind is racing. Her words are romantic and sexy at the same time, and all I want to do is hang on to them for dear life. The larger implications still loom, but now, all I can think about is having her the way I've never wanted any woman, slow and soft and loving.

"I know there's a lot we need to figure out," I say, gently pulling down the cover so I can see her bare body. "And if the wedding is in a few days, I guess we have some time. But what really concerns me is that throb. I'm no doctor, but that sounds concerning."

She moves the rest of the cover off and brings her legs over so she can straddle mine. Without even kissing me again, she moves one hand down. I'm overwhelmed by the sensation of her touching my still wet pussy and her perfect tits just sitting in front of my face. "Based on how wet you are, I'm not the only one with a throbbing issue."

"It seems that way."

"Should we check WebMD?"

"I'm not sure that's a reliable source."

"Hmm, you're probably right." She spreads her fingers across my pussy again before she pulls her hand away. Like always when she's teasing me, I have to stop myself from letting out a grunt of frustration. "Though, baby girl," she says, licking her hand. "I seem to remember somewhere you wanted to take me. Have I made us late?"

I'm too distracted to answer. But apparently, that isn't what she wants because she removes her hand and gives me a stern look. "You have," I say in as steady a voice as I can muster. "But we can get there any time. And I will need to eat before. Someone has made me very hungry."

"If you need to eat, I have some ideas." She leans down and kisses me. She's smiling when she comes back up for air.

"You are insatiable, and it's one of the things I love most about you."

This is the second time tonight that word has been casually thrown about, and even though butterflies are erupting in my stomach, Annie doesn't seem surprised or freaked out. She dips her head so our lips are an inch apart. "This is something isn't it?" she whispers, her lips grazing mine.

"This is something."

"Make love to me." She lifts her head, and I'm not sure I've ever experienced eye contact so intense and connected. Something about it makes me want to capture the moment forever, as if it's too significant to forget. It's as if she's fully giving herself to me but not in submission. Right now, she is offering me her heart. And I'm going to do what I can to fill it.

I move so she falls to the side, and I can climb on top. I push into her, trying to feel as much of her naked skin against mine as I can.

"You feel so good on top of me. I love feeling you like this."

I pull up so I can trail my fingers down her torso. Once I reach her pussy, I don't tease, and I don't linger. I need to feel my hand deep inside her. I need to feel all of her wrapped around me. She grips my back as I slide inside, her mouth parting as she lets out a sweet sigh.

"Yes, baby," she says, lifting her head so she can give me a brief kiss before it falls back onto the pillow. "Like that. Just give me you. All of you."

I push in harder. "You have me." I lean in and take her mouth in another kiss, the kind of kiss I've never experienced. Our lips move tentatively, and I can feel hers quiver. There's no pressure or urgency, but there doesn't need to be. We're just breathing each other in, and it almost feels as if her breath is mine.

As we continue to kiss and I continue to push into her slowly and deeply, she moves so we're side by side. She slides her hand down and mirrors my movements. I push my hips up, hoping to take even more of her hand.

Our foreheads touch as we fuck each other, and our breathing becomes progressively louder. If this is making love, I've certainly never experienced it with another woman. Every part of me feels connected to Annie, as if we're just meeting, while at the same time, our bodies have mapped each other for generations.

"How can you leave this?" she asks in a whisper against my lips. "How can you not be mine?"

I'm too close to an orgasm to process her words. Instead of answering, I lean in and capture her mouth in a passionate kiss. And as our tongues swirl, I push in deeper, and I feel her orgasm hit through the vibration she lets into my mouth. As she grabs my back, my own orgasm follows, and we moan into each other as we climax.

As we come down, our bodies are completely entwined, but neither of us seems to want to move. We stay like that as our breathing evens out. After what feels like ten minutes, she rolls to the other side and turns to face me. "Still hungry?"

"Well, technically, I didn't get to eat anything."

"Poor baby didn't get her sustenance."

"No, but I got something better."

We smile stupidly for a few minutes, and part of me wants to scrap the whole date and stay in bed. But there's still somewhere I want Annie to see.

"Well, this is your date, Choo Choo. What's for dinner?"

"My date?" I say, laughing. "You've directed this entire night. Not that I'm complaining. How about we grab a slice of pizza on our way to the place?"

"A Dawson eating at a pizza joint. That's not something I ever thought I'd see."

"I'm not my brother," I say seriously.

She lightly pulls on my bottom lip. "Don't I know it." As she lets go, she says, "Are you ready to go to this mysterious place?"

"I'd go anywhere with you."

"That was cheesy, Choo Choo. I'll let it slide but only because of that face."

"Glad to know you can't resist it."

She rolls her eyes and throws a pillow at me. "How about you stop talking and buy me some pizza?"

"A slice for Astor Princess, coming right up."

CHAPTER NINETEEN

As we leave the pizza place, Annie looks tentative. But once we're on the street, she slides her hand into mine and links our fingers together. We're in Harlem, so I have no real fear of seeing someone we know, and the small gesture has me smiling. I squeeze her hand before pulling her along. "We're just going down the block."

We're quiet as we walk, and it feels like we've been doing this for years. I have to remind myself that this is our first date and probably a doomed one at that. "Here we are," I say, stopping in front of a building that looks similar to Annie's art studio. It has a warehouse feel to it but a little more inviting.

She looks up. "Ah, so this is the dungeon."

"Not as daunting as one would think, right?"

"Depends on what kind of dungeon you're talking about." She winks.

I drop her hand because the walkway up to the building is narrow. It's clear that the staff hasn't cut the foliage since the place opened about ten years ago.

"I didn't take you for the Harlem type," Annie says.

"You need to stop making assumptions about me based on my last name." My words come out harsher than intended, but her pizza comment also rubbed me the wrong way. I may be a Dawson, but my parents did all they could to keep me grounded.

She puts her hand on my arm before I have the chance to ring the doorbell. "You're right. And I'm sorry. I know you're not like him."

"And he's nothing like my parents. The Dawsons like pizza. And the subway. And normal, everyday things. We're not all Ian."

"I know that." She turns me and places a gentle kiss on my lips. It's so cold that I can see steam between us. But the kiss is so sweet and soft that I forget my annoyance. And really, it's not her fault. I've always been sensitive to people assuming things about my family.

"So do we just ring the doorbell?" she asks when our lips finally part. "There's no knob."

"Yep. Access is a little protected here."

"I feel like I'm part of *The Little Rascals* and the He-Man Woman Haters Club."

Her statement makes me laugh. "The He-Man what?"

Annie rolls her eyes. "We have some 90's movies to catch up on. That can be date two."

"Oh, so we're liking this date? Already thinking about date two?"

"Just ring the damn doorbell." She huffs out a stream of steam. "I'm cold."

I'm still laughing, but I ring the doorbell I've pressed more times than I can remember. A speakeasy window opens in the middle of the door, and a young guy with blue hair peeks out. "Welcome to Atelier. Do you have an appointment?"

"I'm here to see Dorian. He knows I'm coming."

"*Charlie*," he shouts. "Come in!"

The door opens, and we enter a lobby covered in velvet. From the couches scattered about the room to the walls, it's hard to find anywhere that's not sporting the thick red material. Nothing has changed since I was last here, including the worn out check-in desk in the corner.

The doorman shakes my hand aggressively, and now that I'm close to him, I can see that he's not really a man at all. He's college-age, not surprising. The Atelier attracts a lot of young artists. "I've heard a lot about you," he says, still shaking my hand. "You're a legend here. They've covered it up now, but people around here still talk about your graffiti job on the Pratt student hub. That was brilliant."

Annie looks at me. "You graffitied your school?"

"It was a dare," I reply before turning back to the stranger.

"Oh, I'm Bradley."

"This is Annie," I say.

Bradley grabs her hand with the same excitement. "Dorian is around," he says once he lets go. "Let me just text him." He skips back to the desk and grabs his phone.

Annie steps closer to me, pulls on my arm, and whispers into my ear, "Okay, now you have to tell me where we are. Because this room does look like a dungeon."

"I guess you could say it's a community art center. Atelier Populaire. It was inspired by the French art movement. Our own New York house of clashing ideals and social issues." I follow her as she walks around the room and checks out the space. "When it opened a decade ago, it was a workshop for artists who couldn't afford their own space. The back area is still used for that. There's also an area that keeps the Atelier Populaire movement alive by creating political posters. But the place has expanded a lot. They do experimental performance pieces and sometimes even traditional theater. But it's still mostly a secret."

"And you spent a lot of time here?"

"After Pratt, I basically lived here. My best friend at school, Dorian, and his brother, Atlas, started this place. It's where I did most of my art."

"That's amazing. I had no idea this was here."

"He's ready for you," Bradley says. "You can head back through the performance space since there's a show going on in the theater."

I know this center like the back of my hand, so I guide Annie to the right side of the room and a large door. The next room is empty. This is usually where people stand before they're allowed to enter the performance space that changes almost monthly. Over the years, their reputation has grown with certain crowds, and I know they can have a lot of people waiting in this empty room at times.

"Gossip Ends Here?" Annie reads from a red neon sign above the door on the other side of the waiting room.

"Must be part of their recent performance piece." I move through the door. The performance space is dark, and there are three old beds pressed against one wall. The beds are draped in white cloth. A woman occupies each, pretending to be asleep.

Annie screams and grabs my arm because as soon as the door closes, one of the women shoots up from the bed and shouts, "I saw Sarah Good with the devil!"

Immediately after, the next woman sits up and shouts, "I saw Goody Osbourn with the devil!"

"I saw Bridget Bishop with the devil," the final woman shouts from her bed.

"What the fuck?" Annie whispers in my ear.

"I think there may be an active performance going," I whisper back.

"I'm scared. Get me out of here," Annie says louder now.

"Lies! Lies! Lies! Salem lives in lies. Lies! Lies! Lies!" The women keep shouting as we rush to the door on the other side of the room and leave as fast as we can. We both lean against the wall.

Annie looks like she's in a bit of a shock before she bursts out laughing. "Was going through the Salem Witch Trials part of this date?"

"Nope. Not even a little bit. Wow. That was just. Wow. Come this way."

I head down the hall until we get to another door, but before I can open it, Annie puts her hand on my arm. "Please tell me this isn't some reenactment of the Boston Tea Party."

"I promise, it's not." I push the door open to a much larger and brighter room.

"The prodigal artist has returned," a huge voice booms, and a handsome man sprints over to me. He's wearing the same white, fringed leather jacket he's worn since college, which has always looked striking against his dark skin. Before I can even say hello, Dorian is pulling me into one of his usual tight hugs. "Charlie, Charlie, Charlie. My heart. My love. My reason for existing. I've been an empty vessel, and now I have returned to my former self. Hold on a second," he says, releasing me and holding up his hand. "Yes, yes. I can breathe again."

I'm not surprised by his exuberance, but I do laugh. Dorian has always been this way. He's just a loud, proud, overly excitable man. "A bit dramatic there, Dorian," I respond. "But it's good to see you, too. I've missed you. But what the actual fuck did we just walk through to get back here?" I point in the direction of the performance space.

"Ah, yes. *Gossip Ends Here*. Andrea's taken over the performance pieces, and she's into showcasing the plight of women. Did you wait until they got out of the beds and grabbed hands? That's when it gets really weird."

"No, thank God."

Dorian finally notices Annie and pushes me aside. He circles her as he gives her an exaggerated analysis that has me shaking my head. "And who is this angel you brought me?"

"This angel is Annie," she responds playfully, sticking out her hand. He takes it, but instead of shaking it, he kisses it.

"Oh, Jesus, Dorian. Stop it," I say.

He lifts his head and smiles the smile I've seen melt more than one heart over the years. "I may be gay as Christmas, but I can still appreciate beauty when I see it. Humans can be pieces of art just as much as a canvas can. And what a piece you are."

Annie grins at me. "Oh, I like him, Choo Choo."

"Choo Choo?" Dorian comes back over and puts his arm around my waist.

"It's her new nickname," Annie replies. "She loves it."

Dorian lets out a loud laugh, and my whole heart feels like it's filling as I hear it. I've missed him so much. In college, we were inseparable, and besides my family, he was the hardest person to leave behind. "And I like this one, too," he says. "She seems nicer than the last."

"That was years ago, Dorian. Jen's not in the picture anymore."

"Prettier too." He continues to look at Annie as if he didn't hear anything I said.

"She can also hear you," I mumble.

Annie dramatically pushes her hair over her shoulder. "Oh no. Please continue."

He lets out another loud laugh and claps his hands. "Oh, I do like this one. Sassy pants. Charlie needs that. The others have not been up to par."

"Oh, and how many have there been?" Annie asks, directing her gaze at him, but she has an amused expression.

"I don't think I'm allowed to answer that. Gay best friend rules. But Charlie is right. That was a long time ago."

"Annie is an artist as well," I say to him but when I look over to her, the light that was shining so bright in her eyes has dimmed.

"Not really. I don't show or anything. Just a hobby."

"A hobby?" I ask. "Pretty talented hobby to be accepted to SAIC."

Dorian puts his hands on Annie's shoulders. He's always been a touchy person, and through the years, I've gotten used to it. She smiles at him like they've known each other for years. "Angel, you don't have to show to be an artist. Just ask Charlie."

"I thought you've had gallery shows?" Annie asks me.

"Oh, *she's* shown. But I've been taking photos since my mama gave me a plastic toy camera, and I never have. Art is about the creation, not the response." He drops his hands from her shoulders and turns to me. "Shall we? The collection is in the back."

He walks toward the corner and pulls open another velvet curtain. I hear Annie's gasp before I even see what's there, but as soon as I do, I understand.

Dorian's photography is some of the best I've seen from a modern artist. Of our entire class at Pratt, he was the student earmarked for greatness. But Dorian has always been Dorian. He's never had an interest in that kind of attention. Convincing him to show in my gallery has been one of the most challenging negotiations of my career, despite how close we are.

If I wasn't used to his photography, I would have had the same reaction as Annie. And though I don't gasp, my heart begins to race as I stare at a full wall of brightly colored photos. Photos that I wasn't expecting. And it's as if I don't know where to look. There are so many. "Dorian," I whisper. "You told me you were giving me twelve. This is unbelievable."

He moves over to the wall so his back is to us and shrugs as he studies his work. "I'm giving them all to you. I trust you, Choo Choo."

He looks over his shoulder and winks, but I'm not in the mood to play. Annie stands next to him as they look at the collection together. His photos aren't just candid. They're the moments between the moments. He and his camera seem able to capture the truth behind us all. They don't just capture humans; they capture all the tiny things we miss as we live our lives. He captures the emotion *behind* the moment. In every one, I see something unique that will never be seen again.

"Dorian, these are breathtaking. I've never seen..." Annie seems lost for words. "Will you tell me about them?"

"Thank you, angel. This collection is my Harlem. My community. After school, I lost my sight. Every time I looked through my lens, it felt dull, and everything felt forged. Until I came back here," he says, waving his arms around the studio. "And I realized that this community is what I see and have always seen. It's my home. I wanted to capture the place I find more beautiful than anywhere in the world. My heart beats for each one of these faces." He's quiet before he turns to me. "And this annoying woman convinced me the world should see them, too. Or at least the devoid culture of Los Angeles."

"Culture can have a presence anywhere you bring it. And I agree with Charlie. People need to see these." She walks down the line of photos. "Did you know all the subjects?"

"Many I didn't know personally, but they recognized me. My family has been here for decades. But this one," he says, bringing Annie down to the last photo. "This is a special woman."

The woman, probably in her sixties, is laughing as she wipes a tear from her eye.

"Your mother," Annie responds. "I can see the resemblance. You have the same light about you. The same love."

Dorian looks over at me more seriously this time. "I like this one a lot. How long have you been together?"

"We're not—"

"No, Dorian—"

We both speak at the same time, which makes him laugh. "God, you lesbians. You always have so much processing to do." He turns back to the photos. "Well, Ms. Dawson. Do you have what you need, and will you stop pestering me now?"

"You're really willing to put all these in the show? I know this is a big first step."

"It's time for others to see them. Isn't that what you told me, my love? If there was ever a curator I trust, it's you. So shall I put them in a backpack, and away they go?" He knows there is so much more to a gallery showing than that, but he and logistics go together like oil and water. My team will work with him on presentation, shipping, marketing, all of it. But that can wait for now.

I put my arm around him. "Oh yes, put them in some plastic bags and send them via carrier pigeons to LA." He puts his arm around me, and for a few silent moments, we all just study the photos. "They're perfect, babe. Thank you for trusting me."

"Always. Now, enough about me. Are you a New Yorker?" Dorian asks Annie.

"I am."

"Well, you've never seen the real New York art scene. I promise you that. I hope you two enjoy the exhibit."

Annie looks around with a furrowed brow. "There's a gallery here? How big is this place?"

He laughs. "Not a gallery. More like a museum of lost relics. The art that was never deemed good enough at the time. We've collected different pieces over the years. It's a blast from the past of New York's greatest movements." He always speaks like he's some Shakespearean actor, but Annie seems more excited than I've ever seen her.

"Then show me the way," she replies.

"Head through there." He points at another door. "I have some things to finish up here, but I'll see you in the lobby once you're done."

"I know the way." I lace my fingers with Annie's again. "Ready?"

I'll never tire of the expression on her face when she looks at me, a look that's reserved just for me. "Always."

Her words make my stomach flip, and I try not to focus on what she means and instead pull her to the door.

The room is one large space, like the last one, but with softer lighting. There are panels that separate the room into sections so the center can aggregate certain styles or time periods together. But when Dorian called it a "museum," that may have been a bit of an exaggeration.

Annie drops my hand as she excitedly wanders, looking at the different pieces. The room is full of so many things. Paintings, some of which are good and some aren't; sculptures; quilts; posters; and even some random items from New York City bygones. One of my favorite things is an old traffic light from 1917 that was one of the city's first attempts at using them.

Annie looks like a kid as she moves through each section, taking in the pieces and shouting to me like I haven't seen them before. I knew she would love this place as much as I do. And I only took her here because she means something to me, too.

I let her explore as I walk around. There's a section of new political posters in one corner, but other than that, I recognize most of the pieces. But it's not the art or the objects that feel so familiar. It's the smell of the room. It smells like home, and I feel a sense of calm.

This is the art world I wanted Annie to see, not one built around prestige and snobbery. This is real and raw. The artists who created these pieces did it because they loved it, not because they'd get famous or rich; most of them didn't. This place inspires me, and I can't believe I've been away from it for so long.

"Charlie," she shouts from across the room. I go over to what she's looking at. "Where is this from?"

I look at the neon Apollo sign. "That's the original Apollo Theater sign. It was first put up in 1940, I think. They have a new one there now that matches. This was gifted to the art center so that it stayed in Harlem."

"That's so wonderful," she says, looking at the rest of the room. "This whole place is. Thank you for taking me here. I'd say this was a pretty good date." She pulls me in and puts her arms around my neck. Our lips are close, but we don't kiss. We just stare at each other, something we seem to do more and more.

I move my hands to her waist and squeeze. "You think the date is over?"

"It's not?"

"What kind of a woman would I be if I didn't buy you dessert?"

"The horrible kind."

"Then would you like to join me for ice cream?

"In December?"

"I'll keep your mouth warm as you eat it."

"Count me in."

"Let's go say good-bye to Dorian, and I'll take you to the best ice cream joint in New York."

"Lead the way, Choo Choo."

Dorian is leaning against the front desk, talking to Bradley when we emerge from the exhibit. "Angels, how was it?" '

"Wonderful. So much history and beauty in one room. I'm in such awe of what you've done here," Annie says.

"And what kind of art do you make?"

"Portraits. But again, it's just a hobby."

"They're special, Dorian," I chime in. "I've seen them. Better than Clarke."

"Who's Clarke?" Annie asks.

"A woman we went to school with. She's showing at the Whitney right now. And her work is nothing compared to yours."

Dorian nods as he listens. He picks up a card from the desk and hands it to her. "This is my info. We have a collective of artists here. I think you should join. We do showings all the time. Nothing fancy like Ms. LA over here." He nods to me. "I think you should join our little group."

"You've never even seen my work," she says, tentatively taking the card.

"Charlie has. And she has the best eye in the business."

"So she keeps telling me," she says with a smile.

"Call me. Please."

"I will," she says, but I'm not sure I believe her.

"And now we're off. I've promised her some ice cream," I say. Bradley hands us our coats without me having to ask.

"Gerald's?" Dorian asks.

"Only the best."

"Get the maple ice cream. It's divine."

"Thanks for the recommendation," she says before moving over to him. "It was lovely to meet you. Thank you for allowing me to be here."

He places a kiss on both of Annie's cheeks. "I plan to have you back soon." He moves over to me. "And you. I suppose we'll be speaking soon. Business, business, business." He kisses my cheek. "You look well, Charlie. Happy. Whatever has done that," he says, looking at Annie. "Maybe keep it around."

"I'll call you soon." I ignore his last statement since she can hear.

"Stay warm, loves."

Annie gives me that soft smile I crave and reaches for my hand. "Now get me that dessert you promised, and let's get back to that hotel room."

"The hotel? I suppose we *did* already break the rule."

"And they *were* made to be broken."

I take her hand as we leave. And for the first time since my parents were alive, I feel home.

CHAPTER TWENTY

Annie and I sprawl across the bed, trying to catch our breath. We didn't even make it three feet into the hotel room before we were pulling on each other's clothes and falling onto the bed.

"I still can't believe you got chocolate ice cream," she says in a breathy voice.

We're on our backs after hours of more sex or what is slowly starting to feel *only* like making love. Neither of us can seem to move much. I can't even muster the strength to turn my head. "That's what you're thinking about right now?"

"Good thing we fucked because it's almost *all* I've been able to think about."

"Chocolate ice cream is a staple flavor. It's a classic."

"Maybe in 1920. But now, we know better. Who gets plain chocolate ice cream? You didn't even get sprinkles."

"Sprinkles conflict with the creamy texture. Now I feel like you're an ice cream snob. And that is a big red flag."

"I thought you liked me in red?" She turns on her side and gives me a seductive smile.

I let out a sigh as her fingers trail down my hair and onto my arms. It doesn't feel sexual; it just feels intimate, and I've never felt this comfortable with a woman. Not even with Jen at our best. "I do indeed." I close my eyes for a moment. "But I like you in anything."

"You're so cute, you know that?" She gives me a peck on the lips.

"I like this. I like being with you. Did you have fun tonight?" I roll to my side so we're facing each other.

"I did. You showed me a new side of New York. And I'll cherish that forever."

I try not to let my emotions take over when she says forever. "What's the New York that you know?"

"Well, you know about my family. They're snobbier than yours, even though they have no right to be. Everything was strict. Ordered. Serious."

"But you're close with your siblings?" I want to get to know her better. I want to know everything about her. But I wasn't expecting my question to cause such sadness to spread across her face.

"Very close. Zoe was so much younger than Dylan and me. I wouldn't say we helped parent her, but we were huge influences. My parents were never around, so we took care of her a lot. She even slept in my bed every night for about five years. And whenever she cried, it was always Dylan she wanted, not mom or dad.

"It must be so hard for him to be kept away."

"It's heartbreaking for him. We sneak visits every now and then, but it's not the same. And it's hard not to be able to be open about my relationship with him, too. He's to me like Kat is to you. He's my best friend. And I have to keep it a secret from my parents."

"I understand why you're so scared to come out."

"Zoe needs me. I can't just leave her."

"What's she like?"

A smile plays on her lips, and I can see a different kind of affection on her face that she's never shown. "She's sweet. And quiet. Very introspective. Basically, the opposite of Dylan. He is the loudest person I know and doesn't ever stop talking."

"Sounds like Kat."

She laughs. "Very much. They'd get along. But Zoe is sensitive, and like the rest of us, has always wanted to please our parents. But she's a good kid. We used to have so much fun. When she breaks out of her shell, she's really funny and silly."

I play with her fingertips, trying to gather my thoughts. For someone who has lived for her family, I know what this all means and how daunting it can be. But I want to know what she sees in her future. And with whom. "You need to live for yourself, too. She'll always have you."

She nods but keeps looking down. "I know, but it's so much more complicated."

"Would you consider Dorian's offer? I hope you know he was sincere."

"I draw for myself. I don't know if I want to be part of some collective. It's hard enough finding time to do it with my job."

"But you don't need that job. You've never once said it makes you happy."

She sits and pulls the sheets up. In less than a second, the temperature feels like it's dropped ten degrees. "What am I going to do? My parents have basically ensured that my success lies in their company."

"How do you figure? You have an art degree from one of the most prestigious schools in the world."

"It's just a degree, Charlie."

"But you could support yourself. You don't need them. This isn't 1950. You can do anything you want. Your talent needs to be seen. And you've said yourself that you want out of their clutches."

She narrows her eyes. "Is that why you took me there tonight? To push me into the same thing you pushed Dorian into? Is it me you want or my art?"

I'm so confused by the sudden change of mood that my head is reeling. I sit up so I can see her better. "I never pushed Dorian into anything. And I'd never want you just for your art. I took you there because it's special to me, and I wanted to share it with someone who's special to me."

"But not special enough to leave LA for."

I let out a harsh laugh that has no humor in it. "Leave for what? Someone who will never let herself be happy? Who will always lean on a father who doesn't care about her happiness?" I feel exposed so I reach to the floor and grab a T-shirt I can throw on.

"He's not a bad man," she says defensively. "I need to change my life, but my dad isn't some monster."

"Maybe not. But he'll do anything he can to succeed. Not worrying about what or who he takes down in the process, including his own daughter."

"And you know my dad that well?"

"The fact that he's decimating my parents' company and using you to get to Ian gives me a pretty clear picture."

She stares at me, but it's as if I can see all her thoughts flashing behind her eyes. I had never planned to mention any of that. What happens with the companies has nothing to do with Annie or me, and my uncle wouldn't have wanted me to say that. But I'm past caring. This is about us. And if there even can *be* an us. Earlier tonight, I thought that was where we were headed. But she can't seem to get out of the dichotomy of wanting freedom *and* wanting to please her parents for as long as she can.

"That's not true. That's not even what we do." She gets up and puts her pants on. "We invest. We're expanding the hotel group."

"It's not investing, Annie. Ian knows it, too. He's working with your dad to make a whole lot of money from my parents' legacy. And from what I've seen, your dad only cares about two things, just like Ian. Money and prestige."

She puts on her coat, and I don't know how to stop the freight train of drama that just came crashing into this room, but I've clearly hit a nerve with her just like she has with me.

"Will you stop?" I ask when she begins buttoning her coat with a hard expression on her face. "Why are you getting so defensive about something you've already admitted is a problem? I know you love him. But why would you let him dictate your whole life? You're not Zoe's age anymore."

There are tears in her eyes. I get off the bed and go to her. I don't even care that I'm pants-less. I never expected this night to blow up, and it kills me to see her cry. I thought she agreed with all this. But she's conflicted on what her future holds.

"Because he's my father. It's my family. And he's not the man you're claiming he is."

"I'm trying to protect my family, too. Your dad and Ian are trying to destroy it."

"It's not like that."

"It is, Annie. One day, you'll have to face who he is and who you want him to be. And you'll have to decide who you're going to live for."

She gives me a long look as tears stream down her face. "I thought of all people, you'd understand not wanting to lose a father. Don't pressure me into giving up what you've already lost."

I take a step back at words that feel like a slap in the face.

It takes a moment, but her eyes widen as she no doubt realizes what she said. "Charlie, I'm so sorry. I didn't mean that. I'm just defensive. I know you're not pressuring me." She doesn't want to live the life her family has created for her, but there's some barrier she can't break through. Maybe she's behaved the way they've wanted for so long that the thought of evolving is too hard. Breaking up with Ian is one thing, but this seems like something else.

I take another step back, feeling my walls growing with each passing moment. "You're right. I'd give anything to have my dad back. And I guess you have yours. Congratulations."

"Charlie—"

I walk to the door. "I don't think this conversation is going anywhere good. And I have to be up early for the final fittings and some bridal lunch. You should go."

She stands there like she doesn't know what to do, but finally, she nods and walks to the door. "Tonight was the best date I've ever had. Best night I've ever had. I'm sorry I'm not being brave fast enough for you."

"I never asked you to leave your family. And I never gave you a deadline. I just wanted to know there was a future where we could be free."

Her eyes tear up again, and she looks like she's trying desperately not to let them spill. "I've never been brave enough for anything, Charlie. You deserve better. You're special. No wonder I fell in love with you so easily. I'll see you at the rehearsal dinner."

She walks out without another word, and I'm left standing in a daze. What started out as the best night of my life slowly turned into a chaotic mess. I sit on the floor, put my head in my hands, and let the tears that have been waiting to tumble finally fall.

Annie is all I want. She's all I could ever want. But our relationship was doomed from the start, and now it's clear that the barriers between us are only growing impossibly tall.

This rehearsal dinner is going to be hell.

CHAPTER TWENTY-ONE

Even after all the times my parents told us about their romantic wedding at the boathouse in Central Park, my first time being there was for the bridal lunch Kat hosted yesterday. Or the bridal *luncheon*, as Jake's mom annoyingly kept calling it.

My parents told us the story of their wedding so many times, I'm not surprised this is where Kat chose to get married. Central Park was my mom's favorite place in the city. Over the years, it became Kat's, too. My mom loved the park so much that she claimed she'd never move anywhere else because of it. My dad even proposed at the Bethesda Fountain, her favorite spot. Or as he told it, he tried to propose, but on the day, it was under construction. He ended up dropping to one knee next to a bench and a hot dog stand.

My mom tried to take a walk through this park every day, though that decreased the busier she got with the hotels. Kat would often go with her while I opted to stay in my room and paint. Now, I regret every time I said no. I regret all those extra moments I could have shared with her.

As I walk to the boathouse, a shiver runs down my body. If I were ever to get married, I'd want somewhere warm. But Kat has thought of winter weddings as romantic since we were kids, even if it means the rest of us have to freeze. Luckily, I came prepared tonight. I don't care if my large orange parka goes with my outfit. It's not like this is the actual wedding, and I'm choosing warmth over fashion.

I glance at my phone to check the time and see that I'm a few minutes early. Hopefully, that means I can find a much needed drink—or two—before everyone else arrives. My aunt said the actual rehearsal will be quick, and then we'll have a catered dinner in the space. I'll need a drink for both.

I haven't heard from Annie since she left my room, but I haven't reached out, either. Our last interaction is all I've been able to think about. I understand her need to defend her family, even if the criticism is deserved. But she's so conflicted that even if I were to stay in New York, I'm not sure Annie would ever allow us to have the life *we* deserve.

For the past two nights, I've barely been able to sleep. Maybe I was too harsh about her father. She is right; I don't know him. But I know my uncle, and I trust everything he told me. Annie even admitted that Phillip is controlling. It's hard to believe that a man who was willing to cut off his son isn't also willing to tear apart a company to which he has no personal connection.

It's frustrating to see someone as talented and special as Annie throw it away for a family who doesn't believe in her. If I truly thought she didn't want to be an artist, that would be one thing. But she just doesn't know how to be anything but an Astor. I learned long ago that I needed to be more than a Dawson.

As I walk up the long path that leads to the main doors of the boathouse, I try to push the argument and Annie out of my head. This is Kat's rehearsal dinner, and I don't want to do anything that may ruin her moment. But trying not to think about Annie just makes me think about her more. I'm painfully aware that this will be the first time I've seen her with Ian since the family dinner almost two weeks ago. Now that I have held her and fallen for her, the idea of seeing her with Ian makes me sick.

The faster I can get a drink, the better. I take the stairs two at a time and throw the doors open. Unfortunately, every thought I was trying to ignore comes rushing back as I see who's leaning against the wall just inside the hallway.

Annie pushes up as soon as she sees me, and my hasty mission to find a bar is stalled. Convincing myself that we have no future together is futile now. I'm having trouble focusing on anything except how gorgeous she looks. She may be wearing a long black coat, but I can see how short her dress is underneath, and it's hard not to think about how those legs were wrapped around me only days ago. When I bring my gaze up, I'm even more affected. Unlike at the end of our date, her expression is open and warm, and I'm helpless to look away.

"Hey," she says. "I was hoping I'd catch you."

"Hey."

Silence settles over us, but it's not uncomfortable. It's as if we both can't find the words we need. The energy between us is so intense that the air feels thick. As we stand there, her expression becomes so soft and tentative that all I want to do is put my arms around her.

She speaks again first, and it's in such a quiet voice that I take a step closer. "I'm sorry." She takes a couple steps closer to me.

I'm hit with her familiar scent, one that has started to feel more like home than anything else. I close my eyes so I can take it in, and when I open them, Annie is in front of me. "I am, too," I say. "I don't know how things got to where they did, but I am sorry."

"I got defensive about my dad. And my family. Here I am asking you to move back to Manhattan after only knowing each other for ten days. And when you questioned my future, I just snapped."

"It's hard not defending your family."

"Charlie, I wish you knew more about him. I've only told you the bad parts, but he's not all bad. And I work for the company. I would've heard if he was doing anything that would hurt your family. Don't you think I would've told you? I know what your parents mean to you."

"We haven't had a lot of opportunities to really talk, and when we did, we weren't talking business." Being so close and not touching her is an impossible battle, so I look behind me to make sure we're still alone before I take her hand. "Annie, I need you to know that I'm not trying to pressure you to be an artist. If you want to do what you're doing, I support that. I just want you to know that you could. Maybe people haven't told you that enough."

"Nobody has ever told me. Besides professors. But not someone I love." She tightens her grip. "Will you come over tonight so we can talk more?"

"To your place?"

She nods.

"Okay."

She smiles.

I'm not sure how one expression can make me feel so relieved, but it does. "I'm glad you're here. I missed you after you left."

"You did?" The sincerity in her voice makes me want to lean in and kiss her insecurities away. "I don't know why Kat invited me. I'm not part of the wedding."

"Because she thinks of you as family. There's dinner for friends and family after the rehearsal."

She gives me another small smile before looking toward the door and pulling her hand out of mine. When I turn, I can see someone walking up the path. "I better go," she says, but instead of walking away, she looks as if she wants to say more. After a few quiet moments, she shakes her head and starts to walk backward. "I'll see you in there, Choo Choo."

Something about using that nickname after our fight makes my entire body warm. I watch her eyes linger on my jacket. "By the way, I don't know how you do it, but you even make a three-hundred-pound ski coat look sexy."

"Orange must be my color."

"That must be it," she says before finally turning toward the gold double doors that lead into the main room of the boathouse.

"Annie?" My heart is pounding so hard that I'm not sure I can speak properly. More than the end-of-date fight or introducing her to Dorian or even the sex we had before going out, there's one thing I can't stop thinking about from that night. "Did you mean what you said? About falling in love with me?"

Even if it has only been ten days, I'm able to recognize her varying expressions. But the one she's directing at me now feels different. It reminds me of the way my parents looked at me. "From day one."

As I watch her leave, I feel a rush of feelings I don't know what to do with. What I do know is that Annie's not alone in what she's feeling. From the moment she walked into the Runaway and I saw that face, I was hers. And only hers.

Her hips sway as she gets closer to the doors and gives me one quick glance over her shoulder before moving through them.

I'm again feeling a mix of arousal, love, and complete desire. But there are some things that can take me out of a heated moment, even if it's watching someone as sexy as Annie. And the voice behind me does just that: "Charlotte, I didn't expect to see you here so soon."

I cringe before I turn. "Hello, Claudia."

Her eyes narrow. I have a feeling Jake's mom is the type who expects to be referred to as "Mrs. Williams" instead of her first name. But if she's not going to respect my preferred name, she can handle the same.

I wink flirtatiously. "I thought I'd get here a little early to impress you."

She zeroes in on my jacket. If she's trying to hide her judgment, it's not working. "You must be very warm."

"Oh. I am. Cozy as ever."

Our awkward small talk is interrupted when the front doors open again, and Holly rushes in, a wave of cold wind following her. I've never been so relieved to see her; there is only so much Claudia I can take, and that thirty second exchange was my limit. Holly rubs her arms, and when her eyes land on my outfit, she raises both eyebrows. "Heading to the mountains?" She walks over next to me and smiles politely at Claudia.

"Well, I figured this whole thing won't take too long. Heading to Vermont right after. The night skiing is incredible."

Claudia's eyes snap straight back to my jacket, this time a little wider. Holly puts a gentle hand on her arm. "She's kidding. Charlie doesn't even ski."

Claudia gives us both a tight smile. "Well, I'm going to head in and see if they need any help with final preparations."

Once she's through the doors, Holly turns to me. "I think she's fun."

"Yeah, a real hoot. Where's the bar?"

"There is no bar yet. We have the rehearsal first. Then, we get to eat and drink. Have you ever been to a wedding?"

My stomach tightens at the thought of having to face the entire family completely sober. "Yes, but I've never been *in* a wedding."

"Good thing I brought a flask, then." She pulls it from her purse. Her normal energy is a bit low. She looks anxious or upset and like she needs a drink far more than I do. Her eyes keep darting to the front door as if she's waiting for someone.

"Hey," I say, pulling her attention. "What's up?"

"Dad should be here soon. And Ian." Her eyes are now fixed on the front door as she opens the flask and takes a sip. She offers it to me, but her focus doesn't move from the entrance. She is one of the most laid-back and carefree people I know. To see her so serious is unsettling and has my stomach clenching even tighter.

"Holls, what's up?" I pull on her arm, finally breaking her stare. "Come on." I don't know this venue well, but I know where the wedding is taking place, so I know not to head that way. If Claudia and Annie are here, others may be here, too. I pull Holly to the other end of the hall. We can still see the front door, but we can talk more openly. "Talk."

She isn't like me; getting her to share isn't hard. She's the type who likes to process in real-time. "I was helping my mom choose something to wear. She seemed really distracted, not even bothering me with any wedding details, which we both know isn't normal."

I nod as she takes another sip. Once she's done, I grab the flask for myself. For some reason, the tightening in my stomach has only gotten worse.

"Anyway," she continues. "Ian showed up. I was upstairs, so I didn't see him. But he and my dad were shouting."

"What about?"

"I couldn't hear, but I've never even heard my dad yell."

"Did you ask your mom?"

"All she said was that the two of them better pull themselves together before tonight. Ian stormed out, and my dad has been MIA ever since. I think he went to the office. Something is going on."

My legs feel wobbly as I try to process what she's telling me. Ian wouldn't be yelling at my uncle over Annie. This must be related to the hotel deal, and nothing related to that can be good. "They're both coming, right?"

"They'll be here. At least, I know my dad will. Your brother—" She sounds like she's about to say something insulting, but as if on cue, Ian walks through the front door.

He's wearing his typical hooded sweater under a blazer, a style that I've always thought made him look like a preppy asshole. He looks around, then finally notices us. As he walks over, I can see him eyeing my coat, and I'm bracing myself for the dig that's about to come. "Good thing you're gay," he says. "You'd never be able to get a man if that's how you dress for nice events."

"Says the guy who has drawstrings hanging down his chest while wearing a blazer," Holly remarks before looking at his shoes. "Nice boat shoes, by the way."

He glares at her, and if it's possible, his look of disdain is even more potent than it is when he looks at me. Ian and I could be considered friends compared to his relationship with Holly. She never had to play nice over the years like I did. "Oh, Holly. Didn't see you there," he says, acting bored.

"That's concerning. Maybe you should get your eyes checked?"

"If that means I'll see you even clearer, no thanks. Anyway, where is everyone?"

"People are trickling in. The main room is that way." I point, hoping he'll leave.

"Is Annie here?"

That name coming out of his mouth does things to my body, not nice things. He has never deserved to say her name. I wish we were kids again, and I could slug him in the stomach. But that would absolutely ruin this night for Kat. I nod stiffly and do what I can to avoid Holly's gaze.

"And you two? Bringing any dates to the wedding? I won't judge if you paid them to escort you. I'm open-minded like that," he says.

Now I have to put my hands behind my back so they don't do what they want to do.

"How liberal of you, Ian." Holly's voice is fake cheery. "But, no. I'm keeping my options open."

"I hear you do that a lot around town."

"Ian, what the fuck?" I ask. "Now we're into slut shaming?" I can't help but raise my voice. I don't get why it's so hard for him to act like a normal cousin or brother.

Holly returns his jab with a smile. "Well, that's a coincidence. I hear the same about you." She takes a long sip and flashes another smile. "I'm sure Annie would be impressed."

His face hardens, but he offers no rebuttal. It seems Holly is the only one who can scare him into shutting up. Everyone in the family knows that Ian sleeps with as many women as he can, whether he's in a relationship or not. I don't even think it's about the sex. He likes to know he's wanted. His need for approval trumps any sincere feelings he may have.

"Well, excuse me, ladies," he says, putting air quotes around "ladies." "I'm going to go find my girlfriend. I hope you have fun getting drunk like college girls." He gives us both a look of contempt before turning to walk away, but right before he can leave, I call out:

"Ian?"

He turns and acts as if it's the most taxing thing he's done all night. "What? You want to swap jackets?"

I roll my eyes. He's looking to engage, and I'm not giving him that. Not tonight. "This is for Kat. Let's just try, okay?"

He stares. I brace myself for one more dig, but instead, he gives a tight nod. At least, I think it was a nod; his head barely moved.

"How that man came from your parents, I will never know," Holly says. "But speaking of Annie—"

"Not here. We should go in." I start walking, Holly trailing right behind me with a slew of questions ready on her tongue, but we're not going to talk about Annie while the whole family is around.

"Fine, but you still haven't given me details about Wednesday. After this is over, you're mine, Dawson. Let's go to the Runaway. I haven't been in years."

Her mention of that bar causes a new wave of emotion to run through me. There are few places in New York that I've spent more time in than the Runaway, yet now, it only reminds me of Annie and our first night together. "I can't. I have plans."

"Ah. Well, I guess I don't need to ask how Wednesday went, then."

When we walk into the main room, Holly has enough sense to stop talking. Annie is on the other side of the room with Ian, so I do everything I can not to look at her. I'd rather be stuck talking to Claudia for an entire evening than catch one glimpse of Ian with Annie.

To distract myself, I take in the space Kat chose. It's not hard to see why my parents always talked about how special the boathouse is. It's too dark outside to see the lake well, but when they got married here on a sunny June day, I'm sure the views out of the French windows were beautiful. And if Kat wanted her wedding to look like a winter wonderland, she's gotten her wish. Despite the harsh weather on the other side of those windows, this room feels like a warm, intimate oasis. Everywhere I look, there are twinkling golden lights, dark flowers, and candles. Small white trees line the aisle, with elegant gold chairs already set up for tomorrow's guests.

The huge flower archway at the front of the room steals my attention. Stemming from the top of the ceiling, the archway showcases white flowers of all varieties woven together with small lights that shine down on the spot where Kat and Jake will be married. Everything is perfect, and I couldn't imagine a more romantic spot.

Kat is standing next to the archway, talking to her wedding planner. As soon as she sees me, she jumps up and waves like a kid, pointing at the arch. I can't see her like that and not return her smile. At this moment, all my other worries are gone, and I just see my sister, happy as I've ever seen her.

Lena and Juliet are sitting in one of the front rows of chairs, talking to Kat's high school biology teacher. Kat still credits Mrs. Phillips as her reason for loving science, and the two have stayed in touch since she graduated. I couldn't think of a better, warmer person to be marrying my sister and her groom. Luckily, Lena and Juliet don't see me. I feel anxious enough as it is. I don't need their overexcitable energy.

Jake and his parents are sitting across the row, with Jake in the middle, but none of them are speaking. Their family seems more comfortable with silence, the opposite of my family. I'm guessing family dinners at their house are quiet events. Not surprising, since his parents have the personalities of the chairs they're sitting on.

My aunt and uncle aren't here yet, only intensifying the tension on Holly's face as she stands next to me. But I know them. They'll be here. Technically, we have fifteen minutes before the rehearsal is supposed to start.

"Charlie," I hear from the doorway. When I turn, my cousin Logan is hurrying over. As soon as he's within arm's reach, he grabs me and pulls me into his solid frame. "Oh, you can join in, too. I see how jealous you are," he adds, pulling Holly into the hug.

"Hey, Logan," I say when he releases us, and I can breathe again. "Nice beard. Now you really do look like a lumberjack. Very manly."

He laughs and strokes his beard. He has always been the tallest of the family and built like a tree. We've always made jokes about my aunt feeding him protein shakes as a baby instead of milk. But he's a teddy bear; he has none of the bite or sarcasm his sister possesses. "Well, it seems to get me more roles," he shrugs before turning to Holly. "You smell like booze already."

"Judging?"

"Of course not. Can I have some?"

She hands him the flask, and as he takes a sip, I sneak a glance at Annie. She's staring at me. I know I should look away, but my eyes won't listen to my brain. The spell is broken when Ian whispers something to her, making it much easier to turn my attention back to Logan.

"What happened to the kilt?" Holly asks, grabbing the flask again.

He looks at his slacks. "Have you ever tried wearing a kilt in winter? My balls were about to freeze off."

"I'm a woman, Logan." Holly rolls her eyes. "It's the same as wearing a skirt in winter."

"Yeah, but you don't go commando."

"Why did you have to go commando?" she asks.

"It's a cultural thing."

"We're barely even Scottish, Logan."

"Just living my authentic self, Holls. And stop being rude. I'm trying to catch up with our cousin." He swipes the flask out of her hands. "How have you been? Dad says the gallery is going well."

"Don't drink it all," Holly says as he takes a long sip.

"It's going well," I respond, ignoring their bickering. "I met with an artist this week who will be doing a show at my gallery in the spring. It's nice to bring a little east coast flair out west. Holly told me you landed a role?"

"Yeah! It's a new play at a downtown theater. Very avant-garde. I hardly even know what it's about. I have a minor role, but the director is amazing. He's pulled things out of me I didn't know I had. We're in tech rehearsals right now, so it's a lot of work. I'm there all day, every day. But it's fun. It's nice to work instead of going on audition after audition, you know?"

Holly may have more bite, but in some ways, the siblings are so similar. You can ask them one simple question, and they'll give you a saga of an answer.

"That's great." I love Logan, and I'm happy he's finding success. But the last time I asked him about acting, he went through every single method actors utilize to get into character, and I'm too distracted right now to keep this going. "I'm happy you're doing well. I know how much you love it."

"I wish you could be here to see it. But we open the week you leave."

His tone is as light and jovial as always, and I know he didn't mean to make me fall into a pool of swirling emotions. But his comment just reminds me of all the things I'm missing. It's becoming harder and harder to remember why I'm staying in LA.

I risk another look at Annie. I can't think about leaving Manhattan without her being at the forefront of that thought. She's looking at her phone and seems bored while Ian talks to a man that I assume is one of Jake's other groomsmen. "I wish I could see it, too."

"Well, there is one way you can make it up to me."

"And how's that?"

He leans into me, puts his hand on my shoulder, and acts like we're about to hatch some plan like we used to when we were kids. "You're close with Kat, right?"

I shrug. "Close? Pretty friendly. Almost like sisters, I'd say."

"Great! See, I'm walking down the aisle with Juliet." He looks over to where Lena and Juliet are sitting. "Who's great," he quickly adds. "But do you think you could put a word in with Kat and have it changed to Lena?"

Holly smacks his arm.

"Hey!" He rubs it and glares at her.

"You already asked her out, and she said no."

He puts his hands up the same way she always does. "Okay, okay, Gloria Steinem. I just thought she might like the beard."

"Nobody likes the beard."

"Not true. Charlie likes it."

"Charlie was lying."

They both look at me expectantly, and part of me has missed their easy banter. Kat and I like to tease each other, but I'd never be able to have a conversation like this with Ian. Luckily, I'm saved by my aunt and uncle coming into the room. "Your parents are here," I say, pulling their attention away from Logan's beard.

My aunt rushes in like she's an hour late and heads straight to us. She looks anxious and is playing with one of her earrings, a sign that she's upset. I wouldn't have needed Holly to tell me that my uncle is upset, either. I've never seen him so agitated. At my parents' funeral, he was heartbroken, but he kept it together for the family. Right now, he looks like a defeated man.

"Logan, honey. I thought we talked about that beard," my aunt says, but her tone doesn't hold her usual motherly bite.

"I can't cut it, Mom. It's part of my role."

"Are we the last here?" she asks, as if it's the biggest faux pax in the world.

"Yes, but nothing has started yet," I assure her.

"Well, I'll just go check with Kat and see if we're ready." Before she goes, she turns to my uncle, puts her hand on his arm, and gives him a stern look. I know her well enough to know what she's telling him. It's the look we got from her our entire childhood; it meant behave or else.

"What's up, Dad?" Logan asks, oblivious. "You look like you could use this." He holds up Holly's flask. "You should know, it's your irresponsible teacher daughter who brought it. Not this good-for-nothing actor." He points to himself.

His comment seems to break whatever angry spell my uncle is under, and he looks at Logan in surprise. "You are not good-for-nothing, and we love seeing you onstage. I'm very proud to have you as my son." His eyes zero in on Ian.

Logan's face scrunches in confusion as he also glances Ian's way. "Uh, thanks, Dad? I wasn't being serious."

"Give me the flask," my uncle says and grabs it. He takes such a long sip that I wonder how much booze is even left. But Holly doesn't berate him the same way she did Logan. Maybe she knows he needs it more.

Nobody seems to know what to say as my uncle continues to drink, so Holly, Logan, and I casually talk about the rehearsal until a man I've never met—but assume is Jake's best man from Ohio—enters the room. He goes straight to Jake and his parents and sits with them.

"Okay, everyone," Kat's wedding planner, Cassie, shouts from the front of the room. "Now that we're all here, let's get started. We'll practice the procession first. Does everyone know who they're walking with? Go stand with them now."

Everyone moves to their partner.

"Hey, I'm Tim," Jake's friend says as he shakes my hand. "I've heard a lot of good things."

"Likewise. It's nice to meet you," I say, but I'm only half paying attention. I actually don't remember anything I've been told about Tim except that he's from Ohio. I'm mainly watching Annie, who sits in one of the chairs to wait for things to end since she isn't in the wedding.

"Great," Cassie says. "Now, stand next to your partner, and we'll go through who's walking first."

"Can I make one suggestion?" I ask. When Logan looks at me, I give him a wink.

"You have a wedding suggestion? Oh, this should be good," Kat says sarcastically.

"It seems weird to have Ian with Lena. Height-wise, he makes more sense with Juliet. Lena towers over him."

I have so many different expressions directed my way. Kat looks shocked that I even had an opinion on the wedding. Logan is smiling and gives me an overexaggerated wink. And Ian is just glaring, which is my favorite. It's not that he's short, but men like Ian can't stand to feel emasculated in any way.

"You are absolutely right, Charlie," Cassie says as she walks around the room looking at the couples. "Let's make that switch. Great idea."

"She has so few of them, so I guess we should celebrate this one," Ian mumbles as he moves to Juliet.

"Let's all move to the hallway, and we can practice who goes first," Cassie calls. "I'll set up the music so we all know the pace. Tomorrow, the harpist will play, but she's sent us a recording for this."

As we move, Logan and Lena take their place in the line. As he passes me, he bumps my arm and leans in. "Thanks, cuz. You're the best."

"Good luck. May the beard win."

"None of this will be perfect," Cassie shouts. "Let's work on the timing first. Jake, stand with your parents. You'll be the first in. Everybody wait until I give you the go before you start your procession."

I look back, and my sister is glowing. She has her arms linked with my aunt and uncle, and I wish that they all had the same expression, that whatever happened with Ian would be put aside.

Kat looks happier than I've ever seen her, while my aunt and uncle look as if this is a death march.

Cassie calls my name, bringing my attention back to the task at hand, and gives Tim and me the go-ahead to walk. Jake is standing beneath the flowers, and his parents are seated in one of the front rows. As I move toward him, my eyes are drawn to the person they now always seek. And in that moment, I'm overwhelmed so much, I stop walking.

"Are you okay?" Tim asks. "Don't worry, it's just the rehearsal. It's tomorrow that's the scary part, when everyone is watching us."

I know he's trying to be funny, but my head is miles away. I can almost see Annie where Jake is standing. I can feel my uncle's arm in mine as I walk toward her. All I can see is making her mine forever.

I force my feet to keep walking as I push the fantasy out of my head. But when I look at Annie again, her eyes are shining and bright, as if she feels it, too. A future we both want. A future I wish we could find a way to have.

CHAPTER TWENTY-TWO

I don't know what wedding rehearsals are supposed to be like, but I'm pretty sure the members of the wedding party aren't supposed to be glaring at each other during the "ceremony." Cassie does what she can to make things easy and relaxed, but as time goes on, the tension between my uncle and brother becomes palpable. I'm probably not the only one relieved we're finally able to enter the dining room for dinner.

The ambiance is almost identical to the main room, but it looks drastically different from yesterday when we had lunch here. For that, there was just one long table, and the venue wasn't closed to other guests. Tonight, the room is private, and the staff are still setting up for tomorrow's reception. All around the room are large round tables with chairs stacked beside them.

Cassie directs us to two gorgeous tables by the French doors. In the middle of each, the same white flowers from the other room are in bouquets, and I can see some of the lake outside due to the patio lighting. Each table features a white linen cloth, gold chairs, and cutlery that looks like it was made for a queen. If this is how everything will look tomorrow, Kat will be happy. It's the fairy-tale wedding she's always talked about.

As we get closer, I see that each seat has a name card, but Cassie directs us where to go anyway. It must be a wedding planner thing, and she reminds me of Holly. "Bridesmaids and groomsmen at this table." She points to the far table. "Bride, groom, and family at this table."

I'm relieved to see that I'm sitting between Logan and Holly and not next to Annie. I don't think I can handle my uncle and Ian's tension while also dealing with the kind of tension that comes from any proximity to her.

Ian is sitting next to Logan, with Annie on his other side, so I don't even have a good view of her. Hopefully, that will make this dinner easier than our first. My aunt and uncle are across the table, next to Jake's parents. From the expression on his face, my uncle hasn't calmed down at all. Kat sits next to Jake, but she seems oblivious. In fact, I don't think I've seen her stop smiling all night.

"Red or white?" a man asks from beside me. I was so distracted by the family that I didn't even notice the servers begin pouring drinks.

"White, please," I say, not even caring. I just want something to get me through this, and this won't be my last glass.

"Both, please," Holly says, smiling up at the man.

"Lush," Logan jokes and then orders the same.

As soon as the drinks are poured, small salads are put in front of everyone. As people begin to talk and eat, Logan leans in and lowers his voice. "Well, that was fun. Are rehearsals supposed to feel like a party at Macbeth's?"

"That was *such* a lame theater reference," Holly replies, but her eyes are on my uncle. "But, no, something's up with Dad and Ian."

"I thought fighting with Ian at family events was your thing," Logan says to me.

"Not tonight. I'm being good."

"It's about the hotels," Holly says.

Logan takes a bite of salad and makes a face. "It can't be as bad as this salad. Don't they believe in dressing here?" he asks with his mouth full.

"Not everyone likes their lettuce drowning." Holly takes a bite of hers.

This salad debate could go on for a while, so I let my eyes wander. Kat and Jake seem to be in their own world. They've barely touched their food and are staring at each other and laughing about something. I love seeing my sister so happy, but I wish the rest of the table looked the same.

My aunt and uncle are eating in silence. This may be the quietest I've ever seen him at a dinner. My dad could often be soft-spoken and introspective, but my uncle has always been the life of any table, so seeing him this subdued is unsettling. The tension is so tight, I can't imagine it won't snap. But it can't. Not tonight.

Once everyone is done with their salads, including Logan finishing off mine and Holly's despite his earlier complaint, Cassie comes over, whispers something to my uncle, and he stands.

He picks up his glass and taps his knife against it. "I've been asked to say a few words. As most of you know, 'a few' is a hard feat for me." Everyone laughs, but the twinkle behind his eyes isn't there. "But I'll do my best so we can eat in this gorgeous setting."

He pauses and takes a breath. "At such a happy occasion, it may feel odd to bring up the tragedy of life." He takes another breath before continuing. "But we all know there are two people missing who should be here. Yet somehow, it feels like they are. As if they're always here with us. And that's because of the children they raised." He looks at Kat. "Kat, I know your aunt and I are not the people you always dreamed would walk you down that aisle. But we are honored. Watching you grow from the curious kid who could recite every species of bird to the compassionate and brilliant woman you are today has been one of the greatest privileges of my life. Your parents were so proud of you, and so are we."

His voice gets thicker. This is the first time I've heard it like this since my parents' funeral when he gave the eulogy. "I once gave a speech in this room to a couple who reminds me so much of you two. I asked your dad how he knew your mom was the one after just two months. He looked at me like I was crazy and said, 'She was always the one. I just had to run into her.' Well, you two ran into each other. And I can't imagine a couple who deserve each other more."

He looks at Jake. "You are a wonderful man. You've created something special with your clinic, and I know you'll continue to make special moments your whole life. I'd like to welcome you to the family. I know you two will take care of each other. Cherish each other and every moment because we never know what life will deal us." He raises his glass. "To family. The *only thing* that matters."

His eyes land on Ian, and he stares for a moment before taking a sip and sitting down.

Kat doesn't seem to notice the glare because she stands and moves to his chair. "Thank you for being here for me."

He stands so he can hug her properly. I can't hear what he whispers into her ear, but it puts a smile on her face. My aunt also stands and gives her a hug.

"I assume we're getting more than salad, right?" Logan asks as soon as Kat is back in her seat.

"Yes, Logan," Kat says. "I would never starve you. That's the only speech you'll have to sit through. But you better get ready because there will be a lot more tomorrow."

"I'll bring a protein bar." He winks.

Her comment reminds me that I still haven't figured out what I'm going to say tomorrow. Ian and I are supposed to do our own speeches. But I'm not my uncle. I've never been good at public speaking, and I've been dreading it since Kat asked me to be her maid of honor.

"When I get married, we're doing it at a courthouse and going to McDonald's after," Logan says.

"I tried to make that happen, but Kat wouldn't go for it," Jake replies and receives a light slap on the arm from Kat.

"You will not be getting married at the courthouse," my aunt says. "You will give me a proper wedding."

"But you're scary in wedding mode, Mom. Can't I just give you a grandchild, and we call it even?"

"You'll also be giving me one or two of those."

"And Holly? Doesn't she have to pop one out?"

Holly throws her hair over one shoulder. "First of all, *you* wouldn't be popping anything out. The lack of vagina is kind of an issue. Secondly, Mom knows that I'm too good for anyone."

"Your mom has been amazing in wedding mode," Kat says, cutting Logan off from whatever was about to come out of his mouth. I see her eyes dart to Jake's parents, and I have a feeling she's trying to calm the look of shock that appeared on Claudia's face the moment Holly said vagina. "Without Cassie and your mom, none of this would have come together."

"It's easy when the bride is as lovely as my niece," my aunt says, smiling warmly.

"This is a silly conversation, anyway. Logan hasn't had a girlfriend in a decade," Holly says.

"You haven't had a boyfriend *or* a girlfriend in over a decade. Your statistic is worse." Logan laughs at his own joke.

I feel the same envy I felt earlier. Holly and Logan may bicker every chance they get, but I can tell it's not malicious.

"*Mom*, Logan is being bi-phobic again," Holly says in the whiny voice she uses when she's trying to get him into trouble.

"Oh yes, I'm such a bigot." He smiles at her. "You know that whomever you decide to bring to my nonexistent wedding will be welcome. Maybe I'll get married at a Dawson hotel. That's basically free."

"All weddings have expenses," I say. "You'd still need to pay for the staff and food and stuff."

"Says the wedding expert." Holly laughs at me, then turns back to Logan. "Maybe when you find the right woman, you'll lose your hippie attitude and pay for more than a Big Mac."

"I don't think you should plan on a Dawson hotel wedding," my uncle chimes in. "Maybe the courthouse is a good idea."

My aunt puts her hand on his arm, and I can see him take a deep breath.

"Well, I think it makes more sense than any other venue. It's also where I lost my virginity," Logan replies.

"Logan," my aunt says in a stern voice.

My family is not prudish, and I can see both Holly and Kat trying to hold in their laughter, but I can also see Jake's parents looking at Logan as if he just got naked at the table. I know how hard my aunt has tried to keep things easy and civil between the two families this week, but Logan will always be Logan, and he has no censor.

"Sorry, Mom. Just being sentimental," he says, and I can see a small smile on my aunt's face.

"Maybe let's be sentimental about that at a different time?"

"You can kiss that sentiment good-bye, son. There will be no more Dawson hotels to get married at." When my uncle speaks this time, he puts his glass down so hard that everyone looks at him.

"*Not now,*" my aunt says, not even trying to be subtle.

"I'm sorry." He looks at her. "But—"

"*Kat's night,*" she says, as if they're having a conversation we can't hear.

"Okay, what's going on?" Kat puts her drink down. "I'm not obtuse. I know this family. What's been going on?"

My uncle looks at Ian before turning back to my sister with a smile that any Dawson can see is not genuine. "Nothing, dear. Just some business issues between your brother and me. But your aunt is right as always." He picks up her hand and kisses it. "Nothing to discuss tonight." He looks around the room. "Now, where are those entrees? I'm starving."

"What did you mean there won't be any more Dawson hotels?" Kat turns her attention to our brother when my uncle looks at my aunt and then at Ian. "Ian?"

He leans back, and I'm finally able to look at Annie. She seems as confused as Kat, and her eyes are glued to Ian. "Just enjoy your night, Kat," he says. "It's business. You don't need to worry yourself."

"Don't talk down to her like that," Jake says. Kat's assertive, but Jake is always right behind her; it's something I've always loved about him. "There's been something going on all night. Just come out with it now so tomorrow we don't have some Dawson debacle."

"A Dawson alliteration! That's one point to Jake," Logan says. When nobody reacts, he seems to realize this isn't the time or place for his usual humor and sits quietly with his wine.

"Why don't you tell your sister what you're about to do?" my uncle says, looking at Ian.

"It's already done, Neil." Ian takes a sip of wine as if we're talking about the weather.

I've never heard him say "Neil," and I don't think I'm the only one. Even the other table has stopped talking, and all eyes are on what's happening at this table.

"It's not too late, Ian," my uncle says in an urgent tone. "Call Phillip on Monday and pull whatever contract you have."

"I was at the Astors' after I left your place," Ian says. "It's done. I signed."

"Signed what?" Annie asks. "Why were you at my parents'?"

He ignores her and continues to stare at my uncle. My uncle pushes his plate aside, and by the look on my aunt's face, even she knows she can't stop whatever is about to happen.

"Our legal team and the board haven't even received a contract to look at," my uncle says. "How have you pushed this through?"

"This is why Dad didn't leave the company to you, *Neil*."

My uncle narrows his eyes, and I've never seen him look at any of us so coldly. "They didn't leave it to you, either."

"You won't make the decisions that need to be made," Ian responds. "The market has changed. Independence is gone. This is how we keep this family alive."

"You mean this is how we keep this family rich."

"Same thing."

"To you," I interject. "It never was for Mom and Dad."

Ian's eyes snap to me almost as if he has been trying his best not to look at me all night. "Right. They cared about other things, didn't they? Like *art*. I guess we can thank Charlotte for what happened, then."

"Whoa, Ian," Kat says, and she sounds surprised. "What is going on?"

Ian and my uncle both glare at each other for another moment, and it's unclear who will speak first. My aunt puts her hand on my uncle's arm. He grabs it and nods as if he knows he needs to contain things.

"The business model for the Dawson Hotel Group is changing, Kat," Ian says. "That's what's going on."

"Maybe this isn't the best time to discuss business," Claudia chimes in, but she's never been to a Dawson event. Once the train starts rolling, it won't stop.

"What does that mean?" Kat asks my uncle.

"It means your brother is decimating your parents' company. There will be no Dawson Hotel Group."

Kat is silent for a few seconds. "You're selling Mom and Dad's company? Why didn't you tell me? Or Charlie?"

"Charlotte has made it clear she has no desire to be involved," Ian says.

"Or you decided that," my uncle responds.

"What does that mean?" Kat asks.

I sit back and close my eyes. Everything I didn't want to happen tonight is happening. The only saving grace is that my situation with Annie hasn't come out. Though, at this rate, I don't know what to expect. "Uncle Neil, *not now*," I plead, but that only makes my sister turn to me.

"Charlie?"

Kat only has to say my name. Maybe it's a sister thing, but I know from her tone that she's asking me to be honest with her. At this point, I don't know what else to be. Not when she's staring at me with those eyes I can't lie to. I wave to my uncle. "Tell her."

He nods before turning to Kat. "I guess we should start with your parents' will."

"What about it?"

"The company was left to all three of you." He looks at Ian, then me, before turning back to Kat. "Not just Ian. He didn't respect any of their wishes. Not even with the trust. Charlie hasn't seen a penny or asset from what your parents built for you."

The room is so quiet that when the servers begin to bring the entrees, it sounds like a loud clatter. By the speed with which they're doing it, they can sense the awkwardness and want to get out of there as fast as they can.

Nobody touches their food, not even Logan. Kat seems at a loss for what to say.

"Charlotte never even asked about the will," Ian says. "She moved on. About as far away as she could get. She didn't want anything to do with it or this family. Probably out of guilt."

"She didn't have to ask, Ian," my uncle says. "It's a will, and you were the executor. What you did was not only hurtful to this family but illegal."

"What about the hotels?" Kat says, finding her voice. "What does it mean that you're decimating the company?"

Ian lets out a long sigh. "Kat, it's complicated. Let's eat and try to enjoy the night?"

"I have a doctorate in veterinary medicine. I think I can handle complicated."

Ian picks up his fork and knife, slices into the fish, and takes a bite.

"Of course you can understand," my uncle says when it's clear Ian won't be answering. "The Dawson Hotel Group will be acquired by two separate investment groups. We'll lose power over any property we own. Most of our staff and leadership will be laid off. The name 'Dawson Hotel' will go away forever."

"Wait, you signed that contract at my parents' place tonight?" Maybe it's because she's been quiet the entire night, but my stomach does a flip as soon as Annie speaks. Her voice sounds stronger than I've ever heard it when directed at Ian, and she sounds as confused as Kat.

"This has nothing to do with you. We'll talk later," Ian says to her.

"You did this with my dad's company. I have a right to know."

He lets out a harsh laugh. "Well, in that case, you can all thank Annie. It was her who told Phillip that you even knew about the deal."

Her eyes go wide. She looks at me before shaking her head. "I asked him about it because I didn't think it could be true. That you or he would do that to this family—"

"Annie, just shut up," Ian shouts.

I can't stand to hear him talk to her like that. I try to stand, but Holly grabs my arm to hold me down. And as much as I want to fight, she's right. It's bad enough that Kat's night has been ruined. We don't need to add that I've been fucking Ian's girlfriend.

Ultimately, Annie doesn't need my help because a second later, she's standing and pushing her chair back. "I'm sorry, Kat. I don't think I should stay. You look beautiful, and I hope you have the wedding of your dreams. I'm sorry I won't be there to see it." She looks around before her eyes fall to me. Hers are shining with unshed tears. "I'm so sorry," she whispers.

"Stop being dramatic and sit down. This night isn't about you," Ian says, picking up his fork again.

"Which is why I'm leaving." She starts to walk away. "And Ian? Whatever the hell this is, it's over. You're an asshole, and your family deserves better. So do I."

She doesn't make eye contact with me as she walks away. If I wasn't so focused on my sister and the devastation on her face, I would follow. But I can't leave Kat right now, not even for Annie.

"Great job, Ian," Holly says when Annie is gone.

"She'll be back," he says.

Holly scoffs. "I highly doubt that."

Kat is still looking at the door, and when she turns back to the table, she's focused on me. "You knew all this and didn't tell me?"

There is nobody in this world who knows my sister like I do, not even her soon-to-be husband. I know every one of her expressions and her moods, and I've never seen her look like this. Like she's disappointed in me.

"I've only known about the hotel deal for a few days." I know my answer is weak, but I don't know what else to say.

"But the will and the trust? All this time and you never told me?"

"We'd just lost our parents. I didn't want their money. And I know you love Ian. I was trying to protect you."

"I'm not ten anymore," Kat shouts as she stands. "I don't need fucking protection. I need you to treat me like an adult. You've all been lying to me. You should have told me, Charlie. *Years ago.* But I guess you didn't really care. You made that clear when you left me."

"Better there than here," Ian says. "At least nobody else will die."

"That's uncalled for, Ian," my aunt says.

"Why should the person who killed them get anything?" he says louder, shoving his chair back and standing.

"Are you fucking kidding me, Ian?" Holly says.

"We all know it," he says. "You guys won't say it because this family has been kissing her ass her whole life. But it was her stupid fucking art show they were going to. That she *insisted* they attend. I would have left town, too, if I was the reason my parents died."

"Ian, that's enough," my aunt says, and even though her voice is quiet, it does the trick.

I start to shake as his words land. Tears sting my eyes, but I don't let them fall. Ironically, this may be the only thing Ian and I will ever agree on. It *was* my fault they died. I've just never wanted to acknowledge that. Leaving Manhattan was easier than facing the truth: if I had never invited them to that show, they never would have left their event early, and they'd still be alive.

Holly must feel me shaking because she puts her hand on my leg to calm it.

"Your sister never needed to insist on anything," my aunt says. "Your parents would never miss a show. Charlie had nothing to do with their deaths. It was an accident."

"Is that what this is about? You're destroying it all because you blame Charlie for a bad driver that killed our parents?" Kat's voice is louder than I've ever heard it. "Aunt Sandra is right. It was an accident. But if they were alive, they'd be ashamed of the man you've become."

"They were anyway," he spits.

"That's not true." My uncle raises his voice. "Your parents loved you, Ian. But you've gone too far. And your sister—and Annie, for that matter—is right. This isn't who we are."

The room is silent now; not even Ian seems to have a response.

Kat moves closer to him and speaks so quietly, I'm sure the guests at the other table, who are staring at this one like it's a movie, can't hear what she says. "I've defended you our whole lives. Even when you didn't deserve it. But I won't anymore. You've ruined everything they built. Everything they loved, including our sister."

"Kat—"

"No, Ian. I'm done. I don't want you here tomorrow. You're uninvited to the wedding." She gives him one long look before turning. "If you'll excuse me, I'm not hungry anymore." She stares at me, and my heart feels like it's being clenched when I see tears falling down her face. "If any of you want to actually act like my family, I'll see you tomorrow."

She walks out, and the silence is louder than the shouting that just took place. I can feel my own tears, but I do nothing to stop them. Ian may have destroyed this family, but the truth is, I helped.

He begins walking after Kat, but Jake steps in front of him. "Where are you going?"

"To find my sister. Move, Jake."

He doesn't budge. "You've done enough. And not just tonight. I can finally tell you that you're a real piece of shit. I hope the millions you made on that deal make you happy. And don't fucking contact her." He exits after Kat.

Ian stands there with wide eyes. He straightens his jacket as if he was in a physical altercation and walks out, heading out onto the patio and into the dark night.

Everyone looks stunned, but it can't be anything close to the fear I feel. If there was a worst-case scenario, we just about hit it, and I feel at a loss for what my next move should be.

Like always, Holly can read me. She leans in. "Are you okay?"

I shake my head.

"Who are you heading to first? Annie or Kat?"

"Kat doesn't want to see me."

"You know she does."

She's probably right. If it was me, I'd want to be alone. But Kat likes to process things right away. I also need to see Annie. I'm confused about what Ian said about all this being her fault, but more than that, I want to make sure she's okay, too. "Will you text me if anything else happens?"

"Of course."

"So which Dawson is leaving next?" Logan asks in an attempt at lightening the mood, but even his voice sounds shaky.

"Me. I hope that's okay," I say to my aunt.

She nods. But I can't look at her for long. She's put so much time and care into tonight and this whole wedding, and the sadness on her face is heartbreaking.

I give Holly's arm a squeeze as I stand and kiss her cheek. "I'll see you tomorrow."

"For better or worse. Good luck."

I don't say anything as I head toward the main exit. I feel a hole in my stomach that I haven't felt since I was at the hospital, and my parents were declared dead. So much just happened at once, and my head is spinning. The only thing I know for sure is that this family was broken once, and we barely put it back together. I'm not sure we'll be able to do it twice.

CHAPTER TWENTY-THREE

Annie's face as she said good-bye is seared into my mind, but right now, Kat is my priority. I have to try to make things right before tomorrow. In trying to protect her from the truth about our brother, I just ended up hurting her, and she's the one person I thought I'd never hurt in this world. Even if there wasn't a wedding tomorrow, it's time we talked about all the things I've refused to talk about all these years. It's time I acknowledged all the things I've refused to acknowledge. Kat is right; she's not a child. If anything, I've been the immature one.

I stop at the Dawson Hotel so I can grab the folder my uncle gave me a few days ago. It's not that I don't think Kat will believe my uncle; it's that I need to see it as well. And if I'm finally opening this will, I want Kat there with me.

I hop into one of the cabs waiting in front of the hotel and lean back. As the city flies past, I have a moment to think. I can't get Annie's face out of my mind, and in any other situation, I would have run to make sure she was okay. A few days ago, it seemed like the biggest hurdle was that she was with Ian. Now she's not, and it doesn't seem any less complicated, not with her family's involvement in the destruction of my parents' company.

Just another thing I haven't told Kat. But right now, the night before her wedding, I don't know if I can. Especially since I don't know if there is even an "Annie and me" to begin with.

I don't have long to think about it because the taxi turns onto Kat's street on the Upper West Side. I take my phone out so I can send Annie a text. I have no idea where her head is in all this, but she went through something intense tonight, too, and I need her to know I haven't disappeared: *Are you okay?*

I have to put my phone away to pay the driver and slip out, but when I pull it back out, there's a response waiting for me:

I'm fine. I'm more worried about Kat. How is she?

Before I press the buzzer for Kat's apartment, I lean against the wall next to the door so I can finish texting: *I don't know. I'm at her apartment now. But things got worse after you left.*

I figured they would. I'm sorry for what happened.

It's not your fault.

Not all of it.

Her text makes me think back to what Ian said. After our date and subsequent fight, she must have said something to her dad. Based on the shock on her face, I know that if she did say something to him, she couldn't have known the events it would spark.

There's a new text from her: *You must think I'm silly and naive. I guess you were right about everything.*

I try to respond, but my fingers are getting so cold that it's hard to type: *I don't think that at all. You were defending your family. I understand.*

I can see that she's typing, but soon, the text bubbles disappear, and my phone goes quiet. This isn't a conversation I want to have over text, so I send her another message:

Can I see you? I can come over after the wedding tomorrow if that's not too late.

Yes. Come over. Anytime.

The tight ball in my stomach loosens. Things couldn't be messier, and seeing Annie in the midst of it won't help, but I can't stop. Messy or not, I've fallen for her, and I won't be able to think of much else until I see her again. Before I can respond, she sends another text:

Text me when you're on your way. 40 E 75th St.

See you tomorrow, Annie.

I put my phone away and look at my sister's building again. It seems almost comical that I thought it would be possible to come back to this city without incident. The most I thought would happen was that Ian and I would have a few uneasy comments. Now I'm standing under Kat's apartment, wondering how I can mend things with her.

She is the person I've always trusted most. I've never been the most forthcoming person in my family, but growing up, we told each other every secret from the big to the mundane. Yet since my parents' death, I've shut her out.

I feel a throb in my fingers from how hard I'm gripping the file. It seems crazy to be so scared of a few pieces of paper. For so long, looking at this document felt like I was accepting their death. But maybe it doesn't have to feel like that; maybe honoring their last wishes can help heal this family.

I take the cold night air into my lungs once more as I press the buzzer. Jake's muffled voice comes through the intercom. "Hello?"

"Hey, Jake. It's me. Can I come up?"

The door makes a buzzing noise. I push it open and head to the elevator. The door is open when I get there, and Jake is leaning against it. "I was wondering how long it would take you to get here." He folds his arms across his chest.

I lift the folder. "I had to get something from the hotel." I look behind him, but it's dark. "How is she?"

He glances at the folder. As he lets out a long sigh, it hits me how unfair tonight was for him, too, this man who has been so wonderful to my sister. Tonight was supposed to be about both of them, and he's dealing with a Dawson family fight. Again. "She's upset, Charlie. What's in the folder?"

"The truth. Will she see me?"

"It's Kat. Of course she will." He doesn't move, and I can tell he's reluctant to let me in.

"Jake, please. Let me speak to her. Let me try to fix this."

"Two nights free of drama was all we wanted." I've never heard his voice so quiet and cold. I've only ever felt warmth from him. "This family already ruined one of those nights. Don't ruin the next one."

I nod.

He moves to the side. "She's in the bedroom."

I put a gentle hand on his shoulder and squeeze. "I'm really sorry, Jake."

"Don't say it to me. Say it to her," he says, tilting his head in the direction of the bedroom.

I squeeze one more time before heading down the dark hallway. I tap on the door lightly.

"Yeah?"

"It's me. Can we talk?"

"Why are you knocking?"

"I didn't want to interrupt anything."

"What happened to it being the prerogative of a big sister not to knock?"

I smile as she repeats something I used to say when we were kids. The fact that she even mentioned it gives me hope that she'll forgive me. "We're not kids anymore. Privacy is your prerogative."

"Just come in, weirdo."

When I see her sitting on the bed with a cat I don't recognize, I'm not surprised. She is constantly fostering animals. And not just cats. Last time I was in her room, there was a bird. I set the file on her dresser before sitting on the end of the bed. Kat is wearing a set of light pink pajamas. With her makeup off and her wild hair tied in a messy bun, she reminds me of a younger version of herself and the times I would come into her room to talk about anything and everything.

"And who is this?" I ask.

She kisses the cat's head. "This is Jimmy. And Jimmy is very handsome and smart and perfect. Jimmy, this is Charlie. She's here to grovel. Should we let her?" She looks at me. "Jimmy hasn't jumped off the bed like he does when Jake is around, so I guess that means you can stay."

Now that we're making eye contact, I see redness around hers. They may be dry right now, but I can tell she's been crying and by the looks of it, a lot. The disappointed look she directed toward me at the venue is gone, which only reminds me of how pure she is.

She gives everyone a chance, and anger isn't an emotion she likes to hold on to, even when it's deserved.

"I'm sorry your night was ruined," I say.

She gives Jimmy one more kiss before setting him on her pillow. She pulls her knees up and hugs them like she did when we were kids and gives me a long look. "After they died, it made sense that things in the family were hard. But I thought it would get better. It's never getting better, is it?" Her voice catches, and I can see that tears are close to the surface again.

I scoot closer so I can put a hand on her knee. "Our family has always been complicated. Even when Mom and Dad were alive."

"And secretive, apparently. How could you not tell me Ian withheld the trust from you? I tell you everything."

"I thought I was protecting you and your relationship with him."

"Bullshit."

My hand drops. I can count the times I've heard her swear on one hand, yet tonight, she's done it twice.

"You left for LA five days after their funeral. *Five days*, Charlie. How is that protecting me?"

My throat tightens, and I feel tears pressing in, but I swallow them. I have no right to cry to Kat about the mess I've created. "I left out of guilt, not to get away from you."

"You can't possibly believe what Ian said tonight."

"I know it was an accident. But it doesn't change the fact that they got into that accident because they were coming to see me. I asked them to be there."

"They would have been there no matter what. That's who they were. But did it help? Moving to LA?"

I think before answering. If she had asked me that two weeks ago, I would have said yes. Or at least, I thought it had. But since being back, I've felt so many highs that I didn't think I'd feel again. The numbness that settled in at my parent's funeral has slipped away. I *want* to feel again. I want to be part of my family again. "No. It didn't," I say, wishing I had done so many things differently.

Kat's eyes are soft, and the understanding expression causes me to lose my resolve. I take a few steadying breaths as I feel tears start to fall. Kat catches one before lacing our fingers together.

"I shouldn't have left," I whisper.

"Ian should have given you what's yours regardless."

"Can you finally see him for who he is, Kat?"

She drops my hand and shakes her head. "He was wrong in this. In so many things. But it's you that's never seen him."

"What do you mean?"

"I know he's selfish. And his values are way off. But you had a different childhood than he did. And I don't think you even realize it."

"Because he went to boarding school?"

"He didn't even want to go to that school."

"He loved that school."

"Once he was there. But dad was the one who made him go in the first place. He asked not to go."

"How do you know?"

"Charlie, I love you more than anything in this world. I've always cherished our relationship. But you're not the only sibling I have. And you're not the only one who came to my room to talk growing up. Our parents were amazing in a lot of ways. But not always to Ian."

"That's his own fault."

"In a way, yes. He didn't help himself. Especially after high school. But you knew a very different Mom and Dad than we did."

"I don't understand."

"You were their world, Charlie. You got so much of them. Ian and I saw more of our nannies than we ever did them. Remember Marie?"

"Of course. She lived with us."

"In sixth grade, my teacher thought she was Mom. It took her half a year to realize she was the nanny. I know Mom and Dad tried to be there. But often, they just weren't. They would have never missed one of your art shows. Whether you asked them to go or not. Dad didn't even go to Ian's high school graduation."

"So, this is Ian's revenge on them?"

"I don't know what he was thinking. I'm just trying to explain things that you don't see. Ian doesn't hate you, he resents you. He's always been jealous of the relationship you had with Mom and Dad because he didn't have it."

"And that's an excuse to do what he did to their company?"

"Of course not. And that's why I disinvited him to the wedding. He's hurt this family too much now. But he wasn't born evil. He's hurt, and he doesn't know how to handle that."

"Why didn't you ever tell me any of this?"

"Because I don't resent you like he does. I love you. More than anyone."

"You have to believe that if I had known how all this would play out, I would have told you days ago. I didn't want anything to ruin things. I may be older, but I'm an idiot."

A smile appears on her lips. "Only sometimes. Usually, you're great." She is so understanding and good. She deserves so much more than I've been giving her.

"I haven't been a great sister for the last four years. More than anything, this trip has made me see that. I miss you. I miss home."

"And I wouldn't have defended Ian so many times had I known about the trust. I'm not defending him anymore. I just think I know why he feels the way he does."

"The will and the trust didn't mean anything to me, Kat. Our parents were gone. I couldn't get them back. Money wouldn't bring them back. A stake in a company I never wanted wouldn't bring them back. So I ignored it. I left. Because it was easier to be numb than to feel." I stop talking as my voice breaks, and I can hardly see Kat through the tears. I don't remember the last time I cried like this, and now that I've let the tears have their freedom, I don't know how to stop.

Kat scoots down the bed and takes my face in her hands. "I know, Charlie. I know." She wipes away some of the tears, but they're quickly replaced by new ones. "I lost them, too."

I take her hands. "I know you did. And I'm sorry if I act like you didn't."

"You know the hardest part was that I felt like I lost you, too."

Now it's my turn to wipe away her tears. This is not at all how I wanted her rehearsal dinner night to go, with us crying in each other's arms, but it feels easier to breathe than it has in years. This is the Kat and me that I know, and I've gone too long without it. "I'm here, Kat."

"For now."

"Do you want me to stay?" I don't even know what I want her answer to be. I never expected to miss home this much, and part of me hopes she'll ask me to stay. I try not to think about Annie, but she's still in my mind. She's still a huge reason I feel this way.

"You have to make that decision on your own. And it can't be out of guilt. You have to stop that and live the life you want." Her words remind me of all the things I've been saying to Annie. I keep urging her to live her own life, but what have I been doing? I've been punishing myself by distancing my life from everyone I love. From the life I had. It's only now that I realize Annie and I are more similar than I realized. "And maybe stop making rash decisions," she adds. "Just think about what you want."

"Since when did you become the wise sister?"

"I've always been the wise sister."

"Even that time you started a fire in the school library?"

She pulls back her hands and scoffs, causing me to laugh. "It was one book that caught fire, and I was working on a science project."

"Arson in the name of science."

"Need I remind you that my project got first place at the fair?"

"You literally have the ribbon right there." I point to the wall of photos over their dresser. "In your adult bedroom, I might add." She tries to slap my leg, but I pull it up before she makes contact. "And you're still slow."

"Didn't you come here to make me feel better?" She fakes a pout.

The tears have dried, and it feels good just to be us again. The knot in my stomach that has been growing since dinner hasn't gone away. I don't know if it will until I see Annie. But this is a conversation Kat and I should have had years ago, and right now, I feel like the woman my parents raised. "I did." I grab her hand again. "And that science project was very good. Mom and Dad were proud. I remember."

She glances at the ribbon, and the smile on her face is replaced by a frown. "Yeah. They were." She looks back at me with that same expression. "What do you want to do?"

"I think it's time to look at the will."

"I think it's time to get our parents' company in the hands it deserves to be in. Uncle Neil's."

"And how do we do that?"

She reaches over to Jimmy the cat and strokes his head as she smiles. "We fuck some shit up," she says in the singsong voice she always uses when talking to animals.

"Fuck some shit up? Who are you, and what have you done with my sister?"

She turns her smile to me as she continues to stroke Jimmy's head. "I'm a determined Dawson. Let's get their company back, Charlie."

"Let's get it back."

CHAPTER TWENTY-FOUR

I sneak out of my sister's room before she wakes. I haven't looked at my phone to see the time, but I can tell by the soft light peeking through her bedroom window that it's still early. After going through the will together all last night and tentatively planning our next move, I forced her to sleep. She needs her energy today, and we can't fix this situation in one night. I'll see her again in a few hours, but I desperately need to get out of these clothes and shower before I head to the venue to get ready.

I can see Jake sleeping on the couch, so I try to be quiet as I sneak past. It may be unusual to spend the night before your wedding on the couch as your fiancé sleeps in your bed with her sister, but Jake didn't seem to mind, another reason why I love him for Kat. Very few men would be that understanding, but Jake knew we needed that time. He knows how important our relationship is and has always made room for it.

As I hop into a taxi outside their apartment, I feel a mix of emotions. On one hand, I'm relieved that Kat and I aired everything out. I never realized there were so many things about our childhood that I was blind to. As much as I loved my parents, I never even stopped to think about what it was like growing up in our house once the hotel business had really taken off. It's true my parents weren't around all the time, but because they were always there for me, I didn't realize it wasn't the same for my siblings.

There's still so much I need to figure out with Annie, but I feel better about where things stand with Kat. After the wedding of her dreams, I can deal with my mess of a love life.

Once the taxi pulls up to the hotel, I rush to my room to get ready. By the time I shower and answer dozens of texts from Holly and my aunt, I only have an hour before I need to get to the venue for hair and makeup. I figure there's no point in trying too hard with my outfit if I'm just going to be putting on a dress, so I quickly throw on an old Pratt T-shirt and some ripped jeans. Part of me hopes I'll run into Claudia before I get into my dress. I'm sure she'll judge this outfit as much as she judged my coat last night. She doesn't seem like the type of woman to condone holes in pants.

As I'm putting on my shoes, I hear a soft knock on the door, and my stomach does a flip. Considering there's a Do Not Disturb sign, I know it's not the hotel staff. There was something so tentative about the knock that I have a feeling I know who it is. A quick look through the peephole confirms my suspicion, and the calmness I had started to feel after leaving Kat's place dissipates.

I open the door, and for a moment, Annie and I simply stare at each other. The silence doesn't feel uncomfortable, but when she searches my face as if trying to memorize it, the knot in my stomach that had started to loosen tightens right back up. Last night, as she left the venue, her face was full of so many emotions. But right now, she looks like a shell of herself, as if she's trying to push aside her feelings.

"I know I shouldn't be here," she says in a hollow voice.

"I'm glad you are." Without thinking, I pull her into me. After such a long night, all I've wanted is to feel her in my arms again. I can feel a tenseness in her that I've never felt before. I put my arms around her, and only then does she reciprocate, putting her arms around my waist.

As I hold her, something changes. She lets out a sigh and buries her face in my shoulder as if she's trying to hide from the world, and her only solace is me. I can't tell what she's feeling, so I just hang on. Holding her feels like I'm holding something in a dream. Maybe it's because there's never been any certainty with us, but every moment feels fragile and fleeting. And this embrace scares me more than anything that's happened in the last twenty-four hours. I don't want to wake up to see my arms are empty.

"How's Kat?" she asks, moving back. She sets a bag on my bed.

I feel an emptiness the moment we're not touching. I know I can't sit in this room hugging her all day, but it doesn't stop me from wishing I could. Wishing we could crawl into bed, watch a movie, and forget about everything. But today is important, so I do my best not to regret the fact that we're not still embracing. "Better. I was with her all night. I just came back to get my dress."

"What happened after I left?"

"Why don't we sit?" I walk to the bed and sit on the edge as she pushes her bag aside and does the same. "Ian said more horrible stuff, and Kat disinvited him to the wedding. Have you heard from him?"

"No, I don't think I will. My dad hasn't reached out, so I don't think he knows yet. Ian must not have said anything."

"Are you okay?"

She lets out a harsh laugh and pushes some hair out of eyes that seem glassier than normal. I haven't known her long, but it's easy to see that she's not okay. "It doesn't matter how I am. I just did what I should have done months ago."

"It matters to me."

She gives me a long sad look before her eyes go to her lap. "It's my fault last night ended up like it did."

"It's not—"

"It is, Charlie. If I had never probed my dad for info on the deal, he and Ian would have never been tipped off. You would have had more time."

I grab her hand. I wait until she looks at me before I speak. "Last night was Ian's fault. And honestly, kind of my fault. You didn't lie to my sister all these years, I did."

"I understand making decisions to protect your sister," she says, lacing our fingers.

"I know. But this is different from your situation. I was protecting myself, not Kat. I've made a lot of wrong decisions."

"I still don't see why Ian would do this. He had to know he'd lose you all."

"I've never understood my brother. Maybe I should have tried harder."

"Maybe he should have."

Silence takes over the room. I don't have much time before I need to head out, but I don't want to leave Annie.

"I came for a reason," she says, breaking the moment. "It's about the deal Ian made." She reaches for her bag, putting it in her lap. "The other night, I didn't want to believe you about my dad. I should have. After what he did to my brother...I should have known. I was so scared of losing Zoe that I made myself believe he wasn't a monster. I made myself believe that despite what he did to Dylan, he was still my dad." Her voice sounds thick, and the glassiness in her eyes is even more pronounced. "Before I went to college, I had a part-time job helping him. Admin stuff like cleaning out his inbox, scheduling meetings, things like that. Anyway, he is as old-school as they come. He hasn't changed his passwords in fifteen years. Unfortunately for him, I remember them." She opens the bag and pulls out a file. I'm entirely confused as to where she's going with this. She puts the file between us quickly, almost as if the paper will burn her.

"What's in it?"

"All the proof you need about the deal Ian and my dad made."

"What do you mean proof?"

She wipes her face again, and I can tell this isn't easy for her. I've never seen her this strained and anxious. "My dad wasn't just helping Ian facilitate the deal. He was going to be getting a large cut of it. But more than that, he knew it was illegal."

I'm still confused, but she doesn't look like she's done talking so I wait.

She points at the file. "One of the documents in there explicitly shows that he knew about the will."

"My parents' will?"

"Remember how I told you my dad made a bad deal while I was in college that almost ruined our family?"

I nod. That night that seems like months ago now.

"After that, he started doing research on his business partners. His lawyer did his due diligence on Ian. He found out that he wasn't the sole owner of the Dawson Hotel Group. It's all in there." She points to the file again.

"Why would he move forward with it?"

"They'd been working on this deal for over a year when the will was unearthed. That's hours and hours of billable time that my family's company invested. Because my dad was promised a very large cut, he invested our company's money in the upfront labor hours. Ian convinced him that you would never do anything to take the company. My dad made a calculated risk to move forward."

"An illegal risk." My tone is harsher than I want, especially considering how devastated Annie already looks. Phillip Astor may be a crook, but I don't need to tell her that again. "Won't your dad find out you gave me this?"

"That depends on what you and your sister do with it."

The hotel phone rings, breaking the intensity. "Sorry. Wedding day. I should get that." She nods, and I reach across the bed to answer. "Hello?"

"My parents and I will be at your hotel with the car in fifteen minutes. Get your ass downstairs."

"Good morning to you, too, Holly. But if it's going to take you fifteen minutes, I'll leave my room in fourteen minutes and thirty seconds."

"You're annoying. Bye." She hangs up without another word, and the room feels quiet and still again.

I move back down the bed, but this time, I scoot closer to Annie so our legs are touching. "What do you mean it depends on what we do with it?"

Her body language has changed. She sits back on the bed, her hands twisting in her lap. "If you get the company back from Ian, that *will* kill the deal. You don't have to expose my dad."

"The deal could still go forward before then. It's signed."

She looks panicked. "So your plan is to take them both down?"

"I don't have a plan. You just gave me this information. All I want is to get my parents' company back."

"At the destruction of mine."

I try to reach out, but she promptly stands and paces. The embrace we had earlier feels like an actual dream now. "I don't want to destroy your family."

She turns, but she doesn't look defensive. She looks sad and scared.

I move close, but I don't try to reach out again. "Why did you bring me these papers if you don't want me to use them?"

For what feels like minutes, she is quiet, allowing me to get lost in her eyes. And although they're swimming with emotion, I can't decipher what she's feeling. Her eyes are like an abstract piece of art that I can stare at for hours and still not understand.

"Why, Annie?" I whisper. "Why did you bring me that file?"

"You know why."

"I want to hear you say it."

She opens her mouth, then closes it again. Tears fall down her face that she quickly brushes aside. "Because it was the right thing to do."

I can tell that she's trying to harden herself against what she really feels, so I don't push. We're in an impossible situation, and making declarations at this point will only make things harder.

"I know I can't stop you from using it," she says. "I would, if I were in your position. I'm just scared of what it means. For Zoe. And for us."

"Where *does* that leave us?"

She shakes her head and lets out a sarcastic laugh. "Who would have thought it could get more complicated than me being your brother's girlfriend?"

I take her hand. "Where does that leave us?" I ask again, bracing myself for the answer I know is coming.

"You need to figure out your family's move. And I need to be with mine."

"And that's it?"

She lets out a long sigh but puts her other hand in mine and squeezes. "How would this work, Charlie? I date the woman who's going to take my family to court? What do I tell my sister? My mom?"

"Not them. Your dad. And I don't even know what we'll do with that file. I never said I wanted to destroy your family. I just want to save mine."

Her forehead drops to mine. "I know what you need to do. And I'm sorry I asked you not to. I just can't be part of it."

"I don't know how to let you go, Annie. In just a couple weeks, you've become part of me."

She lifts her head and gives me a small smile. "Soon, you'll be back in LA, fighting off models, and you'll forget all about me."

I know she's trying to lighten the moment, but her words feel like a slap. I drop her hands and take a small step back. "Is that how easy it will be for you?"

In a second, she is back in my space. Once I'm staring in her eyes again, she speaks in a quiet, intense tone I've never heard from her. "When I looked up and saw your face that first night in the bar, I had never seen something so beautiful. In that moment, I felt connected to something in a way that not even a piece of art makes me feel. You made me feel alive. You still do. I'll never move on from that." She cups my face. Her hand is warm, and I can't imagine not feeling the soft feel of her anymore.

I close my eyes to savor the moment. I put my hand over hers and press my cheek. "*Annie.*"

"I know."

"This isn't fair."

"I know."

"What am I supposed to do?"

She looks at the clock on the bedside table. "Go. Give your uncle those emails. And then, get your dress on. Have some champagne while you look stunning. And enjoy your sister's wedding."

"And then?"

"Knowing Ian, if this goes where I think it will go, I'll see you across the aisle in court."

We both jump slightly as the hotel phone rings again. "Fuck."
She strokes my cheek. "Go see your sister get married."

The phone rings three more times. I groan as I go to answer.
"I'm coming, I'm coming," I shout into the receiver, not even letting
Holly say anything. When I turn, Annie is at the door. "Wait." My
legs feel unsteady as I walk over, but there are so many emotions
running through me that I feel like I may break. I don't even know
what else I need to say, but letting her leave feels too final. Right
now, what scares me most is forgetting. What if in a week or a month
or a year, I can't remember how her lips feel? Or how it felt to hold
her? I know about loss. And I know that with time, everything fades.

As if she's feeling the same thing, she pushes off the door and
takes the last few steps toward me. Our bodies fold into each other,
and our lips press together. Our mouths surrender to each other and
move as seamlessly as they always have. Kissing her feels easier
than breathing, and I do my best to memorize the feeling as our lips
slow.

When she pushes her tongue into my mouth, I can taste the
saltiness from our mutual tears. The phone rings again, but I ignore
it and wrap my arms around her back, pulling her even closer.

We kiss for another minute. Or maybe it's an hour. I lose track
of time as our mouths take their final breaths together. When my cell
phone begins vibrating in my pocket, she gently pushes away. "The
wedding won't wait for you," she says in a breathy voice.

"I know."

She puts her hand under my chin and lifts my eyes to hers. "I
didn't really give you that file because it was the right thing to do.
I gave it to you because I love you. Take care of yourself, Choo
Choo."

She places one soft kiss on my cheek before she reaches in her
bag and pulls out another folder, this one larger and leather. She sets
it on the bed before walking out without another glance.

My phone vibrates again, but I walk over to the folder and open
it. As I look at a portrait of myself, I gasp, and my legs feel like they
may give out. I sit to steady myself. Annie once left a drawing of
me on this very bed, but this time, it's not a simple sketch from a

hotel pen. Annie created a charcoal masterpiece, which may sound arrogant considering I'm the subject, but it's simply beautiful. She captured the first moment she ever saw me looking at her from upstairs at the Runaway. The lines and shading create an image that looks real, and I'm thrown back to that first night.

She's captured a clear expression of desire on my face. As heartbroken as I am right now, I can't help but smile at the memory. When I pick up the page to take a closer look, I see a note under it. I'm reminded of the first note she ever left me, a note I still have. And once again, this proves that Annie was not a dream. None of this was a dream. I trace each word as I read it.

I will never forget that night or any night since. I love you. Annie

I put the note and portrait down, knowing that if I don't leave, Holly will be up here yelling any second. But my uncle's speech from the night before pops into my head. Every moment I've shared with Annie has been charged with something I've never experienced. Annie was made for me. I just needed to run into her.

I put my hand on the spot she last kissed and close my eyes, wondering how I let the best thing to ever happen to me just walk out of my life.

CHAPTER TWENTY-FIVE

S eems like you and Kat made up." Holly passes me the flask
that she, Logan, and I have been sharing. We're dressed,
but instead of hanging out in the bridal rooms, we're sitting in the
main room where Kat and Jake will get married.

The room looks the same as it did last night, with even more
twinkly lights, and the candles are lit. I take a sip and hand the flask
to Logan, who's sitting in the row behind me. "We did."

"What about Annie?" she asks.

My eyes snap to Logan. "*Holly.*"

"It's fine," he says. "She already told me. I think it's rad."

"Seriously, Holls?"

"Calm down." She grabs the flask from him. "It's Logan. He
doesn't even know how to gossip. So, what about Annie?"

"What about her?" I smooth my dress, even though it doesn't
need it.

"Don't pull that crap with me. Have you seen her?"

"She stopped by the hotel this morning. It's over."

"Just like that? I thought you really liked her."

I close my eyes and will myself not to snap. I've been in a bad
mood since I left my hotel, and the last thing I want to do is rehash
what happened with Annie. Today can't be about that. Even if my
heart feels like it's being squeezed with every breath. "Holly, not
now. It's complicated."

"It's always been complicated. At least she's not your brother's
girlfriend anymore."

Logan lets out a laugh, but when I glare his way, he looks around the room and turns the laugh into a cough.

"Our two families are due for something pretty intense soon and not on the same side," I say quickly. Nobody else is in the room, but that could change at any moment. "Can we drop it?"

"Oh, it's a star-crossed lovers thing," Logan chimes in, once again not reading the room. "That could be romantic."

"Romeo and Juliet died, Logan." I grab the flask and take a long sip.

"Still, Annie's hot."

"Not the point, idiot," Holly says. "I saw the way you looked at her. And I saw the way she looked at you."

I open my mouth again but promptly shut it when my aunt comes in with a "mom" expression on her face. "Logan, what are you doing in here? You're supposed to be with the boys. They're about to do a toast for Jake," my aunt says.

"I'm a sensitive man, Mom. I prefer the company of women." He takes the flask and holds it out.

"Can you three get through one event without that damn flask?" she asks.

"Nope," Holly responds. "Want a sip? You seem like you could use some."

"Once everyone has said I do and there's no sight of Ian, I will gladly take that flask off you."

"You don't think he'll show up, do you?" Logan asks.

"He better not," I respond before looking at my aunt. "Is Kat ready?"

"Yes. And she's asking for you. Holly, why don't you go make sure the rest of the bridesmaids are ready to go while Charlie and Kat have a moment?"

"What room are they in?" Holly moves toward the door. "You know what, don't answer that. I'll just follow the sound of high-pitched giggles."

As soon as Holly is gone, my aunt turns to Logan. "Logan Timothy Dawson, get your cute butt to the boy's room. Now."

"Aw, Mom, you think my butt is cute? Why can't I just marry you?"

"Because our family is complicated enough, you twerp," she responds as she pulls him up and out of the room.

❖

Kat is standing in front of a long mirror when I enter her bridal suite. She doesn't seem to notice me, so I take the opportunity to look at her in her wedding dress. Even with the loss I feel over Annie, my entire mood lifts as I see how happy she is.

When she does a twirl, she sees me and stops. Her smile makes the tightness in my stomach loosen. She looks light and happy, and that's all I wanted for her today.

"You are the most beautiful bride I've ever seen."

"That's a low bar. You've been to, like, two weddings."

"Three, actually. And you definitely top the list." I grab her hand so she can give me a twirl, a move she used to have me do when we were kids, and she got a new dress she loved. "Kat, really. You look like a dream. I wish Mom could see you."

"I do, too. But I'm glad you're here."

"I wouldn't be anywhere else."

She smiles, then gives me a thoughtful look. "I've been thinking about something we talked about last night."

"What's that?"

"I still can't be the one to make the decision on where you live. But maybe you could come back more often?"

"I haven't decided where home is. But I promise, I will be around more."

"Good. Because you know you're, like, my favorite person, right?"

"And you know you're mine, right?"

Her smile grows before it dims. "Will you be mad if I tell you I'm kind of sad he's not here?"

I pull her closer. "Of course not, Kat. He's your twin."

"As much as he hurt me, he's still a part of me."

"I'm sorry it all went down like it did. You deserve better from both of us."

She shakes her head. "No more apologizing. Today is a fun day. Only smiles."

"Only smiles."

"And you never know, maybe you'll meet your soulmate tonight. Have you seen how hot you are in that dress?"

I glance at my dress and shake my head. My sister has good taste, and the simple dark blue dress isn't as ostentatious as some of the bridesmaid dresses I saw in the shop. But I'm not looking to meet my soulmate tonight. That ship sailed out of my hotel room earlier this morning. "Let's focus on getting you hitched, and then worry about me, shall we?"

She takes my hands. "I only say things like that because I want you to be happy."

"Maybe I need to learn to be happy by myself first."

"And when will get you there?"

"I'm on my way. I should have come back years ago."

She smiles widely and squeezes my hands. "Duh."

"Excuse me, ladies," my uncle says, coming into the room. "You both look beautiful. Kat, are you ready?"

I give her a reassuring nod and smile before she looks back to my uncle. "I'm ready."

"Sandra asked me to have you meet everyone out by the main doors," he says to me.

I pull Kat into a gentle hug, conscious not to mess up her dress or hair. "I love you, Kat. I'm so happy for you."

"I love you, too. I expect you to save me a dance later."

"As many as you'd like. Now, go get married."

CHAPTER TWENTY-SIX

Aren't they lovely together?"
I'm usually not one to agree with Claudia, but as I watch my sister take her first dance with her new husband, I have to. They are gliding across the floor and laughing, and they look as happy as I've ever seen them.

"Just lovely," my aunt responds.

"I'm still hungry," Logan says from across the table.

"Shh." Holly smacks his arm. "There's still dessert. Calm down and watch your cousin dance."

"Hey, Charlie." Cassie kneels by my chair. "I thought we would do toasts before we open the dance floor for everyone. Jake's best man will go, then Holly, and then you. Ready?"

My stomach does a flip, but I give her a small nod. This is the part of the wedding I've been dreading. I should have let Holly handle the whole thing. The speeches start as soon as Kat and Jake are back at our table, but most of it is a blur. I hear people laughing throughout Holly's speech, but I'm too nervous to really listen. Soon, I feel a jab in my ribs.

"Charlie." Holly points to Cassie, who's holding a microphone. "You're up. Don't fuck it up."

I've never enjoyed being in the spotlight, which is partly why I always felt more comfortable running galleries than showing my own art. But when I look at Kat's sweet, expectant face, I put all that aside. It's not hard to say what I love about her. "Hi. Um, I'm Charlie."

"Yeah, you are," Logan shouts.

"Thanks, Logan. But maybe slow down on the champagne."

Everyone laughs, which gives me a little more courage. I take a deep breath. "I know most of you, but for those I don't, I'm Kat's older sister. But the saying 'age is just a number' has never been truer than when it comes to Kat and me. I may be five years older, but Kat has taught me more than anyone in my life." I take another breath as I look around. "This world can be cruel. And it can be sudden. And surprising. And heartbreaking. It takes someone special to rise above all that. To see the good in people. To see the light in the darkest times. Someone who's able to heal. And that's my sister. And that's Jake." I look back at them. "I am so happy you two found each other. And that you had enough sense to hold on. I have no advice for you. I don't even know what *I'm* doing."

"That's not true," Kat says, smiling.

I return her smile before I continue. "What I do know is that Mom and Dad would tell you to be kind to each other. And I know you will. Congratulations. I love you both."

I raise my glass, and the rest of the room follows suit, toasting the new couple. As I sit, my hands shake, and I'm not even sure I remember what I said. But Kat must have thought I did okay because she gets up and comes over to me.

"And you thought you would be bad at that." She pulls me into a tight embrace. "Thank you, Charlie. That was perfect."

Jake is next to hug me. "I thought you might fuck that up, but you did well."

"Now, it's time to dance. Don't argue with me. It's my day," Kat pulls me out of my seat and onto the dance floor.

The DJ seems to take the cue as we step onto the shiny floor; the music picks up, and guests begin flooding onto it. Kat grabs my hands and spins me, laughing loudly. Soon, all the bridesmaids have joined us, and I find myself relaxing into the moment. It's hard not to have fun when Kat and her friends are swinging me every which way and laughing their heads off.

After numerous upbeat songs, the music slows, and I feel a tap on my shoulder. "I've had the pleasure of dancing with all the

Dawson women except my eldest niece. Will you do me the honor?" My uncle smiles as he holds out his hand.

"Of course." I slip my hand into his.

He is a great dancer and always has been, so I allow him to easily lead me around the floor. Kat and Jake sway together as they gaze into each other's eyes, and I feel somewhat envious. As much as I love my uncle, he's not the one I wish I was dancing with right now.

"It's been a lovely evening."

"It has. Thank you for being there for her today."

"You don't have to thank me. We're family, Charlie."

"I'm sorry about yesterday."

He shakes his head and gives me a serious look. "No, I'm sorry. That was not the time or place, and I shouldn't have lost my temper."

"It seems everyone thinks last night was their fault." I think back to my conversation with Annie.

"Holly tells me that you and Kat looked at the will."

I check to make sure Kat's not close enough to hear. I don't want her thinking about the will or Ian any more than she already must be. "We did. But there's more we need to discuss."

"What do you mean?"

"I have some emails I need to show you. We'll need to move fast on Monday."

"What emails?"

I lower my voice as he sways me in the opposite direction of Kat and Jake. "Emails between Phillip Astor and his lawyer. Emails between Phillip and Ian. Emails they would not want a court to see. I brought them."

He stops moving. "Come with me." He walks off the dance floor.

I glance at Kat again, but she's in a world of her own with Jake, so I don't think she'll notice. I follow my uncle out the main doors and into the room the groomsmen got ready in.

He closes the door with an urgent look on his face. "How in the world did you get Phillip's emails?"

I knew this was coming, and I still don't have a good answer. But if I've learned anything this week, it's that this family needs to stop hiding things. I don't have to tell him all the details, but I've decided not to lie. "Annie gave them to me."

"Why? Was she copied on them?"

"No, she went into his email account and printed them. I guess she has her reasons for not feeling loyalty anymore."

He wipes his hand over his face, but his eyes are wide. "And what do they say?"

"That Phillip knew Ian wasn't the sole owner of the Dawson Hotel Group. That they pushed the deal forward and intentionally buried that."

"That doesn't surprise me."

"But now we have enough evidence to kill the deal."

"I don't know if we can use those. If Annie wasn't on them, she technically hacked into an account."

"So what should we do?"

"I can have the company lawyer advise us on next steps. But, Charlie, it's not my decision. You and your sister own the company. What do you want to do?"

I take a moment to gather my thoughts. It doesn't take long. The Dawson Hotel group has always been a family endeavor; that's the way my parents wanted it, and that's the way we'll move forward. "This company belongs to the family. Let's have a meeting tomorrow before Kat and Jake leave for their honeymoon. We decide as a family."

He smiles. "Are you asking for a Dawson dinner?"

"I guess I am." I smile back.

"Your parents would be proud of you."

"You think?"

He pulls me into a hug. "I know. Let's get back to the wedding. Cake is coming soon."

❖

Logan digs into his third piece of wedding cake. Right now, we're the only ones at the table, and it feels good to be able to sit and relax. I've been pulled in so many directions tonight with all the friends and family I've had to greet and all the dancing Kat made me do. I need a break.

"This is so good," Logan says with his mouth full.

"How many pieces do you think you can eat before you're sick?"

"I'm not sure. Want to make a bet?"

"I think you'll be done after your fourth."

"Bullshit. I can make it to five."

"If you eat five pieces of cake without throwing up, I'll personally put in a good word with Lena for you."

"Up it to six pieces and get me her phone number."

"Deal."

"You might as well send out our wedding invites now." He takes an obscenely large bite.

"Right, the courthouse and a McDonald's feast. I'm sure she'll be wowed by your romanticism."

"I think any woman would appreciate my thoughtfulness about our future. Weddings are a waste of money and—" He stops as he looks at something over my shoulder. "Forget Lena. I've just seen my new wife. Get me her number, and I'll eat the whole damn cake."

I turn and spot Lily walking toward us in a long silver dress. She looks just as beautiful as she did on the night of Kat's bachelorette party with her long blond hair flowing behind her and her blue eyes as bright as ever. I see what Logan sees. I just don't feel what he feels. "Hey, Lily."

"Lily? What a pretty name." Logan pushes the cake aside. I don't think I've ever seen him ignore food. Not even for a woman.

"Thank you. I take it you're Holly's brother?"

"Logan," he says. "You're very pretty."

She laughs but not in an unkind way. "Thank you, Logan," she says before looking at me. "How about a dance?" She reaches out, but when I don't react, she lets out another easy laugh. "Oh, come on, Charlie. It's not like I asked for your hand in marriage. Just a dance."

Logan stands. "I'll dance with you. Or give you my hand. Whatever you want. Logan and Lily has a nice ring to it, no?"

"Actually"—she laughs—"I was just going to point out to Charlie, that there are very few lesbians to dance with, so she should humor me."

"Oh." He slumps back in his chair and pulls the cake in front of him. He points at me with his fork. "Six pieces and you find me a wife."

When I look back to Lily, her attention is focused across the room. "I thought Kat told Ian not to come?"

"She did." My stomach sinks as my brother stalks toward the DJ booth. Dread fills me as the DJ hands him a microphone.

Before I can move, Logan's rushing across the room. He says something to Ian before he takes the microphone. Ian isn't a small guy, but he has nothing on Logan, who grabs him by his collar, tugs him off the dance floor, and pushes him through the closest door.

"I have to go," I say to Lily and hurry to follow. I find them just inside the long hallway.

"Get off me." Ian pushes Logan away. "I'm giving my damn speech, so move aside."

"No, you're not, dude." Logan is the most cheerful person I know, but right now, he looks like he may punch my brother.

"Will you give me a minute with Ian?" I ask from the doorway.

They whip around. "Are you sure?" Logan asks, looking at Ian like he may do something crazy at any moment.

"I'll be fine."

He sends one more menacing look Ian's way before he walks back into the main room, leaving Ian and me to glare at each other.

When we were teens, he would often lose his temper, and it could take my parents hours to calm him down. Right now, he looks just like that. His chest is rising and falling as if he's just run a marathon, and I can tell he's not in a stable place. He hasn't even changed out of his outfit from last night.

"What are you doing here, Ian? Kat made her feelings clear. Are you trying to ruin her wedding?"

"That's rich coming from you. All these years, you've been the golden child. Now, they'll know who you really are. Then, she can decide who really ruined her wedding."

"Ian. You should leave," my uncle says from behind me.

I turn to find my uncle, aunt, Jake and even Kat, who left her own wedding, standing in the hallway.

"Why should I?" Ian asks.

"Ian," Kat pleads. "Please, stop this."

"Not before I say what I need to say."

"Ian—" my uncle says before Ian cuts him off.

"My turn to talk." His eyes settle on my uncle. "First of all, you're fired, Neil. You are no longer an employee of the Dawson Hotel Group."

"You know that holds no legal weight, son. The company is not yours," my uncle says in a much calmer tone than he used last night.

"I'm not your son. You're fired. Don't ever come into the office. And that's not all. None of you are welcome at any Dawson property. The hotel staff have been notified to call the police if you're caught trespassing."

"Stop being ridiculous, Ian," I say. "You can't do that."

His dark eyes home in on me, and he moves closer. He's trying to intimidate me with his height, but I don't budge. "That especially means you, you pathetic liar," he says in an intense voice.

"*Ian,*" my aunt says.

He doesn't even look at her. "It's Charlotte's name you should be saying like that, Sandra. Not mine."

"Ian. Don't do this now. Just leave," I say.

"Because I'm the bad guy, right?" He looks at each of us before he continues. "Why is that? Because I took over a company Charlotte and Kat never wanted? Because I kept it alive and increased its revenue? I was taking this family places. *Me.* Past the provincial vision our parents had. Who cares what happens to the hotels? I was creating an actual legacy for this family. And what has Charlotte done?" He is smiling, but there is no warmth in it, and the expression only makes him seem more unhinged. "Why don't you tell them?"

"I don't know what you mean," I reply in as neutral a voice as I can muster. I know where this is going, but I have no idea how he found out.

He lets out a harsh laugh. "I took the liberty of going to the Dawson Hotel you're staying at. Without my approval, I might add. You've been evicted. And you'll all love to know what I found on her bed."

"You went into my room? How many laws can we expect you to break this year?" I ask, but even as I say it, my entire body begins to shake. I may have brought the file of emails to the wedding, but I didn't bring everything Annie gave me.

"Here, Kat. This is who your beloved sister is." Ian pulls the parchment Annie left out of his pocket. He's folded it, essentially ruining the piece. He follows it with the note and hands them both to Kat.

She looks at both. Her eyes come up to me in a question, but she doesn't say anything.

"So, Charlotte. Why don't you tell the family how long you've been fucking my girlfriend?"

"Ian, that is uncalled for," my uncle says, taking a step closer.

"Ask her," Ian says. "Ask her if I'm lying."

I can feel everyone's eyes on me, but before I can say anything, Kat steps between Ian and me. "Charlie doesn't need to answer to you. I asked you not to come. You did anyway. You have no regard for anyone's feelings. I don't care what Charlie did. I've always been there for you. I was there when we were born. I need you to be here for me now. And right now, being here for me means leaving."

"Kat—" he starts, but promptly stops when she pushes his chest. I've never seen her raise her hand to anyone. Ian's eyes widen, and he takes a step back. "Ian, if you want to have any relationship with me after this, you will leave now. And let me be the first to tell you that if you insist on trying to run our company like you own it, you will lose that fight."

He stares at her, but not with the same hatred in his eyes that he was directing at the rest of us. He almost looks sad. "I guess I'll see you in court. Sorry if I ruined your wedding." He takes his time to send one more glare at each of us before exiting through a side door.

The silence in the hallway is deafening. I'm shaking so hard that I'm sure it's visible.

"Will everyone please leave Charlie and me alone?" Kat says.

My eyes are glued to the floor, but I can hear them all going back into the main room. My uncle squeezes my shoulder before he leaves, but I hardly feel it with my body as tense as it is.

"Let's go into a room," Kat says quietly.

My breathing is shallow, and I'm afraid of what will happen if I try to move. Kat seems to understand and gently pulls me down the hall into her bridal suite. Once there, she guides me to a chair and sits me down. She sets the portrait and note down and pulls a chair across from me. "Charlie." She touches her knees against mine. "Hey, look at me," she says when I continue to stare at my lap.

I don't know what to say. Everything Ian said is true, and the worst part of it is that I've ruined another day of Kat's that was supposed to be special.

"Is it true? Annie?" Her voice is soft, and she doesn't sound as shocked as I would have expected. I nod, but no words come out of my mouth. "Well, damn, Choo Choo. You want to tell me what happened?"

I let my head drop into my hands. "I'm so sorry, Kat. I'm so sorry I ruined your wedding."

"Hey, I'm married. That happened hours ago. We've eaten, we've danced, we've laughed. Nothing has been ruined. But you need to talk to me. What happened with Annie?"

I take a breath. "Remember that first night I got into town and went to the Runaway?"

"Yes, I remember asking if you met someone, and you said no."

"Well, I did meet someone."

"Annie."

I nod again.

"Why was she at the Runaway?"

"That's a long story."

"Is she gay?"

"I don't know what she would call herself. But we connected. And slept together. I didn't know she had a boyfriend or that it was our brother until the family dinner."

Her eyes widen, and her mouth opens in an almost cartoonish way. "Well, that puts everything into perspective. No wonder you were weird about her coming to the bachelorette party. I assume it wasn't just one time?" She nods to the note.

I shake my head. "I've seen her multiple times. I know it was wrong. And I know what you must think of me."

"You don't know anything. Tell me why you kept seeing her. Was it to get back at Ian?"

My head snaps up. "Of course not. I'd never do that. I just couldn't stop. Annie is...special."

"I would agree with that. And she was always too good for Ian. Are you still seeing her?"

"We ended things. There's no way for us to be together. Not now."

She puts her hands on my lap and leans forward so our faces are close. "Charlie, is it sex? Or is it more?"

I don't even have to think about my answer. This has never been about sex. "It's so much more, Kat. I've never felt like this about anyone."

"Then, it's not over."

I search her face for anger, but all I find is understanding. "Why aren't you mad at me?"

"I wish you had felt like you could tell me. But I see why you didn't. It's kind of one of the craziest things I've ever heard."

"Even crazier than the time Holly dated her therapist?"

"Even crazier than that. Though, they're about the same in terms of ethics." We smile while Kat moves a piece of my hair that's fallen into my face. "If you feel so strongly about her, you should go after her. She loves you. She said it in that note. Are you really going to let her walk out of your life?"

"You just want me to have a girlfriend."

"I do. But you know why I'm not mad? Because I know you. And I don't think you'd do what you did unless you were head over heels for her."

"Our families are going to be in a legal battle soon. How can we be anything?"

She reaches out and picks up the portrait Annie made for me. She's quiet as she studies it. "It's absolutely beautiful. I had no idea she was so talented."

"Her work is sensational."

"So is she," Kat replies, looking up from the drawing.

"So is she."

"Everything is always so final with you, Charlie. But the world doesn't have to be so rigid. Everything can change. We know that more than most people. No door is closed forever. And some things you have to fight for."

"We already have a fight coming up."

"All I'm saying is that nothing is final." She puts two fingers under my chin and lifts. "And keep your chin up, kid."

"You sound more like Mom every day."

"I'll take that as a compliment."

"It is."

She sets the drawing down again and slaps her legs. "Shall we get back to this wedding? I'd say the drama is probably done, but this is a Dawson event, so I won't hold my breath." She moves out of her chair, and I follow. She links her arm with mine as we move toward the door.

"I did bet Logan he couldn't eat six pieces of cake. So the night might take a fun turn yet."

She laughs loudly, and the sound puts a smile on my face. I don't know if there's anyone on earth who deserves a sister like Kat. I know I certainly don't. But I'm grateful I have her.

"Let's see if we can get him to up that to seven," she says as she skips back into the main room.

Most of the people left are my family and close friends, and my smile grows. My aunt and uncle dance, gazing into each other's eyes as if they're the only people in the world. Kat joins Jake at one of the tables and whispers in his ear like they're school-yard crushes. Holly and Logan are flicking napkins at each other and laughing. And as I look at all of them, I have the clarity I need. This is my home. These people are my home. I'm staying in New York.

CHAPTER TWENTY-SEVEN

W hy do you have a gavel?" Holly asks Logan as she enters my aunt and uncle's dining room and sets a salad bowl on the table.

"Because this is a family meeting. I'm making it official," he replies as he reaches for the bowl.

"*Logan,*" my aunt says from the other end of the table. "We're not starting yet."

His hand hovers over the bowl, and he looks as if his mom slapped him. "But the food is going to get cold."

"It's salad, dear. It's meant to be cold. We'll bring the rest of the food out soon. You'll survive."

"That's what you think," he grumbles as he sits back in his chair.

"We'll make this part quick." I pat his arm. "We can start now that we're all here."

"Great," he says, pounding the gavel on the table. "This Dawson Family Meeting in the Year of Our Lord, 2022, has officially commenced."

"Maybe not so loud with the gavel, son," my uncle says from the head of the table.

"I'm just trying to bring a flair of drama to our family, Dad."

"I know, son. And we appreciate it. But don't you think we've had enough drama?" my uncle replies, looking warmly at him. He then focuses on me and spreads his hands. "Your meeting, Charlie."

I look around, not knowing where to start. But when my eyes settle on Kat, she gives me a reassuring smile as she holds her husband's hand, and I know exactly what to say. "Thanks for doing this," I say to my aunt, who cooked dinner. "I know we're all tired from the wedding, and as we all know, some of us were sick all night." I look at Logan.

He grimaces. "I would have been fine if I had stopped at five pieces. Or four whiskies,"

"Anyway, I know I've made a bit of a mess of things." I pause and shake my head. "For the past four years. And I'm sorry for that. Especially to you, Kat."

"We're past that, Charlie," she says. "This isn't your apology tour."

"No, but I still needed to say it. And there's more. Before we get to the legal stuff, I wanted to tell you that I've made a decision. I'm going to stay in New York. At least, for the foreseeable—"

My words are cut off by a scream from Kat. "You're staying?" Her chair falls as she rushes over.

Worried about any other damage she may cause, I stand so I can catch her. "I'm staying," I say into her hair.

When she releases me, tears are falling down her face. I hand her one of the napkins.

My aunt also has tears in her eyes. "That is certainly good news."

"I think that news deserves a toast," Holly says.

I wink. "Any reason to drink."

"This is an extra good reason."

Kat continues wiping her eyes as she goes back to her seat, and Holly raises her glass. "To our family. Back together. Where we belong."

"You're taking my role," my uncle says before raising his glass. "But I couldn't have said it better. Welcome home, Charlie."

"Thank you," I say, smiling.

"Now can we eat?" Logan asks.

"Almost," my uncle replies. "We need to discuss our next move with the company. There are two points we need to address.

Ownership and leadership. As of now, Ian, Kat, and Charlie all own thirty-three percent of the company. And as we know, Ian is the acting CEO."

"More like acting asshole," Logan says, but it's so quiet that I think only Holly and I hear him.

"Let's start with the easy part," my uncle says. "Leadership. Ian has ruined his relationship with Dawson's board of directors. We won't have any trouble getting their support in transferring leadership. I recommend we ask for an emergency meeting tomorrow so we can remove Ian as CEO. Are you comfortable with that?" He looks at Kat and me.

"The employees of the Dawson Hotel Group deserve real leadership," I respond. "You're their leader, Uncle Neil. Kat and I would like to propose to the board that you take over."

"I'm honored. And I would gladly accept the position. But I think we should allow the board to do what they do best. They should decide. It's time we built trust again between that team and our family."

I look at Kat, who nods. "That's fine with us," I say. "As long as they come to the right decision."

He gives me a small smile. Everyone in the family knows the company should be in his hands, but I also appreciate his thoughtfulness and business savvy. "Now comes the question of ownership," he says. "Your parents left the company to all three of you. Traditionally, if we wanted to take over part of that ownership, we'd offer Ian a buyout. But we don't technically need to do that considering the state and federal laws he violated."

"We're talking about a lawsuit?" I ask.

"Our lawyer has looked at everything. There is a buyout provision within the company agreement. My guess is that once you two take over your majority stake and blow up his deal, it'll take some of the starch out of his hoodie. But if not, then, yes. We'd be going to court with him and Phillip Astor."

"And if we don't sue Phillip and just stick to the removal of Ian?" I ask tentatively.

My uncle looks confused. "Why wouldn't we take him to court as well? They put the deal together."

"Because removing Ian essentially kills the deal he signed with Phillip anyway. It holds no legality whatsoever. Why do we need to even touch the Astors? Most of the money that went into that deal came from his company. He's already lost."

My uncle scratches his chin, something he always does when he's thinking hard. "Phillip did invest quite a bit, but he only did that because he knew the cut he'd get. He was very close to destroying everything your parents built. And he's not the only one who invested. Ian has spent quite a bit of Dawson company time and labor on this. We'll want to recoup that."

"This is about our family and getting our company back. I don't see why we need to overcomplicate it," I argue.

"Charlie," Kat says. "Be honest. Why don't you want to sue the Astors?"

"I know," Logan says loudly, raising his hand as if he's in some pop quiz. Holly pushes his hand down, silencing him.

Kat gives me another reassuring smile and nod, and I know I need to be transparent. Because what my uncle is saying isn't wrong: Phillip Astor is a shady businessman, and he almost got away with something drastic. "Because of Annie. This will ruin her family. And her family doesn't just include Phillip."

"Annie," my uncle repeats. "I see."

"Are you in love with her, Charlie?" my aunt asks. So far, Aunt Sandra has let me and my uncle take over this meeting, but that's just who she is. She's quiet until she has something poignant to say, and when she speaks, people tend to listen.

"I am."

She looks at my uncle and smiles, then puts her hand on his. "Some things are bigger than this company. And it's Kat and Charlie's decision. If you want to protect Annie, we'll all protect her."

My uncle leans in and kisses her temple. "I agree. We protect the ones we love."

"For what it's worth, I think you and Annie make a way more attractive couple than Annie and Ian," Logan says.

"I'm not with her, but thank you, I guess."

"Since we're all airing things out, why aren't you with her?" Holly asks.

"We're not airing things out, Holls. We're talking about a lawsuit."

"Yes, but talking about your love life is so much more fun."

"Eating is more fun, too," Logan replies. "Are we done?"

"Almost," I say before turning back to my uncle. "This is not to say that I think this is where the road with Phillip Astor ends."

"How so?"

"I have to assume that whatever deal Ian and Phillip put into place can move forward at any moment?"

"Yes, we'll need to act immediately to have it voided."

"Let's propose a plan to Phillip where he kills the deal himself. If he doesn't, we take him to court. And in exchange for not suing him, we ask him to be a resource for us. Nobody has spent more time with Ian than Phillip Astor."

He considers it and slowly nods. "Kat, are you comfortable with that?"

"As long as I don't have to talk to Phillip," she says.

"Why don't you pass it by Annie and see what she thinks?" Holly asks. "She's free tomorrow night."

"How do you know that?" I ask.

"Because Kat and I are in a text thread with her, and we asked her to hang out tomorrow night. We were going to trick you into it. It was a whole thing." Holly waves like tricking me into a night with Annie was just a casual idea.

I look at Kat. "What?" she asks in an innocent voice. "You're so stubborn. We thought if you two had a drink, you could talk through all your issues."

"We've already talked through our issues."

"Great, then you can talk to her about the company," Holly offers, not even trying to hide her mischievous smile.

"It might be good to get a sense of what his reaction will be from her," my uncle says, smiling like he's in on the plan.

"Did you know about this?"

"Of course not. But I like Annie. And I love you. I think you could be a good match."

"Okay, now we're just talking about Charlie's love life. Can we *please* eat, Mom?" Logan begs.

"I'll get the chicken." She stands. Logan claps like a child.

"You're meeting Annie at eight o'clock tomorrow," Holly says.

"Right." My stomach does a flip that has nothing to do with what I need to say to Annie and everything to do with seeing her again. "And where did you tell her to go?"

Holly and Kat smile at each other, looking way too pleased with themselves. Holly grabs the salad out of Logan's hands and speaks without looking at me. "The Runaway."

CHAPTER TWENTY-EIGHT

C harlie fucking Dawson. Two visits in two weeks. Color me shocked."

"Hey, Darcy."

She grabs a bottle and pours something dark into a glass before I'm even at the bar. As soon as I sit, she slides the drink over to me. "I honestly didn't think I'd see you again. Good wedding?"

"Kat was happy. She left today for her honeymoon."

"Is this your good-bye before you head off to the west for another decade?" She has always been direct, but she doesn't seem angry, just honest.

"Actually, you might have to get used to seeing more of me. I'll be around."

She begins cleaning a glass and nods but as expected, doesn't ask any follow-up questions. "I can't say I'd complain about that," is all she says right before grabbing another glass. "The gang's getting together on Friday at our apartment. You should come. Everyone would love to see you. Alice was pretty bummed she didn't get to see you last time."

"You're allowed to leave this place on a Friday?"

She smiles widely and spreads her arms. "I'm big-time now, kid. I have managers."

"Well, look at you. From barback to bartender to employer of *managers*."

"Yeah, yeah. I'm a real New York success story."

I take the first sip of my drink and relish the familiar burn as it slides down my throat. I take a few more quick sips, and soon, my glass is almost empty.

"Another?" Darcy raises an eyebrow. I nod and slide her my glass. "You seem nervous."

"I'm not."

"If you say so." She continues to work in silence while I try to sip my next drink.

I'm not going to admit it, but I am nervous. My last good-bye with Annie is at the forefront of my mind, and I feel an anxiety I haven't felt before about seeing her. I wish we were here to have a drink like any two women who are attracted to each other, but that's not why I'm here.

I've spent my entire life trying not to get pulled into my parents' company, and now I'm leading the charge to fight my brother over it. I know we're doing what we need to do, but I also know that if my parents were alive, this situation would break their hearts.

I also have no idea how Annie will react to seeing me again when we were so intentional with our last good-bye. It's only been a day since I've seen her, but the distance between us feels vast now.

I look up when I hear Darcy chuckle. But she's looking at the door. "Interesting," she says. "Guess that went well the other night."

I know exactly what she means, and my entire body heats up. Everything feels like it slows when I turn and find Annie walking toward the bar. I can feel the memory of our first night so sharply. The blouse she's wearing may be gray instead of emerald, but even her outfit is similar. And yet, everything feels different this time.

On that first night, I felt drawn to her, an attraction that muted anything I had ever felt for a woman. But it's so much more now. Now, I know who Annie is.

When she reaches the bar, she sets her coat on the stool next to her and sits. Her eyes connect with mine, and the first thing I notice is how much clearer they are than the last time I saw her. "Well, hello, again, Charlie," she says.

"You don't seem surprised to see me."

"It was obvious what your sister and cousin were doing. Choosing the Runaway? They're not that subtle."

"No, but you came anyway."

"You don't seem surprised to see me, either. Were you in on the plan?"

"I only found out last night."

She looks like she's about to say something, but Darcy comes up to us. "Drink, love?" She puts down a coaster.

"Whatever she's having." Annie points to my drink.

"Annie, this is Darcy," I say. "Darce, this is Annie."

Darcy gives her a nod and slides her drink over. "Nice to meet you."

"Likewise. Is this your place?"

"It is. Charlie's been coming here since she was in gay diapers," Darcy replies, putting her elbows on the bar.

"Gay diapers?" I respond.

"I really like it," Annie says to Darcy, both completely ignoring me. "The clientele could use some work, but it's a great place."

"Hey, don't blame the bar for whatever Charlie has done to you. I stopped taking responsibility for her actions with women in 2009."

"What has she done to women?"

"And we're done bonding." I say before she can answer.

Darcy knows more about my past with women than almost anyone, especially considering I met most of those women in this very bar, and I'd rather not go down that memory lane.

"But things were just getting good," Annie says.

"Uh-huh. Real fun." I pick up my glass and jump off my stool. "We'll take these upstairs, Darce."

She just makes a humming noise and begins to wipe down the bar.

"It was nice meeting you," Annie says, grabbing her drink.

"You too. I'll be down here if you need me. I'm both owner and bouncer."

Annie laughs, and it's only now that I realize how much lighter she seems. It's a marked change from yesterday morning when there were more tears than smiles. "Thank you. But I'll keep her in check."

"Something tells me you will."

I move to follow Annie toward the stairs but turn to Darcy again. "Were you always this bad of a wingman?" I whisper.

"Since when do you need a wingman?"

"I don't. Luckily. Because you suck at it."

"She's pretty. And nice."

"I know."

"Then, why are you still standing here?"

"No idea." I start to follow Annie up the stairs, but she's already sitting and looking down at me. She smiles and lifts her drink in a silent toast, mirroring my actions from the night we met.

I don't care if Darcy is watching, I don't move. The first time I saw Annie, I thought her face looked as if it was designed by an artist, and I'll always consider her beauty to be unmatched. But my feelings for her run so much deeper now.

I was living in a lazy fog until I met her, and everything seemed to speed up and click into place. Maybe it took coming back to this bar for that fog to lift completely. I think about what Kat said at her wedding about how I'm always so final about things, and there's truth in her words. Like I told my family last night, I'm coming home to be with them again. But I'm also doing it so I can stop running away from everything that makes me feel.

I wonder what my parents would tell me to do. One of the things I always admired about them was the way they prioritized each other over everything else. I think they'd tell me to fight for her. I don't know how long this company drama will last, but it suddenly feels unbearable. Having no future with Annie has to be a worse fate than any reason we can come up with for not being together.

When Annie tilts her head and pats the seat next to her, I force my feet to head toward the stairs. As I sit, the energy between us shifts, and I can tell by the cloudy look in Annie's eyes that she feels it, too. It was foolish to think we could come here and stick to speaking about business. Now that she's here in person, the company is the last thing I want to talk about.

I don't think I could tear my eyes away from her now if I tried.

"Charlie," she whispers. She looks at me with a desperate expression, as if she's asking me to fix the situation.

"Thank you for the portrait. It was gorgeous."

"Because the subject is gorgeous."

I look at the bar, right at the spot I first saw her, before looking back. "And here we are again. I can't believe it's only been a couple of weeks. So much has happened."

"Do you regret it?"

"I could never regret meeting you. Do you?"

She smiles and shakes her head. "Are we celebrating or forgetting tonight?" She nods to my drink.

"I could also never forget you."

She takes a small sip. My eyes follow her lips as they touch the glass, and like so many other times that I've been with her, my body feels charged, even as I watch her do something simple. "So why did Kat and Holly tell you about tonight if it was supposed to be a setup?"

"Because this wasn't supposed to be a setup."

"No?"

"I was supposed to come here and offer your family a deal regarding the Dawson Hotel Group."

"You mean the one your uncle and my dad worked out this morning?"

"What?"

"My dad told me your uncle called him and explained the situation."

"Wait, he did?"

She nods.

"And what did your dad say?"

"He agreed to work with your family. The deal is dead. He knows he's between a rock and a hard place."

"Why would my family tell me to come talk to you about it first if my uncle was just going to call your dad anyway?"

"Because this is a setup?" she says with a smirk. "My dad said my name came up on the call. Your uncle told him the family cares about me. And that's why you guys made the decision you made."

I nod, not knowing what to say. I'm not upset that my uncle called Phillip and took things out of my hands. I was acting like a middleman anyway, but I am surprised. I thought my family would judge me for falling for Annie, considering how it happened. But they have been nothing but supportive, even encouraging.

"Did you have something to do with that?" she asks.

"Yes."

"Tell me why."

"Because I love you, too."

I hear her let out a breath as she stares into my eyes. "I didn't expect you to say that."

"I love you, Annie. And my family loves you. Well, most of them. Ian might not."

She lets out a sudden laugh as tears reach her eyes. "Charlie," she whispers again.

I scoot closer so our knees are touching and take her hands. I let our fingers lace and feel an instant sense of relief. "I thought I was coming here to talk about the hotels. But the second I saw you, all that seemed unimportant. I don't want to say good-bye. I don't know if I can."

She doesn't try to wipe away the tears that fall down her face. "What about LA?"

"I'm leaving LA."

"You are?"

"I'm not closing my gallery there, so I'll need to make trips. But I'm staying."

"What made you decide that?"

"There are things here that I want in my life."

"Things?"

"People."

She looks like she's processing everything I said, so I stop talking and let her. She brings my palm up to her lips. As soon as her lips touch my skin, warmth spreads up my arm and through my body. "I don't want to say good-bye to you, either."

"I know things will be complicated. I'm not asking you to come out to your family tomorrow. Or even in a month. But I'll wait for you. Even if I have to wait two years for your sister to turn eighteen. Because you're worth it."

"Two years is a long time."

"You're worth it," I repeat. "Besides, I have no idea what's going to happen with Ian and the company. I'll be pretty tied up with that for a bit."

"And here I was expecting a proposal," she says, making me smile with her confident humor.

"How about when you're ready, we start with a second date? And I promise not to trick you into going to an art gallery again. We can do something else. Like a baseball game."

"Do you watch baseball?"

"No, but I know New York has a team."

"Two teams."

"See? You know so much already."

She rolls her eyes, but her smile stays. After the past few days, it feels good to banter with each other. "I loved seeing that gallery. And meeting Dorian," she says. "We don't have to watch baseball."

"I'm glad. But I won't keep pushing the art thing. You should do whatever you want."

"I've done what my family has wanted for so long that I don't even know what that is. But I've been thinking about that group Dorian told me about. Maybe I'll give him a call."

"I have a feeling you'll figure it out."

"Why do you believe in me so much?"

"It's not a task, Annie. I knew the moment I saw you that you were special. Anyone who doesn't see that isn't worth your time." I barely get the last word out before she is putting both her hands on my face and bringing me in for a kiss.

I let out a little gasp that she swallows as she tangles her tongue with mine. We don't kiss for long, but unlike the kiss we shared in my hotel room the day of Kat's wedding, it doesn't feel final. There's something about the hungry way she takes my mouth that promises more.

As my hands tangle into her hair, she pushes her chair back as if my lips burned her. We're both panting, but I can't seem to catch my breath.

"If I keep kissing you, I'll be asking to go back to your hotel again," she says, pushing her hair out of her face.

"To be clear, I asked you," I reply, not able to hide the desire in my voice.

When she casually licks her lips, I have to grab the sides of my chair to stop from kissing her again. "Two years is a long time not to do that again," she says.

"It is."

"Technically speaking, kissing doesn't have to mean dating. Right?"

"Technically speaking, I suppose not."

"And you know, my dad doesn't have a key to my apartment."

I know where she is going, but after all we've talked about, she needs to be the one to ask. "That certainly creates some privacy."

"Want to see it?"

All we've done recently is talk about all the reasons we can't be together. But right now, I don't want to talk. I want Annie. Even if it's only for tonight. Even if it's only for an hour. I'll take whatever she wants to give me.

Instead of answering, I push my chair back and hold out my hand. She has a small smile on her face as she slips her hand into mine, and we make our way downstairs and to the door.

I give Darcy a small wave as she serves a customer. She gives me a nod, but when she sees Annie's hand in mine, I see a smile on her lips.

Annie puts her arm through mine and pulls closer to me as soon as we reach the sidewalk. We only walk a few steps before I stop us, just needing to see her face again, needing to know that this is real.

"Having second thoughts?" she asks.

It's so cold that her cheeks have already turned pink, and I can see her breath in the cool air. I rub one hand against her cheek. "Never."

"Then, let's go, Choo Choo."

I allow her to pull me along as she begins to walk again and soon, she's hailing a taxi. I once left this bar with her and knew we couldn't have a future. But as we face the cold New York air together, and she slips her arm through mine again, everything feels different.

It wasn't just one night, and I don't think it ever will be again.

It's not over. It's not even close.

About the Author

From an early age, Shia Woods enjoyed writing and became an avid reader of literature. Those passions prompted her to earn a degree in journalism. But after years of devouring every queer story she could find, what started as a desire to chase headlines diminished, and she decided to indulge her dream of writing her own stories of love, lust, and passion. When she's not writing novels, Shia can be found hanging out with her family and three high-maintenance chihuahuas in the Pacific Northwest.

Books Available from Bold Strokes Books

A Case for Discretion by Ashley Moore. Will Gwen, a prominent Atlanta attorney, choose Etta, the law student she's clandestinely dating, or is her political future too important to sacrifice? (978-1-63679-617-8)

Aubrey McFadden Is Never Getting Married by Georgia Beers. Aubrey McFadden is never getting married, but she does have five weddings to attend, and she'll be avoiding Monica Wallace, the woman who ruined her happily ever after, at every single one. (978-1-63679-613-0)

Flowers for Dead Girls by Abigail Collins. Isla might be just the right kind of girl to bring Astra out of her shell—and maybe more. The only problem? She's dead. (978-1-63679-584-3)

Good Bones by Aurora Rey. Designer and contractor Logan Barrow can give Kathleen Kenney the house of her dreams, but can she convince the cynical romance writer to take a chance on love? (978-1-63679-589-8)

Leather, Lace, and Locs by Anne Shade. Three friends, each on their own path in life, with one obstacle...finding room in their busy lives for a love that will give them their happily ever afters. (978-1-63679-529-4)

Rainbow Overalls by Maggie Fortuna. Arriving in Vermont for her first year of college, an introverted bookworm forms a friendship with an outgoing artist and finds what comes after the classic coming out story: a being out story. (978-1-63679-606-2)

Revisiting Summer Nights by Ashley Bartlett. PJ Addison and Wylie Parsons have been called back to film the most recent Dangerous Summer Nights installment. Only this time they're not in love and it's going to stay that way. (978-1-63679-551-5)

The Broken Lines of Us by Shia Woods. Charlie Dawson returns to the city she left behind and she meets an unexpected stranger on her first night back, discovering that coming home might not be as hard as she thought. (978-1-63679-585-0)

Triad Magic by 'Nathan Burgoine. Face-to-face against forces set in motion hundreds of years ago, Luc, Anders, and Curtis—vampire, demon, and wizard—must draw on the power of blood, soul, and magic to stop a killer. (978-1-63679-505-8)

All This Time by Sage Donnell. Erin and Jodi share a complicated past, but a very different present. Will they ever be able to make a future together work? (978-1-63679-622-2)

Crossing Bridges by Chelsey Lynford. When a one-night stand between a snowboard instructor and a business executive becomes more, one has to overcome her past, while the other must let go of her planned future. (978-1-63679-646-8)

Dancing Toward Stardust by Julia Underwood. Age has nothing to do with becoming the person you were meant to be, taking a chance, and finding love. (978-1-63679-588-1)

Evacuation to Love by CA Popovich. As a hurricane rips through Florida, so too are Joanne and Shanna's lives upended. It'll take a force of nature to show them the love it takes to rebuild. (978-1-63679-493-8)

Lean in to Love by Catherine Lane. Will badly behaving celebrities, erotic sex tapes, and steamy scandals prevent Rory and Ellis from leaning in to love? (978-1-63679-582-9)

Searching for Someday by Renee Roman. For loner Rayne Thomas, her only goal for working out is to build her confidence, but Maggie Flanders has another idea, and neither are prepared for the outcome. (978-1-63679-568-3)

The Romance Lovers Book Club by MA Binfield and Toni Logan. After their book club reads a romance about an American tourist falling in love with an English princess, Harper and her best friend, Alice, book an impulsive trip to London hoping they'll each fall for the women of their dreams. (978-1-63679-501-0)

Truly Home by J.J. Hale. Ruth and Olivia discover home is more than a four-letter word. (978-1-63679-579-9)

View from the Top by Morgan Adams. When it comes to love, sometimes the higher you climb, the harder you fall. (978-1-63679-604-8)

Blood Rage by Ileandra Young. A stolen artifact, a family in the dark, an entire city on edge. Can SPEAR agent Danika Karson juggle all three over a weekend with the "in-laws," while an unknown, malevolent entity lies in wait upon her very skin? (978-1-63679-539-3)

Ghost Town by R.E. Ward. Blair Wyndon and Leif Henderson are set to prove ghosts exist when the mystery suddenly turns deadly. Someone or something else is in Masonville, and if they don't find a way to escape, they might never leave. (978-1-63679-523-2)

Good Christian Girls by Elizabeth Bradshaw. In this heartfelt coming of age lesbian romance, Lacey and Jo help each other untangle who they are from who everyone says they're supposed to be. (978-1-63679-555-3)

Guide Us Home by CF Frizzell and Jesse J. Thoma. When acquisition of an abandoned lighthouse pits ambitious competitors Nancy and Sam against each other, it takes a WWII tale of two brave women to make them see the light. (978-1-63679-533-1)

Lost Harbor by Kimberly Cooper Griffin. For Alice and Bridget's love to survive, they must find a way to reconcile the most important passions in their lives—devotion to the church and each other. (978-1-63679-463-1)

Never a Bridesmaid by Spencer Greene. As her sister's wedding gets closer, Jessica finds that her hatred for the maid of honor is a bit more complicated than she thought. Could it be something more than hatred? (978-1-63679-559-1)

The Rewind by Nicole Stiling. For police detective Cami Lyons and crime reporter Alicia Flynn, some choices break hearts. Others leave a body count. (978-1-63679-572-0)

Turning Point by Cathy Dunnell. When Asha and her former high school bully Jody struggle to deny their growing attraction, can they move forward without going back? (978-1-63679-549-2)

When Tomorrow Comes by D. Jackson Leigh. Teague Maxwell, convinced she will die before she turns 41, hires animal rescue owner Baye Cobb to rehome her extensive menagerie. (978-1-63679-557-7)

You Had Me at Merlot by Melissa Brayden. Leighton and Jamie have all the ingredients to turn their attraction into love, but it's a recipe for disaster. (978-1-63679-543-0)

All Things Beautiful by Alaina Erdell. Casey Norford only planned to learn to paint like her mentor, Leighton Vaughn, not sleep with her. (978-1-63679-479-2)

Appalachian Awakening by Nance Sparks. The more Amber's and Leslie's paths cross, the more this hike of a lifetime begins to look like a love of a lifetime. (978-1-63679-527-0)

Dreamer by Kris Bryant. When life seems to be too good to be true and love is within reach, Sawyer and Macey discover the truth about the town of Ladybug Junction, and the cold light of reality tests the hearts of these dreamers. (978-1-63679-378-8)

Eyes on Her by Eden Darry. When increasingly violent acts of sabotage threaten to derail the opening of her glamping business, Callie Pope is sure her ex, Jules, has something to do with it. But Jules is dead…isn't she? (978-1-63679-214-9)

Head Over Heelflip by Sander Santiago. To secure the biggest prizes at the Colorado Amateur Street Sports Tour, Thomas Jefferson will do almost anything, even marrying his best friend and crush—Arturo "Uno" Ortiz. (978-1-63679-489-1)

Letters from Sarah by Joy Argento. A simple mistake brought them together, but Sarah must release past love to create a future with Lindsey she never dreamed possible. (978-1-63679-509-6)

Lost in the Wild by Kadyan. When their plane crash-lands, Allison and Mike face hunger, cold, a terrifying encounter with a bear, and feelings for each other neither expects. (978-1-63679-545-4)

Not Just Friends by Jordan Meadows. A tragedy leaves Jen struggling to figure out who she is and what is important to her. (978-1-63679-517-1)

Of Auras and Shadows by Jennifer Karter. Eryn and Rina's unexpected love may be exactly what the Community needs to heal the rot that comes not from the fetid Dark Lands that surround the Community but from within. (978-1-63679-541-6)

The Secret Duchess by Jane Walsh. A determined widow defies a duke and falls in love with a fashionable spinster in a fight for her rightful home. (978-1-63679-519-5)

Winter's Spell by Ursula Klein. When former college roommates reunite at a wedding in Provincetown, sparks fly, but can they find true love when evil sirens and trickster mermaids get in the way? (978-1-63679-503-4)